The House that Florence Left

ALSO BY CHRIS PENHALL

PORTUGUESE PARADISE
Book 1: The House That Alice Built
Book 2: New Beginnings At The Little House In The Sun
Book 3: The House On The Hill
Book 4: The House That Florence Left

STANDALONES
Finding Summer Happiness
Summer In Your Eyes

The House that Florence Left

CHRIS PENHALL

Portuguese Paradise Book 4

Choc Lit
A JOFFE BOOKS COMPANY

Choc Lit
A Joffe Books company
www.choc-lit.com

First published in Great Britain in 2024

Cover art by Dee Dee Book Covers

ISBN: 978-1781898079

For
Sarah, Hannah, Gareth,
Ann, Kevin, Barrie and Sam

CHAPTER 1

The last time Bella Creswell had driven along the lane was when she was eight years old. She hadn't been driving, obviously — that had been her father, who had not been happy about the effects on the car's suspension of the stones, rocks, mud and grass littering the unmade road. Bella, however, remembered being captivated by the canopy of trees hanging over them as they drove, lush and green and tall. She was entranced by the shards of sunlight sparkling through the branches, casting tiny pinpricks of light onto the ground as the family almost bounced in their little red car towards the white house in the distance.

'Why does Florence have to live in the middle of nowhere,' her father muttered. 'Why doesn't she do something about the access? I mean, doesn't she want people to come and see her?'

'You'll have to ask her.' Bella's mother rolled the window down and held her arm outside. 'Oh, that's better.' She breathed in slowly and loudly. 'Actual air, rather than air conditioning.'

'What are those trees, Mummy?' Bella was fishing her notebook and pen out of her bag.

'I don't know, darling.' Her mother turned her head and smiled at her. 'Add it to the list of things we need to find out.'

Bella kicked her legs excitedly and carefully turned the pages until she got to one headed *Things I want to know about Great-Auntie Flo and her house and where she lives*, and added underneath:

1 — What are the trees on the lane?

'I've written my first question,' she announced.

'Could you add, why did she decide to live in the back end of nowhere in the Algarve when she could have lived in a flash duplex near to all the amenities?' Her father laughed loudly, then swore as he swerved to avoid two dogs sprawled lazily next to a gate. 'That wouldn't have happened if she lived in town,' he muttered.

'It's a lifestyle choice, David.' Her mother stroked his arm. 'And we are getting a free holiday and an adventure, aren't we? We would never have gone on that ferry and driven down through Spain and Portugal if she hadn't invited us here. We've seen so many wonderful things already.' She turned around again. 'What do you think, Bella?'

Bella waved her notebook in the air. 'I've got lots and lots of things to find out about when I get back home. I saw so many things, I need to go and do some research so I can understand them.'

'A top researcher already.' Her father slowed the car down. 'Don't worry, girls. When I finally get this car parked outside Florence's house, she gives me an ice-cold beer and I watch the sun go down from one of the hammocks in her garden, I will relax.'

'Yes, that's until you get that old bike out of her shed and go off on one of your rides.' Her mother laughed. 'Or find a golf course, or run down to the sea for a swim, you old fidget you. You'll stay in that hammock for about half an hour before you get restless.'

As the lane curved to the left, her father stopped the car. 'I think this is it?'

Her mother read aloud the directions that Flo had dictated to them over the phone. '*The gate is on the right, almost hidden behind a jacaranda tree. And there is a sign on the left-hand post that says "O Ninho". That's the name of the house.*'

'Yes. We're here. Exciting!' Bella squealed.

'She also said, *Don't bother to ring the buzzer, just drive up as it's not working at the moment.*' Her mother smiled as her father turned the engine on again. 'What a beautiful tree. Pity we can't grow one of those in our garden.'

The family drove in through the gates, and for a moment, they were unable to speak. Bella knew she couldn't find the words to describe how what she saw made her feel. She was, after all, only eight years old, but her parents didn't seem to be able to either.

'Goodness. How beautiful,' murmured her mother eventually.

'Is that it? Is that her house?' Bella pointed towards the tiny white building at the end of the track. Bright red flowers dripped from window boxes next to shiny blue-and-white tiles dotted randomly around the walls.

'I believe it is,' said her mother.

'I flipping well hope so,' said her father.

'It's beautiful.' Bella beamed. 'It's like a painting. No — no — it's like a fairy tale. And there's a chicken, and ducks! And what are those big white birds on that roof?'

'Well, I never. I think they are storks.' Her father sounded uncertain until one stood up gracefully and stretched its long white wings. 'Oh yes. Definitely storks.'

Bella almost screamed. 'Storks, Mummy! Storks. Pet storks. This is going to be the best holiday ever! I'm going to make a list of all the good things that happen when they happen, then I can look at it when I get home when I'm fed up and stuff.'

She opened her notebook again and wrote:

Really good things about Flo's house: storks
Good things about Flo's house: ducks and chickens

Then she saw a swimming pool glistening next to the house and added:

Excellent things about Flo's house: I can swim all day.

* * *

Bella blinked herself back into the present and peered at the road in front of her. 'You'd have thought, Great-Aunt Flo, that someone would have done something about this by now.' She sighed guiltily. 'I'm sorry I never came back. We always meant to, but life got in the way.'

Turning the engine back on, Bella slowly edged the car along the lane, glancing in her rearview mirror at the new houses at end of the main road that twenty-five years ago had been scrub-land and olive trees.

Her phone buzzed beside her, so she stopped. *Are you there yet? Mum x.*

Almost, she messaged back. *I'll be in touch when I've spoken to the solicitor.*

She put it back on the seat next to her and began to drive again, an unexpected nervous churn growling around in her stomach, wondering what the house would be like now that Great-Aunt Florence had passed away. And why she had left it and all the land around it to Bella.

Focusing on the track in front of her as she got closer, she tried to keep the memory of that first childhood glimpse of The Nest in her mind's eye, rather than the new reality of a once-loved house that had been empty and neglected for over a year.

The jacaranda tree was still there, tall and lush and green, the first signs of purple blossom flecking through the leaves. The old sign was still on the wooden post by the open gate. Bella remembered her aunt pointing at it on their first day when they had walked to the beach, explaining what the bold blue letters meant. '*O Ninho*,' she had said. 'It's my little nest. The Nest. And those birds that are painted around the edges

4

are the storks that live on my roof.' She'd touched it, tracing her hands around the letters and smiled. 'Time for a swim, come on.'

Bella shook her head, forcing herself back to the present and continued along the drive.

While she parked, a tall man with hair like a hedgehog's prickles stepped out of a yellow Rolls Royce and waved at her, smiling encouragingly. Bella looked up, took a deep breath, opened the car door and was welcomed by a wave of heat and a loud chorus of cicadas. She braced herself, preparing for the challenge of sorting out the house and selling it so she could go back to her real life with a helpful amount of money in the bank.

'*Bom dia!* Good morning!' The man strode towards her. 'How lovely to meet you, Miss Creswell.' He took her hand and shook it warmly. 'I am so very sad for your loss. I am aware it was over a year ago and the matter of the property has taken a while to deal with, but nevertheless a loss is a loss.'

'Thank you.' Bella attempted a smile. The early-morning start, finishing a report for work on the flight and then the drive to the house had drained her. And she was feeling just a little bit sweaty as the air conditioning in the car didn't work properly. 'We were all very sad.'

'She was a real force of nature.' The man smiled again. 'I am so sorry. I should have introduced myself instead of assuming you knew who I was. I am Ignacio. I am here on behalf of your aunt's *advogado* to hand over the keys.'

'Thank you for meeting me here.' Bella glanced around. 'I'm sorry I'm a bit late. I had to find a quiet corner of the airport so I could connect to the Wi-Fi and send some information for work. My out-of-office is now on and I just wanted to arrive here and get straight on with it instead of finding my way around Lagos to stock up on supplies — I haven't been here since I was a child.'

'Oh, it's changed a lot over the years.' Ignacio's phone buzzed. 'That's my reminder — I am sorry to rush you but I am teaching a yoga class in forty-five minutes.'

'Yoga? I thought you were a solicitor.'

'I earn extra money by meeting clients for the solicitors. And I do airport runs. And teach tango . . . but mainly I am a yoga teacher.' His grin grew even wider. 'At the age of forty-nine, I decided I needed a change of course so began to study it. And here I now am, doing the thing I love at a retreat called the House on the Hill.' He sighed happily. 'And as a result I met the love of my life, Minnie. We are to be married next year.' He laughed. 'I didn't mean to give you my life story. But this place, you know . . . You watch it, you'll be in love in no time.'

Bella shook her head. 'Oh no. I'm not looking for love. I want to make my life easier, not more complicated.'

Ignacio put his hand over his mouth. 'I'm sorry. That's inappropriate, given the circumstances. This must be hard for you.' He touched Bella's arm kindly. 'You must come and join us, if you enjoy yoga, of course. I like to work. And—' he looked at his car, '—I brought my old and cherished Rolls Royce that I used to use for weddings here because I feel both you and your Aunt Flo deserve the sense of occasion that brings.'

'Oh — how lovely.' Bella managed to get the words out, trying to mask the sudden urge to cry.

Ignacio looked at the floor and shuffled his feet, cleared his throat and patted her on the shoulder. 'I am also a trained counsellor, but I'm not very good at that, so I don't do it anymore. I have a tendency to speak before I think. Which isn't good for counsellors if I'm honest.'

Bella breathed in, breathed out, opened the car door again and took out a bottle of water. 'I'm a bit dehydrated,' she mumbled, taking a long gulp. 'I am also nervous. I didn't know what to expect. I don't know what I'm meant to be doing. And I don't want to let Flo down.'

Ignacio nodded, handing her a large padded envelope. 'When she left her house to you she knew what she was doing.'

'What was that?' Bella took the package.

'I don't know.' He laughed. 'But you know Flo!'

But I don't, she thought. *I don't really know her at all.*

Ignacio put his briefcase on the patio table. 'Well, as you are here now, shall we deal with the paperwork?' He opened it and took out a pen and a file. 'You need to sign for the keys and the car and go through a few other things.'

'Ah yes, the car. What's it like? I'm banking on it being driveable — I've only got the hire car for a week as it's so expensive.'

'It's a Fiat Punto. She bought it only three years ago. Barely driven, bright red. She loved bright colours.'

'Ah. I didn't see it in the driveway.'

'It's in Hugo's garage. He moved it to keep it clean and safe. He'll drop it round when it's convenient for you.'

'That's very kind. Who's Hugo?'

'He's your next-door neighbour. He and Flo were very close. He'll be along to show you around and how to switch things on — you know. He's been keeping an eye on things. He popped in earlier to meet you but because of your delay in getting here he had to leave.'

'Oh dear. My job is quite demanding so I had to make sure everything was in order before I signed off.' She felt an unexpectedly nervous lurch in the pit of her stomach. 'I rarely have more than five days off in a row. So this long break is something of a challenge.'

Ignacio smiled kindly. 'Well, you are among friends here, so we will support you for as long as you are here.'

Bella felt tearful again. 'Gosh, I'm tired. It's making me overemotional.' She cleared her throat. 'I'd better head into Lagos to buy some food.' She attempted to fight off the tears by trying to sound businesslike and purposeful.

'Oh, don't worry about that.' Ignacio waved his hand at the house. 'Hugo brought you a few things to keep you going for tonight at least. I think he's left them in the kitchen. And we have written a list of people who can help you with various things if you need them.'

'That's very, very helpful. I love lists.' Bella's eyes began to feel heavy. She wondered if any of the beds were made up inside so she could just fall into one and doze off.

Ignacio handed her a pen. 'If you sign here, here and here—' he pointed at a form '—I will get out of your hair and you can rest.'

She allowed the house to come into full focus now, noticing tiny pockets of grey brick dotting the chipped bright white walls, swathes of grey dirt around the faded blue windows and dry brown stems where the bougainvillea had been, except for one green shoot, fighting for light. Four of the tiles had fallen to the ground next to the front door.

Ignacio picked them up, shaking his head sadly. 'At least they aren't completely broken, just a bit around the edges.' He sighed. 'Are you planning to stay long?'

'As long as it takes. But hopefully not too long.'

'As long as it takes for what?' Ignacio frowned curiously.

Bella felt tired again and sat on one of the patio chairs. 'I don't know.' She almost laughed, looking up at him. 'I was so surprised that Great-Aunt Flo left this to me that I haven't had time to process it. All I know is that I have to do something with it.' She looked around. 'Mend it or something?'

'And sell it?' Ignacio sat down opposite her. 'The will stipulates you can't sell it or rent it for at least six months — and you have to use the sum of money left to make it better — whatever that means. Do you know what that means?'

'Honestly? I haven't a clue. And I need to get it sorted — can't have an empty house in another country to worry about.' She could feel her voice beginning to rise, so took a breath and tried to control it. 'My company have let me take all my holiday and I'm going temporarily part-time in three and a half weeks so I can work from here and do whatever needs to be done. And then go home.'

Her eyes began to feel heavy with fatigue. 'I'm usually very organised. I make lists, I tick tasks off, I plan ahead, I do my research, I think about things before I decide. But . . .' She shook her head and tried to smile. 'On this occasion I couldn't do any of that. And no, I don't know what—' she made an inverted comma sign with her fingers '—"make it better" means. But I'm going to sell it. If the market is bad, I may rent it out for a while. Not holiday lets though. Too much work.'

Ignacio nodded. 'We want to make life easy for you, so you can meet the challenge ahead feeling strong.'

'Challenge?' Bella signed the documents and looked back at him. 'Are you sure you don't know what she meant by "making it better"? I mean, did she leave a list of things I had to do?'

'No — we checked. Exactly as it said on the will — make it better. She wrote it a long time ago. I don't think it would have got past any legal adviser these days.' Ignacio took the pen from her.

'It needed to be quantified. Does someone come and check after six months to see if I've made it better? And if so, how do they measure it?' Now her voice was sounding whiny and tired.

'I think perhaps Flo thought you would know when it was better.'

Bella stared at him. 'Really? I met her when I was eight. I could be the most untrustworthy person in a room of . . . I mean a city of . . . or a . . .' She could feel her mind almost fuzzing with fatigue. 'Or . . . full of untrustworthy people . . . Oh, I give up.'

Ignacio smiled. 'Everything will become clear, I'm sure — once you've had time to rest.' He looked into his briefcase. 'Ah, yes. We found this in the file of her old paperwork — we think it got mixed up and left there by accident.' He took out a small print with storks painted around the edges and words in pink. 'It was made for her by our friend, Alice.'

Bella read it and looked at him. Then she read it out loud:

The amble by its very definition does not have to have an actual firm destination, often fizzling out in a café, on a beach, or in a shop en route. Although it isn't really en route as you are not actually going anywhere. You are ambling.

'I can't remember the last time I ambled anywhere. I always have a firm destination.' Bella looked at it, confused.

'Always? Even when you go out for a coffee or a walk?'

She smiled. 'A coffee shop is a firm destination. And when I do my walks for my step count I always plan the route.'

'Perhaps you will learn the art of ambling here.'

'No.' Bella said firmly. 'I've got too much to do and too little time to do it in.'

Ignacio didn't say anything. Then he closed his briefcase and picked it up. 'I hope to see you soon, Bella. If you need anything, just ask.' He walked back to his car. 'Hugo will be along tomorrow.'

Bella smiled at him and watched as he drove back along the track to the road. Then she took the keys from the envelope and opened the door.

Light flooded the darkened room.

She stood in the doorway for a moment. The space was homely and cluttered, with knick-knacks covering most of the surfaces. A bright pink sofa took pride of place next to a small table painted with mosaics, with four dusky-blue wooden chairs placed untidily around a dirty white table and a large chest of drawers hid in the corner next to the stairs.

She walked inside, particles of dust hanging in the air illuminated by the sun, a dry, musty smell filling the room. She spun slowly around, remembering again that holiday all those years ago, when the house was filled with life and people and noise.

Sitting on the sofa for a moment, Bella mentally began to go through the list of things she needed to sort out before she could get the house in shape. But she felt herself sink into the sofa, as if it was encouraging her to take a nap. Her mind began to fuzz over again, so she forced herself to stand up and walk up the stairs, hoping to find a welcoming bed to rest in for a while.

* * *

Bella rolled onto her back on top of the bedsheet. Her aunt had painted large orange roses on the ceiling, their green stems tangled elegantly around one another. She raised her arm, waving it slowly in the air, tracing the lines with her finger, wondering how Flo had done it. 'I saw that film with Charlton Heston where he was Michelangelo, and he was lying on his back on a kind of structure. It was Charlton Heston, wasn't it?' she murmured, glancing next to her absent-mindedly, to see what Gino thought. Then she remembered he wasn't there. He hadn't been lying on any bed anywhere near her for over a year now. Looking at the clock she worked out that as it was 3 p.m. in Portugal, he would quite probably have just climbed out of a bed somewhere in San Francisco. Maybe his. Maybe not.

But wherever he was he would be on his phone working, or his laptop, doing deals and making money. Because that was the most important thing for him, above all else — including, Bella had realised a little too late, her.

'I don't care!' she shouted, then trained her focus back on the ceiling and counted to ten, breathing slowly, forcing him out of her mind. 'I'll ask Google and research it myself.' She sat up and padded along the cool tile floor to the landing, down the stairs and paused next to her luggage. She remembered the food that Hugo had left in the kitchen and decided to prioritise that instead.

Opening the cool bag, she took out some ham, cheese, orange juice, two ready meals — one macaroni cheese and one chilli con carne, three tomatoes, a loaf of bread, some margarine, crisps, hummus and water. Plus three bottles of white wine.

Making a mental note to thank Hugo, she put all of it in the fridge apart from the bread and dips, rummaged around in the cupboards till she found the plates, then took her snack out onto the terrace along with a brown envelope marked 'Helpful information'. The heat wrapped itself around her this time, the cicadas quiet until she scraped a chair towards the table, which they accompanied with loud screeching again as if she was a conductor waving an insect choir into song.

She dipped her bread into the hummus and gazed at the landscape, trying to compare what she saw now with what she'd seen when she was eight. But all she could conjure up was snippets. Flo standing in the garden with a canvas and easel, with Bella next to her with her own, using her brush to paint bright swathes of colour across the paper. Her father pushing her in the homemade swing hanging from the tree behind the house, her mother screaming when she jumped into the unheated swimming pool for the first time.

Bella stood up and walked around to the kitchen door. The tree was still there; the swing was not. The swimming pool lay empty except for drifts of leaves and other litter she didn't really want to identify.

Back at the terrace Bella sat down again, slightly deflated. She knew there was a lot to do to the house, but she hadn't the energy to work out what. It would all have to wait until tomorrow, she decided, as that was the most sensible thing to do. She took another bite of bread and dip, then opened the envelope and rummaged through the leaflets and flyers advertising builders, takeaway delivery, hairdressers, painters and decorators, restaurants, gardeners, and people who looked after pools.

Inside was also an A4 typed page, with information about local shops and other amenities, with a photograph of a yoga, mindfulness and dance studio called The House on the Hill. Underneath, Ignacio had written:

> If you want some rest from all of the house business, this is a great place. This is where I work with my fiancée Minnie. She runs it with her niece, Layla. It is a very well-established and popular place. Ignacio.

Deciding that keeping up with her yoga was a good use of her time and needed to be scheduled into her days, Bella looked at the phone number, then remembered she needed to ring her parents to tell them all was well — in so far as she had inherited a dilapidated house that needed a lot of love and probably a lot of attention, and she had already realised that she didn't know where or how to start. Her heart fluttered uncomfortably, understanding, for the first time in a very long time, what being outside her comfort zone felt like.

She took her empty plate back into the kitchen and grabbed her mobile phone from her bag. The phone wouldn't connect, so she moved around the kitchen then every room, trying to find a signal, before stepping outside and waving it in the air as if she was holding a net to catch good telecommunications reception. This tactic never worked, she knew that, but she always tried it just in case.

Bella sighed, knowing she had to call them or they'd be worried. She decided to drive down the lane towards the new houses in the hope she may get some signal there. Grabbing her keys, she jumped in the car and drove it to the main road, climbed out and rang her mother again. This time the call connected.

'Bella!' her mother shouted. 'I was worried something had happened. Is everything all right? You arrived hours ago. Your father said not to worry, but I do!'

'There's no signal at the house, Mum.' Bella leaned into the car and took out her drink. 'And I had a nap just after I arrived as I was so tired. I should have rung before I did that, but I just sat on the bed, and the next thing I knew I woke up.' She took a long gulp of the water. It was very warm.

'Ah, of course.' Her mother's tone sounded calmer immediately. 'Are you all right? Has the signal gone?'

'I just had an unexpectedly hot drink.'

'So—' her mother's voice lowered '—how is it? Falling down? Half falling down? Absolutely gorgeous?'

'Needs some love and care. Not sure how much yet.' Bella's attention was caught by a stork soaring, serene and elegant, above her. 'But it will all be all right. I'll go into town tomorrow, sort

13

out the internet connection and start to research house repairs and renovation.'

'You don't have to do it all yourself. You can't learn how to repair everything with YouTube videos.'

'I won't,' Bella lied.

'You've never done DIY in your life. And, you know, you could just sell it as is. Let someone else sort it out.'

'I can't, Mum. I have to make it better . . . whatever that means. And now I'm here. It feels wrong to leave it like it is. I'll have more idea of what to do once I've been here a few days. It'll be all under control very soon.' She almost shouted the last few words, as if she was trying to persuade herself as well as her mum. 'How is Dad today?' She had been asking that question almost every day of her life since she was nine years old. But the anxious knot in her stomach she felt every time the words were uttered still came.

'He's good today. The new medication seems to be helping.'

'That's good. How are you?'

'Oh, I'm OK. I'm always OK if he's OK. I've got some extra shifts at work too for the next couple of weeks.'

'Well, don't overdo it. I can help with money.'

'You help enough already, Bella. And we are grateful. But spend some of it on yourself.'

'You're my mum and dad and I want to spend it on you.'

Her mother paused for a moment. Bella knew she had decided not to argue. That short conversation had been repeated regularly over many, many years. And it always ended the same way.

'I don't like to think of you out there on your own in that house,' her mother said eventually. 'Is it still so remote?'

'No need to worry, Mum. The guy who handed over the keys — he knew Flo, told me an old friend of hers — Hugo or something — is next door and happy to help.' As she said the word 'help', Bella's mind began to churn with a list of all the jobs she may have to do before selling it.

'Oh yes . . . We met Hugo when we came over — I don't suppose you'd remember — his family have lived next door for

14

ever. It's nice to know he's still there. They owned that lovely café by the beach.' There was a pause. 'Maybe you'll meet a young nice man there, Bella, to help you get over that—'

Bella interrupted her before her mother could say 'Gino' and voice her negative opinion of him. She didn't want to be reminded of her massive lack of rational judgement when she had first met him, how she had ignored all the 'red flags' her mother had mentioned periodically. 'I'm here to sort the house out, Mum, and come home. I won't have time to meet a nice young man . . . and anyway, I don't know where I would find one.' She almost laughed.

A dog barked in the distance at the sound of a car backfiring loudly, making Bella jump. 'I'd better go. I haven't unpacked yet. I'll call you tomorrow. Love to Dad. Bye.'

She ended the call, then logged onto her work email account to check that the report she'd sent from the airport had arrived.

There were no messages.

She began to type.

Bella here. Just checking the report I sent arrived. I was on dodgy Wi-Fi at the airport when I filed it. I need to take it off my list of work tasks.

An answer arrived immediately.

Hi, Bella. I sent the acknowledgement earlier. It must be hovering in cyberspace. Lil Mulvaney.

Sporadic phone signal so maybe that's the problem. As long as I know. Bella

Is the weather lovely? Lil

Nice and warm, Bella responded. *I'll mark it as done in the diary then. Enjoy the rest of your day.*

She got back in the car and headed to her new, albeit temporary, home, took her work diary out of her bedroom drawer and entered the report as completed.

CHAPTER 2

Tiny pinpricks of light dotted the room, scattering along the floor and up the walls. Bella gazed at them absent-mindedly for a few moments, reluctant to get out of bed, partly because it had taken her a long time to get to sleep. Her flat at home was next to the corner of the A3214 and the lack of traffic noise here in the middle of the night made her uneasy. Getting out of bed and walking downstairs would also remind her that she needed to get out her pen and paper and go around the house noting what needed to be done. And then she had to get all of it done. Or some of it at least.

Something clattered noisily to the floor in the kitchen, which was all the motivation Bella needed to jump out of bed and rush onto the landing.

'Is anyone there?' she shouted, her heart beating uncomfortably fast. As soon as the words were out of her mouth she wondered what she would do if someone answered. Or if no one answered. She crept down to the living room and padded quietly along to the kitchen door, which she had left open overnight.

A fluffy black-and-white cat was standing on the worktop with its face in the tub of hummus, which Bella was sure had had the lid on when she'd gone to bed.

'What? Who are you?' she asked the cat, trying not to laugh.

The cat briefly looked up at her, then turned back to the food. She picked the animal up from the worktop gently and put it on the floor. 'Not terribly hygienic, is it?' she muttered. The cat glanced at her again, then wiped its hummus-encrusted nose with its paw.

'How did you get in?' she asked it sternly, just as another fluffy black-and-white cat climbed through the cat flap, which she hadn't noticed the previous day. 'Hello. And you are?' She laughed, watching the cat walk to the utility room and sit down expectantly.

Bella followed it. 'You don't want me to feed you, do you? I haven't got any cat food, and anyway, you really should go home for your breakfast.' Opening the back door, Bella peered outside, partly to check there weren't any more cats on their way. There weren't, but a large Labrador was bounding along the lane, barking, followed by a man's voice getting progressively louder and yelling repeatedly, 'Deidre, come back! Come back!'

Realising she was still in the T-shirt she had worn to bed, Bella hurried back inside and pulled the knitted dress she had worn to the airport in her backpack, assuming the dog and the man may be paying her a surprise visit, then she went back outside.

A stocky man with grey hair tied back in a ponytail was trying to put on a lead.

'Hello. Can I help you?' Bella stood assertively on the terrace.

He looked up. 'Good morning! You must be Flo's long-lost relative. Sorry about Deidre. She clearly sensed you were here and wanted to say hello.'

'Hello, Deidre.' Bella waved at the dog, then spoke to her owner. 'I'm Bella. Are you Hugo?'

He walked over to her and shook her hand. 'No. I'm Will Phoenix. Good to meet you. I live around the corner. I'm glad someone's finally in Flo's place. I was getting worried it would fall down.'

17

'Oh, goodness. I hope it doesn't need that much work.' Bella glanced back at the house.

'Ha, no — I mean it probably needs some TLC. Someone to live in it. It was always so full of life when Flo was around. She was always hosting gatherings.' He glanced over the top of her head for a moment. 'I haven't been here since just after she died.'

Deidre began to bark, her tail wagging excitedly.

'I see the cats have moved back in.' Will smiled and pointed at the front door, where the animals were now sitting.

'Moved back in?' Bella stared at them.

'Flo's cats. I took them in when she died, but they'd come back here every day. Now there's a human here, I expect they've decided to stay.'

'But I can't have pets. I don't know how long I'll be here. I can't have any ties to the place. No responsibilities apart from the house . . .' Her voice trailed off.

'I'll try to keep them, but they are cats after all. And if you go, I expect they'll move back in with me.' Will checked his watch. 'I have to go. I do the occasional airport pick-up job, and today's an early start.'

'But . . .' Bella was looking for the right words. 'Cats will complicate things. What if they don't want to go back to you?'

She tried to work out where she would put them on her list of things to do to the house. What if she sold it and people who didn't like cats moved in? Or who had allergies to cats? 'I wasn't expecting to look after animals. I hadn't even considered it as a possibility.'

'They'll be fine. They've managed for the past year.' Will tickled Deidre's ear. 'If she turns up again, just don't feed her and she'll head back to me when she's bored. What she is, is very nosy.'

'Right, well . . .' Bella looked at the dog and tried to sound enthusiastic. 'It will be lovely to see her. I'm just not used to pets.'

'They've obviously decided you could do with some company.' Will took a card out of his pocket and handed it to her. 'If you need anything, my number is there. I know Hugo has

18

promised to help, but it's good to have more than one person to call on.'

'Thank you.' Bella took it. 'I really don't think I can keep them. I'm not here for long.'

'You're not keeping them, Bella.' He laughed. 'They're keeping you. Got to be going.' He began to walk away, then turned back. 'They're called Yin and Yang, by the way.'

'Which one's which? Although I don't know why I'm asking as they can't stay.' Her voice began to rise. 'Sorry. It's just a bit unusual, that's all.' She tried to sound calmer than she felt.

'No idea. They're always together, so I just say, "Yin and Yang" and they both arrive. See you.' He waved and began to walk away, dragging a reluctant Deidre with him. 'I've fed them already, so don't let them emotionally blackmail you into giving them more food,' he shouted. Then he turned back again. 'I know a good gardener if you need some help getting the land back up to scratch.'

'Do you know when Hugo will be around at all?' she called after him. 'I need to go out but I don't want to miss him.'

'Just get on with your day. He'll be around when he can.' He checked his watch and began to almost trot down the lane.

Bella looked at her own watch. 'I'm very grateful to Hugo for his help, when he arrives. But I'm on a tight schedule over the next few months, so I can't start my time here hanging around for—' She realised she was talking to the cats again, so stopped and went back into the house, followed by her new pets. 'Did he say land?' she asked Yin or Yang. 'I forgot there was land.'

She stared at them for a moment, then laughed. 'Suppose it's better talking to you than to myself, which is what I do at home.'

The cats meowed, then lay down at the bottom of the stairs. Bella stepped over them. 'Before I add "land" and "you" to my list of things to think about, I'm going to have a shower and unpack. That's what I'm going to do.' She waved her finger at them. 'But as you weren't on my list of things to do, Yin and Yang, don't get too settled. I mean it.'

* * *

After a cold shower, Bella decided to prioritise going through the notes she'd been left to find out how to heat the water. She opened the wardrobe door, sneezed for what felt like half an hour and added 'duster' and 'air freshener' to her shopping list. Then she took out a notebook and on one page wrote: *Cats x2 — what do I do with them when I go?*

Then she walked outside to find the land that Will had mentioned.

At the back of the house was a field with orange trees clustered together at the far end and what looked like some old vegetable beds and tangles of weeds and wildflowers scattered across the rest. She looked at an overgrown pond next to some fencing and sighed. It was covered in green algae.

A donkey brayed in the distance. Bella tried to locate where it was but couldn't find it.

She lingered for a moment in front of a grubby white outbuilding with a blue wooden door, but decided against opening it and went back inside, adding *'Land — do a proper inventory'* to her list. Deciding to investigate the narrow stairs curling up from the landing, she opened the door at the top, wondering why it hadn't been locked and mentally adding *'Find key'* to her list, then stepped onto a terrace that stretched the length of the roof.

'Oh' was the only word her mind could come up with as she stood in the sunlight. In the distance, over the trees and sand dunes she could see a long, curved stretch of golden beach. 'Meia Praia,' she murmured. 'I remember it.' She spun around slowly taking in the view, from the red rooftops of Lagos to the mountains to the north, to a crisp blue lagoon to the east. She glanced down. Dead leaves had gathered in the corners of the terrace and a thin layer of dust and cobwebs covered the floor.

Deciding to add *'Clean roof terrace'* to her list when she got downstairs, Bella looked up again. Someone was flying a blue-and-red kite over the beach. She smiled as it danced in the breeze.

* * *

Driving slowly down the narrow lane towards Meia Praia, Bella passed a small café at the junction onto the road. Her eyes widened as she turned right towards Lagos, the water glistening like a sea of diamonds rippling out towards the horizon, the sand a sunlit gold, the distant outlines of the city buildings glowing silver. She smiled, realising that Ignacio had been right — there was much more of Lagos than last time she'd visited. Switching the air conditioning off, she opened the windows so the salt-scented breeze would billow through the car.

Pulling up at a zebra crossing, she watched a couple walk towards the beach and was briefly consumed by an urge to take off her sandals and walk along the warm sand too. But she needed to buy food and, anyway, it was only April so the beach was probably not very warm.

You can do that after you've felt the sand between your toes and paddled in the waves. It was as if Flo was talking to her, and Bella's internal voice began to sound just like hers, lilting and Welsh, with a laugh waiting somewhere to burst out. *You've got a few weeks off before you have to start working again. You haven't got an urgent deadline. The sun is shining, the birds are singing, and it will take half an hour to buy your food. Go on. You know you want to.*

Bella laughed, and a sliver of the stress of the past few weeks drifted off, swept by the breeze into the distance. A flock of birds fluttered through the sky, and she imagined them carrying away the shock she'd felt when the letter arrived from the solicitor telling her she'd inherited Flo's house, the confusion about why, and the worry about how to deal with it without damaging her career. And the sadness about the loss of someone she had met so briefly, but whose vibrancy and love of life she had never forgotten.

She blinked, watching the flock soar towards the cliff, then inland, and visualised them dropping all her worries into a forest, where they would disperse into the trees and somehow change into positive thoughts; and then she stopped, realising that the idea of letting things go is to let them go, not give them an onward story — and that her imagination had provided quite a lot of stuff for those poor birds to carry away.

Rain began to patter on the windscreen, a huge rogue cloud in the shape of a balloon settling above the beach. The couple hurried back across the zebra crossing. Sensible shopping it would be.

* * *

Following a speedy visit to the supermarket, Bella drove home and unpacked the shopping. She then fed the cats, who had been studying her with interest as she moved around the kitchen. 'I think you're part of the estate then,' she said, stroking them both in turn. 'Yin, or is it Yang? This is a temporary friendship, though. So don't get too attached.'

Turning on the tap, she put her hand under the water. It was still cold, so she grabbed her phone and attempted to connect to the internet. She couldn't.

Frustrated, Bella peered outside. The sky was now a bright, almost incandescent blue, with no clouds in sight. She grabbed her bag, strode onto the terrace and began to walk down the track that led to the beach lane, in search of a café with an accessible internet connection.

She followed the sound of music drifting softly over the dunes, trying to work out what the song was, then took off her sandals and smiled as the sand warmed her feet a little. Turning a corner, the end of 'Try a Little Tenderness' merged into Etta James singing 'At Last' and she paused for a moment. A man was brushing the wooden deck of a café, humming loudly to whatever tune he was listening to on his headphones, which didn't sound like what was being played out of the speakers.

On a chalkboard leaning against the railings at the top of the steps was written:

Casa de Lopes
Produtos locais frescos

Fresh local produce
Aberto — Open

Free Wi-Fi
Paredechecarseutelefone
(esse é o código)
Translation: stop checking your phone! (that's the code)

Bella smiled just as the man took his headphones off and turned towards her. *Um . . . l*, she thought, as he scratched his very attractively unshaven face absent-mindedly, and said the first thing that came into her head. 'Do you have any tables free?'

The man looked at her, his face serious. 'Let me think—' he looked around at the empty café '—We may be able to fit you in.' His face softened. 'Sit anywhere you want. What would you like?'

'A latte, please.'

'A *galão* it is. Coming up.'

'A what?' Bella couldn't quite understand what he said. 'I meant a latte.'

'Yes. *Galão*.' He looked at her, his face expressionless.

Bella stared at him for a moment 'But I meant a—'

'It's the same thing.' He interrupted, smiling. 'Milky coffee in a glass, on its way. You'll like it. It's better.'

Bella half-smiled as he carried the broom inside. *Ah . . . a comedian*, she decided, then looked around for the best place to sit, choosing a low sofa with a view of the sea.

She heard him shout, 'Julian — *galão* for outside. Delivery has just arrived.' She tried to connect to the internet and stared at the screen, watching the line across the Google site edge very, very, very slowly from one side to the other and wincing slightly every time it seemed to move backwards, as if it had gently collided with railway buffers.

A young man placed a glass in front of her. '*Galão*,' he mumbled quietly.

'Thank you.' Bella looked up, but all she could see was his back as he hurried inside.

Taking a sip of the coffee she leaned back and gazed into the distance, watching seagulls surf the breeze over the beach as fluffy white clouds drifted across the horizon.

Turning her attention back to the phone, she saw the internet signal still locked halfway across the screen, so stood up, held it in the air and waved it around as if it was a flag. It still didn't connect, so she stepped back and held it in front of her, then descended the steps, edging slowly backwards, staring at the screen as she went, ready to stop moving as soon as she got a signal.

'Oh, come on . . .' she mumbled irritably. 'Oh—'

The line had moved very slightly further forward, and so she took another step backwards, and another, and then another. 'Nearly . . .' she muttered, trying to hold the phone even higher above her head — which was irrational, she knew, as that's not how you connect to the internet — then stepped back again, but this time put her foot in what felt like a box, lost her balance, fell over and landed flat on her back.

'Oh!' Bella heard a man's voice moving closer. 'What happened? Are you all right?'

She looked up as he knelt down next to her. It was the man who had shown her to her seat. His face was backlit by sunlight, which looked a little like a halo.

'I was trying to connect to the internet.' Her voice sounded high and thin and a bit pathetic.

'Is your head all right?'

'I think so.' Bella managed to sit up and found herself staring into his chocolate-brown eyes. She was temporarily unable to speak.

'I'm worried you have concussion,' he said after a long pause.

'No. No.' She dragged her gaze away and tried to focus on standing up. 'I'm OK. Just embarrassed.' Longing to be able to pull herself to her feet from a seated position like the rest of her class in yoga, she quietly rolled over onto her knees.

He held out his hand. 'Let me help.'

But she was already clambering clumsily to her feet, embarrassed.

The man stood up too. 'I see you still have your mobile phone in your hands.'

'Ah.' Bella looked at it. 'Still no signal.'

'Can I ask you something?' His voice was serious. 'If you had managed to get a mobile phone signal when you were holding your phone above your head, how were you going to use it to communicate?'

Bella managed a smile. 'That is an excellent point. The pursuit of the signal temporarily got hold of me and I seem not to have thought it through.' She sighed. 'In fact, I sound a bit irrational, don't I?'

She glanced down at her feet, which were covered in a bright red substance. 'Is that blood?' she said slowly, trying not to panic.

'Tomatoes,' the man replied flatly. 'I was carrying my delivery into the kitchen, and I'd put that box there to take home.'

'Ah.' She stared at her feet. 'Thank goodness it's not blood. I'm sorry. I've ruined your tomatoes. Unless you're using them for passata or a sauce?'

His expression didn't change.

'I'll pay for the tomatoes,' she said, her embarrassment ramping up a notch.

He shook his head. 'I shouldn't have left them there. Well, you are around the back of the kitchens and there's no one here normally except employees. But I shouldn't have left them there.'

'I need some hot water and can't get the system to work so I thought if I could look it up on the internet, I'd get it to work and actually have a warm shower rather than a freezing one, and I saw you had Wi-Fi so thought I'd have a coffee at the same time and kill two birds with one stone.' Bella realised she hadn't taken a breath so stopped talking.

'Why don't you call the owner of the place you are staying?' The man spoke calmly as if he was talking to a child. 'They'll get it to work for you.' He picked up the box.

'I am the owner. Very new.'

He turned to look at her curiously. 'You are living here now?'

'Oh . . . No . . . I don't really — just temporarily.' She closed her eyes briefly to try to organise her thoughts. 'Do you have a hose or something? I need to wash my feet. I feel I may attract a horde of flies on my way home.'

A phone rang from inside the café. 'I have to go.' He pointed at a bucket and some watering cans propped next to the wall. A hose was hanging up behind them. 'This will help?'

'Boss!' Julian the waiter waved at him from the kitchen. 'It's that call you've been waiting for.'

The man sighed apologetically. 'No rest for the wicked. The chef and my bar manager will be arriving soon too, so I have to get on. Are you sure you are all right?'

'Yes, yes. Just—'

'Boss . . . They are in a hurry!' shouted Julian again.

The man shook his head, nodded at Bella and hurried inside, closing the door behind him.

'—a bit embarrassed,' she said to the door, then turned on the tap and pointed the hose at her tomato-caked feet.

* * *

Back at the house, Bella decided to get to work and put some saucepans on the stove to heat some water. The cats weaved around her legs, purring and chirping, so she got some newly purchased cat treats out of the cupboard and put them on the floor, stroking their fluffy tails as they ate. 'My mother would say you must have been sent to me by the universe to provide pet therapy, Yin and Yang.' Yin or Yang meowed at her. 'But I personally don't believe in all that. I really don't. It's nice to have you here though.'

She poured the water into a large bucket with some cleaning liquid, went outside and began to wash down the garden furniture, planning on moving inside to work on the living room when the midday heat got too much or it started to rain — the weather was confusing her today.

After a couple of hours she stepped back and admired her work, the chairs, benches and tables now a gleaming silver. She decided some little plants would look nice there and made a note to do some internet research and see what would grow well — once she'd sorted the internet out, reasoning that a bit of bougie dressing-up would do no harm when potential buyers visited. The cats climbed up onto a seat each, yawned and stretched out. The early-afternoon heat was acting like a sedative for all of them, as if they were in a well-lit sauna. The cicadas began to screech loudly, just as a bead of sweat trickled down Bella's back.

There was still a hammock to be cleaned hanging invitingly above the patio. It looked grubby and forgotten, but also comfortable. The cats' eyes were already closed, and she decided a nap would suit her too, so she climbed in and leaned back to recharge her batteries before starting on the living room. Closing her eyes, she began to rock gently, accompanied by the comforting sound of cicadas and birdsong.

* * *

The clatter of a saucepan woke her, and she sat up suddenly, forgetting she was in a hammock, which rocked dramatically then dropped her onto the floor.

'Oh, God,' she mumbled. 'Where the hell am I?'

At the same time a familiar male voice shouted, 'Are you OK?'

She looked up. A tall, dark and handsome man was hurrying towards her. 'I think I startled the cats and one of them knocked something off the table. I'm so sorry.' His voice was deep and warm and he sounded slightly worried.

Bella's brain slowly cranked into gear. *Ah, oh, right. I'm in Portugal, and is that the man from the café? Oh no . . . the man from the café. The last time I met him I was flat on my back covered in squashed tomatoes.* She felt her face turn red.

He held his hand out to help her up, and she took it, dragging herself to her feet. 'I'm OK. Thank you. I dozed off.'

'We've met before haven't we?' He smiled at her sheepishly.

'Yes . . . Have you come to ask me to pay for the tomatoes? I'm happy to pay, really. I did ruin them and you are running a business.'

He put his hands up in front of him. 'No, no . . . My name is Hugo. I'm your neighbour. I've come to say hello and see if you need any help to get settled.'

Bella stared at him for a moment. 'You're Hugo? I thought you were older. I'm sorry, that sounded bad.'

'Older?'

'I assumed you'd be older. It's just I was told you were an old friend of my aunt's and as she was older, I assumed—' She stopped talking and took a breath. 'I've just woken up and I sound strange, don't I?'

'I've known her — knew her — for ever. I live next door. I was born there.'

'Was your father called Hugo?' Bella wanted to make sure she'd got the right information.

'Yes he was. And his father too. My family had very little imagination regarding names.'

'Ahh . . . I obviously took the word "old" literally.' She blinked slowly. 'I'm still sounding strange, aren't I?'

She was waiting for him to say *'No, not at all'*, but he didn't.

'It's my night off so I was walking home and thought I'd see if you needed help. I assume the hot water isn't working. The buzzer on your gate isn't working either. I hope you don't mind me just walking in. I may have been a bit rude earlier. I apologise.'

'Rude? Were you?' Bella didn't know him at all, so didn't know whether he had been rude or not, but the idea of hot water and a warm shower was worth more than making him feel bad about it.

'Your aunt was a great neighbour. She looked after us. We looked after her. And you are family, so I promised I'd keep an eye on the place if anything happened.' He stopped talking suddenly and knelt down to stroke both of the cats. 'Hey, you two. Moved in already?' He looked up at her. 'You have to stay and not sell it, or what will these two do?'

His face was expressionless. Bella couldn't work out whether he was serious or not, so ignored the question. 'Would you like something to drink? I've only got water, orange juice or wine, though.'

'Thank you, but I'm fine. I run a café. I have access to food and drink all day long.'

'Oh yes, of course.' She smiled at him. 'Thank you for popping over. I really appreciate it. I honestly have no idea what I'm doing.'

'Shall we?' Hugo's expression changed as he followed her into the house, and he stood in the doorway for a moment. 'Every time I come in here I feel her absence.' He looked at the floor and cleared his throat. 'I know where everything is.'

He opened the door to the anteroom behind the kitchen. 'I'm not surprised it's not working,' he shouted. 'It's been switched off outside. Probably Flo did it just before she got in the ambulance. She was very thorough.'

'Ah, OK, thank you,' she shouted back, then filled the kettle. 'Can I use electricity in here?'

'Yes.' He walked back into the kitchen. 'So, you are now fully functioning as far as electricity and water is concerned.'

'Thank you.' Bella tried to make eye contact with him, but he pulled his sunglasses down from the top of his head.

'I'd better be going. I have to feed the chickens.' He opened the kitchen door and stepped outside.

'Well, thank you again.' Bella followed him.

Hugo glanced back and nodded, then hurried down the path to the road.

At least I've met my neighbours — unless there are more, she thought. Next she would make a schedule of what needed to be cleaned, mended, replaced or thrown away, which would give the water enough time to heat so she could have a warm shower. She sighed, realising that her excitement about the hot water said a lot about her life at the moment.

Hugo suddenly stopped and turned back. 'Are you going to sell it? I know I was joking earlier, but—'

'Yes. Or at the very least long-term rent if that's the best way temporarily.'

'Money, money, money.' A frown flitted across his face. 'It's not the most important thing. That's what I tell them when they come knocking.' He walked towards the gate again.

'It is if you haven't got any,' she said to his back, wondering who was going to come knocking. And why Hugo had turned from friendly to not quite so friendly in the space of less than a second.

CHAPTER 3

Having collapsed into bed the previous night following another bout of cleaning, Bella woke to a cat squeaking into her ear. For the year after Gino left there had been no morning noise inside her flat, only that of bin lorries and buses outside. Opening her eyes, confused, she managed to remember where she was and that two cats were now living with her.

There were the regular morning messages on her phone from colleagues and her boss sent at 8 a.m. in their work group chat. She absent-mindedly tried to read them, then remembered she wasn't technically supposed to be at work, just as the signal disappeared. Bella looked at the screen, contemplating going in search of some internet again to check the progress of some of the projects she had handed over. The cat began to hit her face with its paw, so she gently moved it out of the way and put the phone down.

Climbing out of bed, she put on a wrap and walked downstairs, the cat running in front of her. 'Aww, Yin or Yang, you're very sweet.' The other cat was sitting by its food bowl. 'Are you hungry, Yin or Yang?' She took the food out of the pouches and spooned it into the bowls. 'I've got to go out for a moment to find some mobile phone connection so I

31

can answer those messages from work. You never know, I may have missed something and I need to check.'

Someone knocked on the door. 'God, what time is it?' She looked at the clock on the wall. 'Eight thirty? Bit early.'

She stepped out of the kitchen into the hallway and shouted, 'Who is it?'

'Hugo.'

'Hugo?' She opened the door. 'Hello.'

His dark hair was wet, curling down towards his neck, his sweatshirt scattered with damp spots and he wasn't smiling. Bella felt an unwanted and confusing urge to move closer to him, but she held onto the door and stood still.

'I've delivered Flo's car. I've left it in the driveway. I drove straight through because of the buzzer-on-the-gate-not-working issue.'

'Thank you. I've added it to the list of things to fix.' She stepped aside to let him in, deciding that it was best to be friendly despite his sudden change of mood the day before. She smiled at the little red Fiat that was parked next to her rental car. 'Would you like a tea or coffee? I'll put the kettle on.'

He looked like he was going to say no, but nodded and almost smiled. 'A glass of water would be nice. I've just been for my morning swim and then rushed around here before work. My throat's a bit dry.' He followed her into the kitchen. 'You have been busy already I see. All the dust has gone.'

Bella handed him a glass of water. 'Some of it has gone.' She leaned against the cupboard and folded her arms. 'Small steps, I suppose.'

'If you put it on the market it would go in a flash.' He sipped the water. 'And you could leave it to the new owners to clean and renovate. I understand things will change.' He looked around the room. 'I have to apologise for yesterday. I'm just very sad because being Flo's neighbour was a privilege and a pleasure and I miss her every day.'

Bella nodded, trying to work out what to say. Flo was simply the whisper of a happy memory for her, part of another, more carefree life long, long ago. The one that changed in the space of a minute, when she was a child. 'It must be difficult for you,' she said eventually.

'For you too.' His expression warmed.

Bella tried not to notice. 'It's a practical difficulty, to be honest. I can't sell for six months according to the will, and I have to "make it better" before I do anything.'

He shook his head. 'Flo — a one-off right to the end. What about the long-term rental option? Is that realistic?'

'Not really. It's too much of a tie. Too much responsibility. But I need to find out what the estate agents say, I suppose. It could be a short-term solution. At least that is all tangible and measurable. It's much easier to write "tangible and measurable" in a list than "make it better".' She put her hands in the air and used her fingers to make inverted commas.

'I'm here. I always promised Flo I'd make sure everything was done properly if anything happened.' He smiled. 'I'm surprised that's not in the will.'

'Thank you. I'll bear that in mind when things have settled a bit.'

'Just remember. When you sell, be careful. Take advice about the buyers.'

'OK. Is there anything you need to tell me?' She tried to read his face, but he was already heading for the door.

'Actually—' Bella followed him '—Where's the storks' nest? I remember one when I was here when I was eight. Years ago. But I loved it so much I put it on my list of things to research when I got home!'

He looked up to the roof on the outbuilding. 'There were storks. There was a nest on the chimney over the outbuilding. But not since your aunt died. They left. It's strange really . . . Storks are protected in Portugal, you know. If they were here and you sold the place, the owners would have to get special permission to knock that down.' He turned away again. 'I'd better go.'

'Ah, OK, I see,' she said.

33

He glanced back. 'Not that you'd want to knock a place like this down. It's unique. If you need anything else, let me know.' He walked down the track and onto the road.

Bella watched him. She knew he was attractive, but she didn't want to know really. That was the last thing she wanted. Although, she decided, she was allowed to find him attractive on an intellectual level, but was not allowed to actually feel that attractiveness.

She bit her lip and took a breath, remembering how she found Gino attractive on every single level, with every part of herself. Then a tiny, familiar, lonely ache began to overwhelm her, pushing her onto the patio to escape it. Bella took a deep breath and closed her eyes, trying to enjoy the scent of orange blossom and sea.

Hugo's words floated back into her consciousness. *The owners would have to get special permission to knock that down . . .*

Not sure I really want anyone to knock any of it down, actually, Aunt Flo, she thought, listening to the breeze ruffle through the trees. *Especially as I'm going to have to put all this work in to make it better.*

Bella opened her eyes and went back inside to get ready, determined to sort out the internet so she could access her spreadsheets and get on with the job she had come to Portugal to do.

* * *

Bella parked the Fiat close to the supermarket near the marina and walked past the boats, the riggings rattling in the wind, dark grey clouds rushing across the sky, covering up patches of bright blue as they did, the sun occasionally peeping shyly through the gaps. It felt as if someone was flicking a light switch on and off.

Heading over the marina footbridge to the avenida, which stretched the length of the river as it flowed out to sea, she took big, fresh breaths of air and hurried along the cobbled path, almost laughing as the wind pushed her forward, forcing her to walk faster. Pausing for a moment, she took a map that had been in the information pack out of her bag and studied it, then crossed the road and walked past a carousel towards a square, where a large statue of what she assumed was a king stood next to a café outside which a busker was setting up a microphone and sound system.

A wisp of a memory fluttered through her mind. Of stalls of trinkets and jewellery, people walking and laughing and music and dancing on a warm summer's night many, many years before. And there was Flo in a bright red dress, her auburn hair tied up casually with artfully escaped curls snaking down her neck. 'Let's get you a hair braid, Bella, shall we? And maybe a henna tattoo. But don't tell your parents it was my idea.'

Bella sat on a bench, the snippet fading to a black-and-white memory again, staring at the birds flitting along the branches of a tree. She thought about her aunt and how she would feel about Bella and her plans. *What do you want me to do with your house, Aunt Flo? All I wrote down before I came out here was 'How to Make it Better' and 'Information on Selling'. But I don't know how to measure 'better'.*

The busker began to strum his guitar. Bella stood up and, as she walked to the next square, burst out laughing when she realised he was singing, 'There Are More Questions Than Answers'. She shook her head, giggling, then began to search for the building with the lime-green tiles, where, the instructions had said, *'The mobile phone shop is opposite and you can get information on setting up the internet there.'*

Stopping off in the square for a drink on the way back, Bella scrolled through her phone for information about storks, wondering why they were protected. Logging onto a site called 'I Love Storks', she read through the information and took a screenshot of a paragraph she found at the bottom.

Under decree law 140/99 storks and their nests are protected in Portugal. The law protects them against the disturbance,

removal or destruction of their nests outside authorised peri-
ods. Permission to remove the nests has to be requested from
the ICNF (Institute for Nature and Forest Conservation).
The ICNF are responsible for stipulating if, how and when
any nests can be moved.

Despite the fact that there were no storks at her aunt's house, in the spirit of 'you can never have too much information', she would add it to her spreadsheet once she got access to it. She left some money for her drink and got up. On the wall behind next to the exit was a poster advertising the House on the Hill, Ignacio's yoga, mindfulness and dance studio in Lagos. She took a photo of it and decided to add it to the list of things to research when she got home too. When the broadband had been connected.

As she walked off her phone pinged several times. There were three voicemails from work, a couple of WhatsApp messages and some texts. Bella squinted at it and sighed as she read the first text:

I know you made it clear on the handover that you weren't
available for any calls for three weeks, but no one can find
the final report for the board you did before you left. HELP!
Joanna.

The second one read:

Final report missing — where is it? Kirk

The third one read:

Apologies for interrupting your Portuguese sojourn, but we are
all running around like headless chickens here. Not like you
to leave without every t crossed and every i dotted. So, where
is the financial report? Lil P.S. we're all missing you already
and it's only the first full day of your break!

Bella felt her jaw clench irritably, so she crossed the road and sat on the wall along the river, deciding not to listen to the voicemails or look at the messages as she knew they'd all be the same. She called Lil.

'Hi.' Her colleague sounded very flustered. 'I'm so sorry. I know your out-of-office is on, but we've got this board meeting in three hours, and I need to read the report before I go in.'

'I've filed it in the F drive, where I always do.' Bella tried to sound assertive and calm at the same time.

'Is it?' Lil started clicking a keyboard very loudly.

'Yes . . .' Bella listened patiently.

'Oh my God! It is. Why couldn't we find it?'

'I can't answer that, but I'm glad you've got it.' Bella began to amble along the avenida towards the footbridge over to the marina.

'I think we all panicked because you've gone so quickly. Even though you'll be working from there soon but . . .' Lil's voice started to rise. 'We can't do without you, Bella.'

'That's good to know. But yes you can.' Bella laughed. 'Honestly, it's all there. Just have confidence.'

'Before I go,' Lil sounded like she was gathering files from a desk — Why didn't you answer our messages straight away? You always do. It sent us over the edge I think.'

'There's no internet connection at the house as yet and only sporadic mobile phone signal,' Bella replied.

'Oh my God, you'll go mad. You without instant access to the internet.' Lil guffawed, then coughed. 'I've got to go. Enjoy the rest of whatever it is you're doing.'

'Thank you.' Bella smiled despite herself and put some coins in the hat of a Charlie Chaplin living statue as she walked past. 'I won't go mad without it. Just a bit irritated.'

Lil lowered her voice conspiratorially. 'I think you should have a holiday romance. Get on Portuguese dating apps immediately.'

'I'm not on holiday, Lil. Business trip. I mean—' Bella felt her face turn red.

'We came up with that list, didn't we? After Gino.'

'Well . . .'

'I don't think connections are about lists though. I think you meet someone and there's something you maybe can't identify and you go from there.'

'When I thought about Gino after the list we made he pretty much ticked every box. It wasn't just rational, it was instinctive too.'

'He's in San Francisco now though.'

Bella hesitated for a moment, trying to think of a response that would make sense of that. In the end she said, 'Yes, but—'

'But?'

'I like men who are organised, ambitious, respectful.' Bella mentally ran through her list again. 'Optimistic, fit, financially independent, sexy, attractive.'

'Well, you can't quantify the last two, can you?' Lil laughed.

Bella began to laugh. 'I thought you had to rush back to work for that meeting.'

'Yes, I do. Look after yourself. Bye.' She put the phone down.

Bella thought of the note Gino had left on her pillow after he'd cleared his things out of her flat.

It's been a blast. But you're so work oriented I can't see a future. Bye, Bella. G x

Said the man who was glued to his computer from 7 a.m. till 10 p.m. every day, had been her first thought.

It was as if you'd left six months before you'd actually left, was her second thought.

I felt at the end you were just a lodger, was her third thought. *A very tidy and contained lodger who used to complain if I left a dish unwashed or a slipper discarded, or a T-shirt left on the bed. No wonder I disappeared into my work.*

And then she started to cry.

* * *

Bella spent the afternoon cleaning the kitchen cupboards, standing on chairs to disperse cobwebs in dusty dark corners, eventually clambering down after trying unsuccessfully to prod a large cobweb away. Then she began to move the pink-and-lime chest of drawers out from the wall, somehow hurting her shoulder as she did.

'Ow!' Pain shot around her back. Out of the corner of her eye she thought she saw something move, but when she looked again, she couldn't see anything.

The cats appeared in the doorway. Bella slid to the ground and looked at the ceiling. Yin and Yang wandered over to her and sat at her feet.

'I need to stretch and relax. I need yoga,' she told them, pulling herself up from the floor using the furniture. She picked up her phone from the table. There was still no signal, so she grabbed her bag, put on her sunglasses, locked the door behind her and headed towards Hugo's café and the elusive Wi-Fi.

Pink blossom hung from the trees lining the track to the road, the spring sun glowing welcomingly, warming her back and relaxing her aching muscles. Music drifted from the café and she heard voices talking animatedly, growing louder as she got closer.

Turning onto the pathway to the sea she realised that this time, she wasn't the only customer. A large group of people were drinking coffee, studying maps, scrolling through information on their phones and talking animatedly. Their tables were strewn with binoculars and sun hats, with multicoloured walking poles lying on the floor around them.

'Hello, neighbour. Are you taking up birdwatching?' Hugo had put a tray of drinks down on a table.

Bella smiled, wondering that if she saw him often enough, he would become less handsome due to familiarity, then decided to look up the psychology of that once her internet was connected. 'Is that what this is?'

'It's spring, so great for birds. The estuary over there is a haven for the ones that are flying back from North Africa. It's like an avian airport hub like Heathrow or Frankfurt.'

'Ah. Maybe I'll get one or two interesting species in my garden.'

'I hope you don't.' Hugo walked over to her and said quietly, 'You'll be inundated with twitchers if they find out.'

'Twitchers?'

'Birdwatchers. It happened to me a few years ago, and to your aunt and Will. Some of them camped overnight.' He grimaced. 'Without our permission.'

'Oh dear.'

'What would you like to drink?' His face was serious so Bella wasn't sure if he'd found the episode funny or not.

'Just a latte please.'

'*Galão* coming up!' He nodded and walked away, pausing at another table to collect some plates.

Bella took her phone out of her bag, connected to the internet and booked herself a yoga class for the following morning, then scrolled through a list of estate and lettings agents to get an idea what kind of price she might get for selling or renting the house, taking screenshots of a few for reference.

Hugo came back with her drink and put it on the table.

'Maybe the twitchers could tell me about storks,' she said.

'If you ask them any questions about any kind of bird they will talk to you for ever and I will never get my tables back.' His face was unreadable again.

'I just want to know what would happen if the storks ever came back.'

'Unlikely. But if you sell it's not your problem, is it?'

Bella detected a slight frown. 'I'm only trying—'

A customer caught his attention. 'Excuse me,' he said, turning away to talk to them.

'—to gather information. It's what I do,' mumbled Bella.

Finishing her drink, she left the money on the table and decided to walk down to the sea before going back to the farmhouse. She took her shoes off and sighed as her feet touched the sand. It was cool and soft, so she wiggled her toes and set off, pausing occasionally to admire her footprints. Picking up some shells on the shoreline she breathed in the fresh, salty sea air and gazed at the sea, remembering.

Her father was standing waist deep in the water, laughing at her mother, who was attempting to catch the waves with a boogie board. Bella floated around on her back, watching the clouds drift past, until her father began to splash her.

'Dad!' Bella giggled, managing to stand up before attempting to pick up some water in her hand so she could throw it at him.

'Useless,' he guffawed, as she jumped and accidentally trickled it over her own head.

'She's just trying to surprise you with a different approach,' her mother said kindly.

Bella held up her arm and banged it onto the surface of the water, then pulled it out. 'I'm dragging the sea out,' she squealed, pushing it towards her dad. Then he picked her up, kissed her on the cheek and dropped her with a splash. Bella sank, immersed in the water, the world suddenly muted, until she burst out of the waves, shaking the sea out of her hair.

A droplet of rain touched Bella's face, followed by a steady pitter-patter as it hit the sand, dragging her back to the present. *Before the accident. Only a few months before. Is that why you got me here, Aunt Flo? To remember our last holiday before Dad got hurt? Because I had to grow up very quickly after that.*

She looked at the sea again to try to find her eight-year-old self, as the rain grew heavier, holding her arms out. She looked up at the sky, enjoying the feel of cool water, then turned and ran back to the path, allowing her hair to get steadily more wet, her clothes to cling to her body. By the time she reached the café, she was drenched.

'Oh dear, that was a sudden shower.' Hugo watched her as she took cover.

Bella laughed. 'Actually, it was surprisingly lovely.' She glanced down at her sodden trousers. 'I'd better be going.'

He looked at her, half amused. 'Can I lend you an umbrella?'

Bella turned her head to the sky. The rain showed no signs of stopping. 'Thanks. But I may as well give in, so no. In for a penny, in for a pound.'

'Your aunt loved walking in the rain.' He shook his head and smiled.

Bella nodded then hurried down the steps and along the track towards the house.

Standing under the terrace, she fished her keys out of her bag and watched her clothes drip into a satisfying puddle under her feet, then jumped up and down to shake as much moisture off them as possible. Looking around to check no one could see her, she took off her clothes and walked into her house, leaving them in a damp pile outside. 'Would have ruined the floor,' she told the cats, putting the keys on the table next to the door, where she had left the picture Ignacio had given her.

The amble by its very definition does not have to have an actual firm destination, often fizzling out in a café, on a beach, or in a shop en route. Although it isn't really en route as you are not actually going anywhere. You are ambling.

Bella looked at it for a few moments. 'As soon as the internet is connected I'll have absolutely no time for ambling,' she explained to it.

She walked up the stairs to the shower, her mind filling with a list of things she needed to do with every step, slowly leaving behind the eight-year-old Bella that had briefly reappeared in the rain.

CHAPTER 4

The House on the Hill stood just back from the road, perched above Lagos and the long, curved sands of Meia Praia beach. Bella drove into the car park and got out of the car, rolling her shoulders to try to get rid of the ache in her neck that had worsened overnight.

A small dark-haired woman in an expensive suit scurried down the steps, waving goodbye to someone inside. 'I have an appointment with a client in an hour,' she was saying. 'I probably shouldn't have come to the class.'

A woman of a similar age to Bella followed her. Bella admired her long, wavy, lustrous red hair, absent-mindedly touching her own, remembering that she hadn't had time for a visit to the hairdresser because she had been so busy making all the preparations to travel to Portugal.

'The meditation class is supposed to make you less stressed, not more, Elena.' The woman's voice was soft and calm and measured.

'Maybe I'll come to an evening next time. It's not relaxing having to bring my work clothes with me to change. I'm always in a hurry.' The woman climbed into her car. 'Tell Minnie and Ignacio that I'm going to Rio Formosa for some birdwatching on Friday if they want to join me.'

'I didn't know they had started birdwatching.'

'They haven't. But if I keep asking, I will wear them down.' The woman chuckled, then closed the door and turned the engine on.

The lady with red hair turned her attention to Bella. 'Hello. I'm Layla Garcia. Is this your first visit to the House on the Hill?'

'I'm here for the advanced Ashtanga Yoga. Bella Creswell. Did I hear your friend say Ignacio?'

'Yes — he teaches here. And welcome!' Layla beamed at her. 'It's in Studio One. If you follow me, I'll show you.'

The House on the Hill smelled of patchouli and lavender. Bella felt like she'd just opened her eyes after a particularly relaxing massage. 'What a lovely building,' she said, admiring the cool, grey-tiled floor and the plants dotted artfully around the hallway and up the staircase.

'Thank you. It belonged to my grandparents. I live here actually — most of the time. My partner Luke lives next door so when he's around I sometimes live there too.'

'It's a beautiful setting.' Bella glanced around as some Latin music began to pump from another room, before the door was slammed firmly shut.

'Zumba class.' Layla smiled. 'So, are you on holiday or a resident?'

'I've just inherited a house from my great-aunt, Florence Creswell, so I'm over for a little while to sort it out.'

'Flo?' Layla touched her arm. 'We were all so sad when she died. She used to come here every week.'

Ignacio strode out of the yoga studio. He was dressed in cream sweatpants and a T-shirt with a small the House on the Hill logo on the collar.

'Ignacio. This is Bella. Flo's niece. She's inherited her house.'

Ignacio grasped her hands. 'Welcome, Bella. How lovely to see you again! I'm glad you chose us for your yoga and mindfulness. Your great-aunt would have recommended us anyway, so . . .' He trailed off.

'I'm sure she would have.' Bella didn't know what else to say.

'Have you fallen in love with your great-aunt's house and decided to live here now?' His eyes lit up.

Bella shook her head, smiling. 'No — I'm going to sell it. I can work remotely for a few months if need be while I sort it out, but I'm not staying.'

'You won't have any problem selling. Or even renting.' An older woman with cropped white hair tinged with pink highlights rolled out into the hallway on a swivel chair from another room.

'Minnie. This is Bella, Flo's niece. And this is Minnie, my aunt.'

'Nice to meet you.' Bella smiled again, wondering if she was the only person in Lagos who didn't know her Great-Aunt Flo very well. 'I haven't spoken to any agents yet about it. I've only been here a few days.'

'Well, available land is being snapped up. I'll bet you get some developers after you for that. They used to plague Flo.' A phone rang in the office. Minnie ignored it. 'A house in only half an acre of land a few doors from Elena has been bought and they are building three luxury homes on it. Can you believe it!'

She rolled back into the office as Ignacio nodded gravely. 'They should be building affordable homes, you know. Or at least not just luxury villas worth millions of euros. I believe it's important to bring investment in, but people are being priced out of the area. It is a conundrum.'

The main door opened behind them and Layla's face lit up. 'Hugo! Do you need any help?'

'Yes please — I've got three more crates in the van.'

Bella turned around. Hugo stood in the doorway, carrying a box of oranges and wearing long grey shorts and a grey baseball cap. Sunlight flooded in behind him, framing his body in a glow. She remembered opening her eyes and seeing his face backlit after falling over the first time she met him and felt her face go a little red.

45

'Can someone help me carry them to the kitchen? I've got another delivery along the beach and I'm running late.'

'I've got ten minutes before class.' Ignacio walked over to him and took the crate. 'You get the others to the door, and I'll take them in.'

'Have you met your new neighbour yet?' Layla pointed at Bella. 'Flo's great-niece!'

'Ah.' He looked surprised. 'Yes, we have. I hope you dried off quickly last night.'

'I did. And had a very hot shower. Thank you.'

'Good.' He paused for a moment as Ignacio opened a door at the back of the hall. 'Better get going.' Hugo nodded and rushed outside.

'Lovely man.' Layla whispered to Bella.

Minnie poked her head around the office door. 'What were you two up to last night that you needed to dry off AND have a hot shower?' She raised her eyebrows.

Bella laughed, slightly embarrassed as Ignacio walked back through from the kitchen. 'Nothing — I've literally been here for less than a week. I don't move that fast.' She felt her face redden again.

'Ah, so you like him then?' Minnie smiled at her mischievously.

'I haven't even thought about it.' Bella said a bit louder than she intended.

'Don't be embarrassed. Everyone likes Hugo.' Layla touched her arm. 'It would be unusual if you didn't. Shall I show you to the room, even if it's just to get away from these two?'

Bella nodded gratefully, glad to get away, because, they were all right, she did find him attractive. But the last thing she wanted was a flirtation with her great-aunt's next-door neighbour. It would just complicate things.

Layla opened the door. 'Actually, if you're on your own, we are all heading down to Hugo's this evening to celebrate Ignacio's birthday. It'll be at seven, and you're more than

46

welcome to join us. Any friend — or relative — of Flo's is part of the family.'

'Oh.' Bella hesitated for a moment before deciding she would be better off out of the house than sitting in it alone with only her racing mind for company as she wondered what bit of the house to deal with next. 'Thank you. It is very quiet there at night. I lived in the middle of London and the silence is, in my opinion, much less relaxing than police sirens and screaming. So, a bit of company would be nice.'

'Do you dance at all?' Layla turned the light on in the studio, picked up a bottle of lavender essence and sprayed it around the room.

'Around my handbag?' Bella said uncertainly.

'We've got a DJ booked. Minnie rather likes to trip the light fantastic — salsa and tango-wise anyway. But you can just listen if you don't want to dance.'

Bella felt herself relax a smidgen. She hadn't realised she'd been so tense until she'd sensed the tiny releases of negative energy triggered by the most unexpected things — the cats, for one. The running through the rain on the beach. And now this.

'I need to get going on that spreadsheet as soon as possible.'

'Spreadsheet?' Layla pushed her long hair behind her ears.

'Did I say that out loud? I like things to be ordered. How I file my research. I'm a financial markets researcher in the city. And I've not done it for a few days, so I feel I'm drifting a bit.'

'Oh. I LOVE lists!' Layla laughed gleefully as another pupil pushed the door open and walked in.

Bella's phone pinged in her bag, so she took it out and checked it. 'At last,' she said. 'My internet is being connected tomorrow. Normal life can return, as can all the information about Flo's house I emailed myself before I came out!'

'Hello, all!' Ignacio banged the door open and strode inside. 'The class will start in ten minutes. In the meantime, grab a yoga mat from the store over there and get yourselves comfortable. And—' he picked up a remote control and pointed at the sound system '—remember this . . .'

'Special' by Lizzo began to blast around the room.

Layla raised her eyebrows. 'He likes to start his classes by playing uplifting music with a strong message. This one mainly for the past two months.' She laughed. 'Better go. Hopefully see you this evening.'

* * *

Feeling refreshed and slightly more relaxed after the class, Bella drove into town to have a look in some estate agents' windows. She crossed the road along the river and studied the photos of properties on sale in the window of the first one she saw — a mix of luxury villas, traditional cottages and high-spec apartments. None looked quite like the Nest. Hovering in the doorway, she decided not to go in, telling herself that once she'd got going on the spreadsheet again, she would have all the right information to ask the correct questions in order to get even more information.

A clock struck eleven in the distance, and she decided to stay for a while, because, she reasoned, when she got back to the house, she would need to get back to work, and her muscles were clearly grateful for the relaxing yoga class, so why upset them again so quickly?

Turning right away from the main road, Bella walked past a low, white abandoned building covered in artwork, the beginnings of orange bougainvillea starting to bloom through the almost non-existent roof, then rejoined the avenida next to the petrol station and looked around. *Which way next?* she thought. *Up the steep, cobbled street on my right or carry on along to where the road climbs up the hill. And why can't I make up my mind?*

Noticing a woman coming out of a shop eating what looked like a *pastel de nata* she decided to get one for herself and went inside, scanning the others in the display case.

'I'll have a *pastel de nata*, and . . . one of those.' She pointed at another cake.

'The orange roll?' the woman asked.

48

'Yes please.' Bella smiled.

'It's warmer today,' the woman behind the counter said, picking up the cakes and putting them in the bag. 'I think it'll be colder and wetter for the next day or so. But we need the rain. You never know at this time of the year. It can be hot, it can be cold, it can be wet, it can be dry, it can be windy.' She laughed. 'Sometimes all in one day.'

She put the bag on the counter and tapped the prices into the till.

'It's really lovely whatever the weather.' The sight of the cakes had put Bella in a better mood.

'It is. Soon it will be very hot, and all the visitors will come.' The lady pointed at the numbers on the till. 'Cash or card?'

'Card.' Bella waved her phone at the card machine. 'Thank you,' she said. 'What is that in Portuguese?'

'*Obrigada.*'

'*Obrigada,*' repeated Bella.

'*Até a próxima vez.*' The woman smiled. 'Until the next time.'

'*Até a próxima vez.*' Bella waved at her from the doorway, stepped onto the street and took a bite out of the pastry.

Her focus would come back once the internet was connected and she could compile her lists, she resolved, heading across the road to enjoy the breeze, then striding westwards towards the tiny fort at the head of the river. She took another bite of the pastry and wondered if, actually, her focus would come back if she just ate more cake and therefore more sugar.

And then she stopped. *You're ambling,* her inner voice whispered.

'No,' she announced to the empty path in front of her. 'I'm doing some research.'

* * *

The man from the telecoms company arrived at 2 p.m. and left at two thirty, after which Bella took her laptop from its

49

case, plugged it in, and connected it to the internet. She almost leaped to her feet when she clicked on Google and didn't get a little circle going round and round slowly and endlessly.

'Right.' She rubbed her hands together as the cats jumped onto the table and watched her log onto her emails, find the one she'd sent herself with the spreadsheet called *'Great-Aunt Flo's House'*, and download it. Taking a deep breath, she opened it, feeling she was welcoming an old, familiar and very sensible and focused friend into the house. She opened the section labelled *'SELLING'*.

There were three tabs named *'POSITIVE'*, *'NEGATIVE'* and *'TO DO'*. Under *'POSITIVE'*, she had written: *House owned completely by me — no mortgage.*

Next to that were other subheadings named *'Financial'*, *'Legal'*, *'Quality of House'*, *'Quality of Land'*. In the section called *'RENTING LONG-TERM — BACKUP PLAN ONLY'*, there were three tabs named *'POSITIVE'*, *'NEGATIVE'* and *'TO DO'*. Under *'POSITIVE'* she had written: *House owned completely by me — no mortgage.*

Next to that were other subheadings named *'Financial'*, *'Legal'*, *'Quality of House'*, *'Quality of Land'*. Bella liked her spreadsheets to look exactly the same so she could compare her notes easily.

Yin or Yang stretched, putting a paw onto the keyboard. Bella scratched the cat's ear and gently moved it away. 'Where shall I put you?' she said gently.

She filled in the positive sections in the general sections under both renting and selling and wrote: *Cats — what will happen if other people live here — will they stay, will they be welcome?*

She looked at it for a moment, decided it didn't make sense, so added another tab labelled *'Miscellaneous'* and added the cats to that.

'I'll work it out,' she muttered, opening the other section titled *'Things to do'*, then closed it again quickly. 'Later.' She shut the laptop and stood, deciding it was time to get ready for her impromptu night out. 'Better than staying in with all this noisy silence!' she told the cats.

* * *

She stared at herself in the bathroom mirror, mentally adding giving it a good clean to her to-do list as she rubbed a clear patch in the middle with her fingers. Her hair looked lank and lifeless, and her eyebrows needed some care and attention too. She sighed, wondering whether she could be bothered to go out, as it was obvious she needed more than twenty minutes to look like she belonged at any kind of celebration at all.

Rummaging around her make-up bag, she pulled out her tweezers and plucked her eyebrows, then put on her make-up. Pulling her hands through her hair, she tried to make it look a little fuller and less flat, then attempted to cover the clear patch on the mirror with dust and stared at herself again. *Much better*, she thought, as she could barely see herself through the dirt.

She put on a long blue jersey dress, sensible black shoes and a patterned silk scarf, walked downstairs, found a torch in a kitchen drawer in case she needed to light the way along the lane, and grabbed her bag. She opened the door and stopped, catching a glimpse of herself in the small mirror in the living room. 'I can't go out with this hair. I just can't,' she announced to Yin and Yang, who were now fast asleep on the sofa, then ran back upstairs and searched through her luggage for something to tie her hair back with. Moving on to the chest of drawers in case she'd already unpacked something and put it away, she pulled out the bottom drawer and noticed a little yellow velvet bag. It wasn't hers.

She opened it, deciding that as it was Flo's she would have to investigate its contents anyway. Inside were some bright and colourful necklaces, bracelets and decorated hair bands. Bella smiled, feeling as if she'd accidentally bumped into Great-Aunt Flo.

Picking out a bright blue Alice band, she could almost see Flo standing in the middle of a room surrounded by people, pushing her back to that holiday again. Flo had stood in front of a large mirror in the spare bedroom, twirling around in a blue dress with a wide white petticoat underneath, swishing it to and fro, laughing while Bella sat on the bed watching her, longing to twirl around in a swishy dress too. 'Here you are.' Flo had handed her a pink Alice band '—you're a bit small to wear my clothes, but try this.'

Bella had jumped off the bed and taken it. 'Thanks, Auntie Flo,' she'd said, putting it on and standing next to her aunt in front of the mirror.

'I think we're ready to go out now. Your mum and dad are waiting downstairs, and I think your father is hungry. Grumpy hungry. And so, we have to hurry so we can make sure he gets food in his tummy.' Flo had rubbed her stomach and licked her lips.

Bella had squealed in delight, and Flo had adjusted the hairband on her great-niece's head. 'There you are. Perfect.'

Bella touched her hair, back in the present, wondering which long-forgotten memories would arrive out of nowhere next.

An old photograph pushed to the back of the drawer caught her attention as she put the velvet bag back where she'd found it. She pulled it out of the drawer gently and examined it. It was a photograph of Flo and a handsome man with jet-black hair. They were standing under the tree next to the gate outside the house, gazing into each other's eyes and laughing. Bella smiled. Flo looked so happy. She turned the photo over. On the back, her aunt had written, *Me and F. Our special place*.

She put it back where she'd found it, deciding sorting through old photographs and knick-knacks was not at the top of her list of things to do, and walked into another bedroom to find the mirror, put the band on her head, fiddled with her hair for a moment and went back down the stairs.

Outside, the moon hung in the distance, casting a shimmering glow over the trees, the only sound the constant roar of the sea. Switching on her torch she headed down the track to the lane, pausing under the jacaranda tree next to the gate. Tall bushes and tree branches blocked the moonlight so she looked steadily at the floor as she walked to make sure she didn't trip over, still not at ease with the lack of people, traffic and sound of sirens.

As she got closer to the beach, the sound of laughter and music grew louder. The car park was full, and Bella stood for a moment, mesmerised, as she watched the movement and blur of colour inside.

Ignacio waved at her and weaved his way to the entrance to beckon her in. 'You came!' he shouted. 'Come on. I'll introduce you to everyone. Well, not everyone. I don't know everyone. I told people to bring one friend each. So, some I don't and some I do.'

He took Bella's hand and guided her in as the music changed to the conga, and several people jumped to their feet.

'Oh, this is a bit early in the night for this,' he shouted, as he got swept away. Bella stood watching the line snake around the room until someone grabbed her and latched her onto the back. She laughed, surprised, and giggled as Layla and Minnie jumped up behind her and joined in.

Dancing past the kitchen, she locked eyes briefly with Hugo, who was standing in the doorway holding two trays, calmly waiting for the conga to finish trailing past. Something close to a smile flickered across his face. Bella decided he had a nice smile, even though it lasted for less than a second, and wondered what he would look like if he was laughing.

And then the music stopped.

'Come and join us over here.' Layla sat down and patted a chair next to her.

'This is Elena, our accountant, and Jorge, her nephew, who's in finance.'

They both said hello as she sat down.

'Over here is Duarte da Silva — family friend.'

'Hello.' Duarte leaned forward. 'You are Florence's great-niece?'

'Yes, I am.' Bella was expecting him to ask if she was going to sell the property or say something about selling the land.

But he didn't. 'Wonderful woman. Sorely missed. How are you finding The Nest?'

Julian the quiet waiter placed a drink in front of her. 'Everyone gets a free *copo de vinho verde*,' he mumbled, then walked off.

'Thank you.' Bella looked back at Duarte. 'I've only been here a few days. But it's lovely so far. Needs a bit of TLC.'

'I'm sure you'll give it what it needs.' He picked up his drink. 'Here's to Flo, and here's to you, Bella.'

'A toast to better times for the Nest,' said Layla, and they all picked up their glasses and took a sip, then put them down.

'Your aunt was very interested in my Living Statue charity festival.' Duarte leaned forward and smiled.

'I think she was just being polite.' Minnie turned to Bella. 'She was very kind and empathetic. And,' she said more quietly, 'understood Duarte's — how shall I describe it — need to constantly have new things to aim for. He basically has what is known as ants in his pants.'

'I heard that, Minnie.' He laughed so loudly, everyone grinned. 'She said it was an excellent idea. She and Hugo were setting up a charity and I said this would be a good way of raising money and awareness.' Duarte picked up his phone and scrolled through the photographs. 'Very left field, she said.' He held up a picture so Bella could see. 'I'm planning on doing it next year. In the meantime, I'm honing my craft.'

'Oh.' Bella studied the photo. He was posing on a plinth in a black Elvis wig.

'I'm practising his dance — you know, the swivel-hips one — for when people put coins in the hat.' Duarte smiled.

'I thought you were focusing on producing films?' Minnie nudged him playfully. 'Or is this the general life of a billionaire, one passion after another?'

'Films take a long time. I'm doing this to give myself a creative boost in the meantime. And take the stress away from my property portfolio. And as for the record company, well . . .' He closed his eyes for a moment and rubbed his temple. 'I donate a lot of money to charity, but I also take the coins people put in my hat and take them to the soup kitchen or the charity shop.' He looked over at Hugo. 'The charity Flo was working with Hugo on was for children from deprived areas of some of our cities to get experience in environmental work.' He put his phone down. 'It all got paused when she died. I think she helped encourage him along and he's lost momentum. We all did. Maybe by next year he will have regained his motivation.' He turned back to Bella. 'I hope you will come to the event. It will be all day.'

'I won't be here next year, I'm afraid. I've got a lot of commitments at home — work, my parents — so I'll be back to my London life by then.'

He patted her hand kindly. 'Everyone says that.'

Elena put her drink down just as the DJ put on 'Oye Cómo Va'. 'Ah a cha cha cha,' she said, standing up. 'May I borrow Ignacio, Minnie?'

'Go ahead.' Minnie leaned back in her chair and took another drink. 'I do love this place.' She glanced at Hugo, who was leaning by the bar watching the party. 'And Hugo. He needs someone new in his life. Honestly, the irony of who his ex went to work for.' Bella felt herself being scrutinised. 'He needs a wonderful woman who isn't prone to deceit or unkindness.'

Bella's mind was racing with questions, but Jorge stood up before she could ask any. 'Would you like to dance?' He held his hand out to her.

Ignacio and Elena cha-cha'd past. 'I can't dance like them. But I'd like a dance.'

'No one can dance like them!' Jorge laughed. 'Let's just move around in time to the music and hope for the best.'

Bella nodded and took his hand. 'Thank you. It's nice to let my hair down a bit — it's been a while!'

For the next hour she managed to relax, enjoying the atmosphere and getting to know Flo's friends better. When the music changed to 'I've Had the Time of My Life', the whole room almost erupted into mass singing and dancing. Everyone stood up, and Minnie and Ignacio appeared to be channelling their inner Baby and Johnny. Minnie made a run at Ignacio, who dodged out of the way rather than catching her and holding her above his head. They both doubled up in laughter, and Bella began to laugh too. Then out of nowhere, a wave of tiredness swept over her. She put a hand over her mouth so no one could see her yawn and decided to slip out quietly. She picked up her bag and walked towards the door, waving goodbye to the people who had been sitting around her.

The breeze caught her as she stepped outside, a wave of salt, sand and fresh, clear air washing over her. The moon had inched behind the clouds, leaving a few stars twinkling in the gaps between them, briefly bright in the looming darkness. She watched the white crust on the crashing waves thundering onto the beach, and thought about what she would normally be doing on a Wednesday night in April. Watching passers-by on the street below is what, she realised, wondering what the man in the blue bobble hat who walked his dog past her flat every night at eight thirty was listening to on his headphones, or the lady who nipped to the convenience store opposite like clockwork at 9 p.m. every day of the week would be buying today — a bottle of milk, several bags of crisps, or a box of wine.

A blast of 'Despacito' burst out of the bar as the door opened behind her and was muted as it banged shut.

'Can I drive you home?' It was Jorge. 'The streetlights stop well before the lane to your great-aunt's house. I mean your house.'

'Oh. It's fine, thank you. The walk will do me good.'

'Not if you fall in a pothole in the dark — the track is a challenge to walk on, isn't it?'

Bella hesitated, then gave in. 'Yes, you know. You're right. That's really kind of you.'

He smiled and pulled his hand through his wavy fair hair. 'I didn't know your aunt but from what I hear she would have wanted us to look after you.'

She climbed in and did up her seat belt.

'I have only been here a few months. My aunt Elena knew someone who was looking for a financial expert and I decided I wanted a change from Lisbon.' He started the car and began to drive. 'So if you need any advice before deciding what you need to do regarding the house, just ask. Portuguese law is different from UK law in these things probably. I'm happy to give you some pointers.' He shook his head. 'At least you'll have an idea before you get involved with solicitors and paying them for advice!'

'Oh.' Bella smiled at him. 'Thank you. Haven't quite hit the ground running on that. Thought I would.' Her voice trailed off.

'You have been here less than a week.'

'I suppose.'

'And given the time it took to sort out your great-aunt's affairs, you have only very recently found out about this new responsibility?'

'Yes.' Bella glanced at him, warming to his kind face and comforting voice.

'Here we are.' He turned right into the lane and slowed as he drove down the track to the house and up the driveway. 'I want to protect the suspension.' He laughed.

Another thing to think about, thought Bella. *The state of the car . . .*

'I know a few parties who would be interested in buying. So, if and when you're ready, I can put you in touch with them.'

He stopped the car outside the Nest. It was pitch black except for the light the car headlights threw out onto the ground, illuminating the few steps to the front door.

'I forgot to put the light on inside before I left.' Bella sighed, getting her keys out of her bag. 'I live in the centre of London and it is never ever completely dark.

'There are probably security lights. ' Jorge got out of the car and walked around to open her door. 'The switch is probably in the utility room. Just check through the instructions on how to use them in the welcome pack Ignacio gave you.'

'Right!' Bella got out and held her hand. 'Thank you.'

He kissed her on both cheeks. 'This is Portugal,' he said. 'No handshakes necessary between friends.'

'Of course. I'll get used to it.' She walked to the door. He got back in the car and drove away, waving, once she'd opened it and turned on the porch light.

'Nice man,' she told Yin and Yang, who wandered over to greet her. 'Now to bed in my very quiet house.'

Pouring herself a glass of water she leaned against the sink, the silence almost deafening, interrupted only by the ticking of the clock on the kitchen wall and the roar of the waves. An animal squealed outside.

'Oh . . .' She shivered, looking at her phone and taking it to the living room. She sat for a few minutes trying to reconnect it to the internet, put on an ambient natural rainforest soundtrack to cover the quiet and occasional real natural noise outside and stood up. As she did, she noticed something scurrying up the wall behind the chest of drawers and leaped to her feet, screaming.

'What are you?' she shouted, rushing into the utility room and grabbing a broom, which she held in front of her, ready to deal with whatever was hiding in the living room. The cats watched her disinterestedly, then ambled out into the kitchen. A gecko ran along the wall and disappeared behind a clock.

'Geckos in the house!' She turned to the cats, who were sitting by their bowls. 'What do I do?' She looked at the wall again and saw another, smaller one scurrying down to the chest of drawers. She froze, her heart thumping, wondering whether there were any more hiding in any other rooms.

She stood with the broom in her hand pointing at the wall for a minute or so, unsure of how long she should stand guard. Feeling exhausted, she decided to take refuge in her bed and deal with her new guests in the morning. So she ran up the stairs, still carrying the broom, pulled the bedsheets open to check there was nothing there, knocked the wall a few times with the broom, cleaned her teeth very, very quickly, and climbed into bed, wrapping herself up in the sheets as protection.

CHAPTER 5

Bella woke as soon as it was light, opening her eyes and scanning the walls and ceiling to make sure there were no more skittery uninvited guests, rolled over to check there was nothing under the bed, then gingerly got up and hurried to the bathroom, after which she picked up the broom and tiptoed down the stairs.

Taking a deep breath, she pulled the chest of drawers away from the wall, then jumped back, in readiness for doing something. Although she had no idea what she would do. She liked geckos — when they were outside, that is. She had never imagined a day when she would be sharing a house with them.

'Of course I wouldn't,' she said to Yin and Yang, who had both jumped off the sofa and were doing their early-morning stretching exercises. 'I lived in London. Although I have no idea what I was sharing my flat with, to be honest.'

After a few moments, Bella decided any geckos were firmly in hiding, so pushed the furniture back into place and went into the kitchen to make a cup of tea.

She carried it through to the living room, sat down at the table and opened her computer so she could put her thoughts in order ready for a day of thorough research about house prices.

She sighed and took a gulp of her drink, her fingers hovering over the keyboard. Then she dramatically began to type, adding to *Positives* under all the headings: *Jorge can offer advice — more info soon.*

Then she set up a separate folder in preparation for the advice he would offer to be summarised and placed succinctly in the correct place.

One of the cats jumped on her lap. 'Right, Yin. Or Yang. I'm going to have a proactive day. Off to the beach for a morning walk to get the mind juices going, then into town to blitz estate agents. And—' she picked up her phone and opened a language app she had downloaded the night before she'd flown out '—immersive Portuguese for as long as the phone signal holds out.'

She set off down the track, enjoying the birdsong, and wondering why the quiet was wonderfully relaxing during daylight and somehow terrifying at night. With each step, she tried to work out a trail around the city, based on a list of estate agents she had made, and the time it should take, factoring in a couple of coffee breaks along the route. She reminded herself as she did that she was here to do a job — dealing with the property and, in a few weeks' time, her own paid job — so that just because she was staying in a kind of holiday idyll, she shouldn't allow herself to be sucked into enjoying herself too much. Because that's how she kept on top of all her responsibilities at home — timetabling everything, including rest and relaxation.

She put her earbuds in, connected to the 'Learn Portuguese at your own pace' app and switched it on.

'Good morning,' said the voice. '*Bom dia*. Repeat.'

'*Bom dia*,' said Bella.

'Good afternoon. *Boa tarde*. Repeat.'

'*Boa tarde*.' Bella smiled.

'Good night. *Boa noite*. Repeat.'

'*Boa noite*,' echoed Bella. Climbing over a dune, she knelt down to do up an untidy shoelace.

'Hello. *Olá*. Repeat.'

She stood up. '*Olá* . . .' She stopped. '*Olá* . . . Oh . . .'

Hugo was striding out of the sea, shaking the water out of his hair in what Bella thought was a very movie-star-like way. And wearing a well-fitted wetsuit in, she decided also, a very movie-star-like way. Pausing on the sand, he turned back to face the shore and began a series of yoga moves.

'How are you? *Como está?* Rep—' The signal dropped out halfway through the word.

'The café . . .' She realised Hugo had seen her and he was now walking towards her shouting something, but his words were swept away by the breeze.

Bella stood still and waved. 'Hello. What? I didn't hear,' she shouted.

Hugo arrived at the bottom of the dune. 'The café isn't open yet,' he yelled.

'I know. I'm here for a bracing walk. Isn't the water very cold?' She didn't know what else to say as he came up to her.

'That's what the wetsuit is for.' He almost smiled.

Bella found it attractive and told herself to stop finding it attractive. *Although to be honest, it has been a while,* she thought, trying to remember the exact date when Gino had left — physically rather than emotionally.

'How about I make you a coffee anyway?'

It's just a coffee. Bella's sensible inner voice made an appearance. *Just, you know, remember that he is your neighbour — temporarily. No emotional stuff. Repeat: no emotional stuff.*

Bella smiled at him. 'Oh, thank you. That will set me up nicely for the day.'

Just, well, don't find him attractive. OK? Her inner voice was trying to sound assertive.

Hugo turned to walk towards the café and Bella watched him go.

'Oh, right, that's easy. Not.'

Bella realised she'd said that out loud.

'I didn't quite catch that?' Hugo looked back.

'I said . . . um . . . At this time of the morning the beach is very . . . attractive?' she couldn't stop her voice trailing upwards uncertainly.

'Attractive.' He smiled. 'That's . . . I suppose . . . Yes, it is. Beautiful. Gorgeous. Entrancing.'

He paused, waiting, Bella decided, for her to say something interesting.

'Magical, mysterious. Sandy?'

Hugo laughed loudly and continued to chuckle as Bella followed him back to the café.

He pushed open the door. 'Shall we sit out here? It's sheltered and we can still enjoy the fresh air.' He picked up two padded seats and put them on the chairs. '*Galão*?'

'Milky coffee in a glass like a latte, *galão*?' Bella grinned and sat down.

'Coming up.' He went back into the café while Bella sat and stared at the view. It felt still and full of life at the same time, the beach curving elegantly along the bay, the golden rocks of Ponta da Piedade glowing at one end, the cliffs above Alvor at the other, the sky a light, steely blue above the waves. Seagulls danced across the water, lifted by the air, and an ocean liner glided along the horizon, out towards the wide Atlantic.

'If I could paint that view and hang it on my wall, I would.' Hugo put her drink in front of her and sat down.

'It is rather glorious.' She picked up the glass. 'Do you go for early-morning swims every day?'

Hugo was now in jeans and a T-shirt. 'When I can. Life can get a bit busy, so when I've got time I come down. All through the year.'

'I'd love to swim in the sea myself, but I'm very much a warm water person.' Bella glanced at him. His hair was still damp, curling down to the top of his neck, just above a tattoo of what looked like the sail of a boat. She wondered what the rest of it looked like, then shook her head. *That kind of thought is not allowed. Have other thoughts.*

'Are you OK?' Hugo leaned towards her.

'Yes, a fly or something was buzzing around.' Bella took a long gulp of her drink. 'So, how long have you had the café?'

'For ever. It belonged to my parents. The house next to yours is my family home. I was born there and I grew up there. So, for me I have been there for ever too.'

'So, you always knew my great-aunt then?'

'Yes. She helped me to change the smallholding to be more sustainable. It always needs more work, but she was very supportive. She was helping me with a charitable venture too. All about the land.'

'I live in a flat in the middle of a city.' Bella turned her attention to the sea again. 'I buy everything with the environment in mind. But, well, I don't even have a balcony. There is a shared garden though. It's nice . . .' She trailed off, thinking about the things she'd left behind. There wasn't much. Not even a pot plant.

'So, if I was strange with you the first time we met, I apologise.' Hugo stood up and held out his hand. 'Both your aunt and I have been under pressure from developers over recent years — some ethical, some not. I understand you need to do what you need to do. Let's shake on that.'

Bella got up and took his hand. 'Yes. Of course,' she murmured, momentarily staring into his deep, chocolate-brown eyes.

They both sat down. 'When you said some weren't ethical . . . ?' Bella took a sip of her drink.

'There is a shortage of affordable housing. Like in a lot of places. And luxury villas bring in money, I know. But it has to be in keeping with the surroundings and some people don't care.'

'You still haven't defined unethical.' Bella picked up her drink again.

'Before the storks left there was one who would have knocked the whole place down without getting the right permission. He told your aunt. She kept saying "the storks are here, you can't do anything to the house anyway", and he'd tell her it didn't matter. They'd keep it quiet. Don't need to tell anyone.'

'But now the storks have gone?'

'After your aunt died. It was strange . . . but . . .' He looked at her. 'Mother nature, eh? And, you know, I don't think anyone would get permission to build on the land here — I don't think it's good building land. But still they try. Maybe they think the regulations will change.'

A clock chimed eight in the distance. 'Right, I'd better get going.' Hugo stood up. 'Take your time. And I'd like to show you the smallholding so you can see what is next door to you.'

'Of course.'

He opened the sliding doors. 'Tomorrow morning? It's my day off. Sort of. Around ten? My accountant is coming around at ten thirty so it will be a quick look, but as we're neighbours, I'd like you to understand what I am about.'

'Works for me,' Bella agreed. She wanted to understand that too.

CHAPTER 6

Hugo strode out of the waves, his body glistening in the sun. Pushing his hair out of his eyes he looked up and smiled, waving at Bella as she sat on the sand. 'You should come in,' he shouted. 'It is beautiful.'

Bella moved towards him, unable to stop herself, drawn by his positive energy and . . . 'Shh,' she whispered. 'You'll frighten it off.'

'Yes, shhh,' whispered Hugo. 'Has no one told you that silence in these situations is imperative . . .'

Bella opened her eyes, stuck halfway between her dream and something else entirely.

'What?' she said out loud, sitting up.

No one said anything. She laid back down again and glanced at the clock. It was 6.45 a.m. Eating cheese late last night had been a bad idea. Rolling over, she closed her eyes and tried to get back to sleep.

'Can you see it?'

Opening her eyes again, Bella pulled the sheet over her head, wishing people wouldn't talk so loudly at the bus stop early in the morning.

Then she sat bolt upright. She wasn't in London. She was in an old farmhouse at the end of a track in the Algarve. 'That was an actual voice, wasn't it?'

Yin and Yang lay fast asleep at the end of the bed and didn't reply.

'Yes. Yes. Over there. It's beautiful, isn't it?'

The voice was outside the house.

Clambering out of bed, she ran downstairs, her heart racing, then grabbed a mop from the cupboard and crept to the front door just as she heard footsteps outside.

Brandishing her mop she opened the door and pulled herself to her full height, trying to look as fierce as possible, while attempting to not hyperventilate.

A man in a white hat and blue shorts was holding a pair of binoculars and staring through them at something in the distance.

Bella tried to quell the shakiness in her voice by shouting. 'Who are you and what are you doing in my garden?'

He jumped and turned around, accompanied by disappointed chattering nearby.

'It's gone now.'

'For goodness' sake.'

'Where do you think it's flown to?'

'Near Hugo's house? He'll never let us close.'

'Why did you do that?' The man with the binoculars was looking at her, his face red and angry.

Bella held the mop up as if it was a spear. 'What? I've opened my front door at just after six thirty in the morning to find a load of people trespassing on my property.'

'Your property?' The man looked confused. 'Nobody lives here.'

'Clearly they do. I do.' Bella counted the number of strangers who were standing in a cluster near the gate. There were twelve of them.

'But Flo passed so long ago. We thought the place was empty and was going to be sold to developers.' He took her

67

hand and clasped it. 'I'm so very sorry. I'm Hans Karlsson. We are the local birdwatching group.'

'Right.' Bella watched the others as they all bowed their heads, apparently in embarrassment.

'There were reports of a very rare migrating bird in the area, and we tracked it to your garden.'

'It's gone now though. Because of the noise.'

Bella looked at the group. 'Who said that?' She waved the mop again. 'You frightened the life out of me.'

They all looked at the ground again.

'Did you know Flo?' Hans seemed to be trying to calm the situation down.

'I'm her great-niece. She left the property to me.'

'Ah.' He waved at his friends. 'This is Flo's great-niece. This is hers now.'

A murmur of appreciation rippled through the group.

'This area isn't protected but it is so close to the Alvor Estuary that sometimes we used to come and camp in the garden overnight in the spring to see what birds we could see.'

'Oh, did you?' Bella's heart had stopped racing and she leaned the mop against the wall.

'It is such a magical place. We were so worried that someone would come along and buy the land and build all over it.'

'I'm selling the house, probably, but not to just anyone.'

'Ah. OK — just be careful with who you deal with then.'

'Elena did tell us we shouldn't be here,' a woman said loudly. 'We should have listened.'

Hans shook his head. 'She does tend to fuss though, so I ignored her.'

'Well maybe next time, listen.' The woman's voice grew louder. 'I only came because clever clogs here—' she pointed at a man with a walking stick standing next to her '—said he was going to drive. And I didn't want him to have *another* accident.'

'I am so sorry.' Hans sighed. 'We get very excited sometimes.'

'Shall we go to the estuary anyway?' the woman suggested. 'It'll be awash with amateurs.' She almost spat the words out.

'But at least we won't be trespassing. And the bird has gone now so it's not worth hanging around near here.'

Everyone nodded and murmured then, at the same time, waved, turned around and walked collectively down the track.

Hans shook her hand. 'Thank you for your understanding.' He watched his friends go. 'Sometimes I think we've been looking at wildlife for so long, we all look like a flock of birds too when we're together.'

Bella laughed, following their progress as they disappeared around a corner. 'It's nice to meet you, Hans. Even if the circumstances were a little strange.'

He nodded. 'I hope we didn't frighten you.' His face was serious again.

'Not too much.' Bella picked up the mop. 'I'll take this in and start the day again I think.'

Hans nodded then walked down the steps, waving as he got to the track, and followed his friends towards the beach.

A flutter of leaves and branches behind her caught her attention. A large black bird with feathers flecked with electric blue stretched its wings in a tree at the side of the house.

'Oh hello,' she whispered, sitting on the step. 'Where were you hiding? Don't worry. Your secret's safe with me. I won't tell them you were here.'

She looked at the light pink blossom in the tree opposite, then winced as the memory of what she'd been dreaming about came back. 'Oh no. Oh dear. I'm due at his house at ten.'

Inside, she sat down at her computer, and calmed herself down by adding monthly electricity and water costs to her lists of financial facts and wrote: *Find out how far the house is from the natural park — will this impact the value — I need to know so I know the estate agents are providing accurate valuations* — to her list.

She closed the laptop, got up and made herself some breakfast, her mind now ordered and settled. Then she put her headphones on, clicked on her Portuguese language app on her phone, and listened to it while loading the dishwasher.

* * *

Bella stood next to the gate to Hugo's house, trying to work out how to open it. Or whether she should ring a bell first. If she could actually find a bell.

'You have to pass the test before you can go in.' Will was ambling down the road following Deidre, who broke into a run when she noticed Bella.

'I think I've failed already.' Bella leaned down to stroke the dog, who barked happily then sat down.

'He really should cut back that hedge.' Will pulled away some greenery to reveal a buzzer next to a small brass bell. 'So, in case the electricity isn't working, just ring both.'

'Oh, OK.'

'If the electricity is working the gate will open automatically. If it isn't, Handsome Hugo will meander down the track to let you in.'

Bella pushed the buzzer then rang the bell. 'What happens if he's not in? How long do you wait before you decide to go?'

'How long is a piece of string?' Will laughed. 'Pot luck.'

'And why Handsome Hugo?' Bella already knew the answer but thought she should ask.

'The obvious. And that's what your great-aunt used to call him. Now I have to be careful that I don't call him Handsome Hugo to his face.'

Deidre stood up and walked away.

'It's OK, you don't have to wait. I have an appointment pre-booked.' Bella tried pushing the gate. 'I'll ring again.'

'Anyone been round trying to get you to sell yet?' Will followed his dog.

'No. Would anyone really do that?'

The gate clicked open.

'There were certain parties getting a bit pushy not long before your aunt died. She was getting very annoyed actually. Your place is just at the edge of where the building controls start — you can't build closer to the coast, you can't build closer to the marshes and behind is a flood-plain. And because of the birds, the land further along is protected. It's the perfect spot as far as some people are concerned.' He shouted as he hurried away, 'Just take your time and don't let anyone pressure you.'

'Oh . . . OK. Well, I only take logical and principled decisions based on a range of economic and practical factors,' she said to his back. 'So, no one will pressure me.' Will had already disappeared, so the last sentence was directed into thin air.

Bella walked into the garden, shutting the gate firmly behind her and began to walk up to the house, past orange trees, three goats, a few chickens and a donkey. The house was yellow and blue, surrounded by a host of spring flowers. A cow mooed in the distance. Bella wondered how big Hugo's place was.

A familiar-looking cat walked towards her, followed by another one. 'What are you two doing here?' she said, kneeling down to pet Yin and Yang.

'They like to be around you, obviously.' Hugo was walking down the steps towards her.

'Lovely place you have here.' Bella glanced around appreciatively, trying to admire Handsome Hugo in a detached way, as you would a painting, rather than wanting to run her hands through his hair, and . . .

She coughed and shook her head in an attempt to reconnect with her sensible self. 'In fact, it seems perfect,' she said loudly.

His face lit up. 'It's who I am. The café is what I own, and I have a manager to look after that. But this—' he turned around in a circle, his arms outstretched '—this is where my heart is.'

'It's . . . it's . . .' Bella couldn't seem to find the words. In her head, she was rambling. *You've got a great job, your own flat, you are a very able and competent woman.* Her inner voice was sounding slightly frustrated. *Now, spit it out — anything — don't let this whole 'Handsome Hugo' thing get in the way. Come on. Come on . . .*

'Really nice,' she said eventually, following him to the back of the house, where a grove of orange trees stretched into the distance.

'I have a dream.' He turned to her. 'I want children to learn about the environment here — learning about sustainable farming, wildlife, the sea.' He smiled. 'It's all here. I just need to start doing something about it.'

Bella nodded enthusiastically. 'That sounds absolutely wonderful.'

'Your aunt was helping me with an idea for a charity too, but . . .' He looked at the floor for a moment. 'I also want to start an agricultural collective.' He sounded like he was forcing himself to sound bright and upbeat. 'To supply local restaurants with seasonal vegetables and fruits.'

'You really have a lot going on.' Bella said, buoyed by his enthusiasm.

Hugo began to walk. 'There is an old barn over here.'

Bella followed him through the trees to a dirty white one-storey building. 'I just need to do something with this, make sure there's parking for school buses and that kind of thing.'

'So, this charity Aunt Flo was helping with?' Bella stared at the building and tried to imagine it being used again. 'How far along were you?'

'Oh, well, I had drawn up plans for the building and what I would offer, and we had come up with a strategy to start raising money. We decided it would have a charitable arm, and a business arm to make money. We thought we could market that to large businesses — hospitality, tourism, maybe get small groups in to understand our land and how it works. And that could help fund the educational side of it.'

'That sounds amazing.' Bella smiled at him.

'We had submitted the paperwork to give it charitable status but then when Flo died, I left it. I didn't follow it up.'

'That's a pity.' Bella thought about Flo's house and how it had been left empty, almost frozen in time, since she'd gone. Glancing at Hugo, she realised that the charity was almost the same. 'I'd love to see more of the land around the house.'

'Of course.' Hugo beamed and walked ahead. 'Follow me. I get so carried away sometimes not everyone realises that I'm passionate rather than just going on and on and on about it.'

Bella couldn't remember the last time she had heard the word 'passion'. Certainly not in anything anyone said at work. A word Gino frequently used was 'drive', she remembered. And 'ambition'. But never 'passion'.

'It's an ambitious project.' Hugo had stopped walking. 'Here.' He opened his arms expansively. Lemon trees clustered around vegetable beds covered with netting. Further away were more trees, and several water butts and a large, long greenhouse. 'My great-grandparents on my father's side moved here from the Azores many years ago and began to cultivate the land. A lot of what they planted is still here — although we have had to adjust over the years.'

'I didn't realise the area was so big.' Bella was looking at the trees, but wanted to watch Hugo's face, which lit up as he described his home.

'It's a lot of work. We also have orange trees, almonds and figs, plus beetroots, onions, cabbages and lettuces. I learned to farm from my family, to respect the land and the wildlife.' He stopped talking. 'It has my heart.'

Bella couldn't speak for a moment, the only sound birdsong and sea, finally realising that when Gino had said the word 'ambitious' it had felt cold and hard. But she only now knew that because when Hugo uttered it, it felt full of life and fire and passion.

A car horn beeped repeatedly in the distance. They looked at each other as if they'd been woken from a dream. Hugo checked his watch. 'Oh, Elena — my accountant — is early I think.' He looked at Bella apologetically. 'I'm so sorry. She's usually late.'

'It's OK. I've got to do more research. Busy day. Lovely to see the place.' Bella hurried after him as he walked back towards the house, the car horn continuing to beep.

'She's not usually this impatient. Or early.'

Bella remained silent, confused by what she was feeling. Which was quite a lot. Her rational inner voice was calmly telling her, *He is undeniably attractive, and of course, a man that loves the environment, owns a café, swims in the sea all year round and does yoga on the beach would turn anyone's head. But you've only just arrived in Portugal. Maybe all the men here are like that.*

Her other side, the one she hadn't seen for a while, was feeling like a teenage girl.

And this wasn't a good idea. Bella had work to do. She couldn't allow her head to be turned by her neighbour. She breathed in a heady mix of sand, sea and the smell of fresh oranges. This was not a smell you got in central London unless you'd bought a diffuser.

As Hugo ran up the steps to his house, Bella noticed a guitar lying next to a hammock. 'Do you play?' she asked.

'I dabble. I was in a band when I was in college. But I've not got the time to do anything like that these days. Some mornings I pick it up, with every intention of playing something, but then just put it straight down again. Like today.' He pressed a button and the car horn stopped beeping. 'Gate's open.' He smiled at her again, his eyes crinkling at the corners.

'Well.' Bella held out her hand. 'This was lovely. Brief but lovely.'

'Maybe another time when I don't have so many things to do in one day.' He shook her hand and caught her eye.

Bella looked down, searching for the right words which she wanted to sound friendly, enthusiastic, yet slightly businesslike and totally devoid of any emotion or attraction.

'Got to go. See you soon.' She turned around and walked towards the gate, taking deep, sensible breaths.

A car sped up the drive past her and she thought she saw Will and Deidre in the back as it came to a sudden and very dramatic halt next to the house.

Elena climbed out, waving at Hugo. 'I found this man on his knees in a ditch.' She shouted. 'He couldn't stand up. And his dog was barking. I couldn't leave him there, so I got him in my car. You'll know what to do, won't you Hugo?'

Bella hurried back to the house in case she could help as Hugo opened the passenger door. 'What happened, Will?' he said calmly. 'Can you move?'

Deidre jumped out and started barking again, then whining, then barking, so Bella walked over and knelt down next to her. 'It's OK,' she whispered. 'We'll sort it out. It's fine.'

The dog sat down and sighed. Will began to speak. 'I saw a log in the road and decided to move it out of the way, and when I was down there I saw a flyer in the ditch. So I tried to pick it up, fell in the ditch, my back seized up and my knee made a funny noise.' His voice was strained and breathless.

'I don't know how I got him in the back of the car.' Elena looked at Hugo. 'That was the right thing to do, wasn't it?'

Hugo smiled at her. 'I'm sure it was, Elena. Why don't you go into the house and get yourself some water. And bring some out for Deidre and Will too.'

'I've got an airport run this afternoon.' Will was still on all fours in the car.

'Let's get you to a doctor,' said Hugo, still calm.

'Stupid flyer,' moaned Will. 'I only tried to pick it up because it was asking for land. There's a few stuck to trees along the roads nearby.'

'Land?' Hugo peered in the car.

'It's on the floor.'

Bella stood up. 'Can I do anything to help?'

Hugo picked up the piece of paper. His face clouded over as he held it up.

Terreno procurado para potencial nova habitação.
Remuneração generosa

Land wanted for potential new housing.
Generous remuneration.
Call (00351) 913 213 902

Elena ran down the steps towards them with a bowl of water and a drink for Will. 'Here.' She tried to hand the glass to him.

'I can't pick it up,' he moaned.

'Oh . . .' Elena paused for a moment, then climbed in next to him. 'Here,' she said gently, holding the glass to his lips. 'It might fall on the floor, but some may get in your mouth.'

Bella noticed Hugo putting the flyer in his pocket. 'Let's get him to the hospital. Can you take Deidre, Bella? Elena, you can drive, and I'll set the satnav.' He walked back into the house, came out with his phone, put his wallet in his pocket and locked the door.

'OK,' Bella agreed.

Elena clambered out of the back of the car and into the driver's seat, while Hugo got in next to her and slammed the door. 'Just shut the gate after you and it will lock automatically,' he shouted over the car engine.

Elena did a speedy three-point turn and drove out towards the road. The car disappeared from view and Deidre whined and looked at Bella. She realised in all the commotion she'd forgotten to ask Hugo what to do about geckos in the house. But, if she was quite honest, that was less to do with what just happened with Will and more the result of her distracting thoughts when Hugo was giving her the garden tour.

'Well,' Bella said. 'Um . . . shall we go? For a little walk?'

Deidre's tail wagged happily as she followed Bella down the drive and back to her house.

* * *

Bella did a sweep of the living room to check for geckos then sat down at the table and opened her laptop. Deidre lay down next to her, and the cats placed themselves either side of the computer like bookends. She clicked onto her spreadsheet, needing some order after the events of the morning.

Deidre sighed and looked up at her dolefully.

Bella looked down at the dog. 'Oh, I haven't got dog food. I haven't got a lead. And I don't know if I can leave you? I've never owned a dog. Please forgive me.'

Deidre's tail wagged again as she was talking to her. Bella searched for *'Can dogs eat cat food'* on the internet. She made sure she typed the year in afterwards to ensure the advice she got was up to date.

Dogs can eat cat food if absolutely necessary but it's best to avoid making it a routine part of your dog's diet. Dogs and cats have different nutritional requirements.' Deciding this was the best piece of advice, she relaxed slightly, poured some water in a bowl for the dog just to feel like she was doing something, then found a Dido playlist to put on as relaxing background music and began to research prices for the selling of property. There was nothing like the Nest in the local area, so she searched for some within twenty kilometres, then for other newer ones nearby to get some kind of average.

'Here With Me' came to a close as Bella finished making her list, shut the laptop and stretched her arms above her head. All was in order. 'Time for a little break,' she announced.

The animals stirred at the sound of her voice, and all three turned their heads to the door as the bell rang.

'Oh! That was quick,' she told Deidre. 'You'll be home again almost immediately.'

Opening the door, smiling expectantly, she found Jorge instead.

'Hello.' He nodded. 'My aunt sent me a message about your neighbour. And asked to check in on his dog?' He loosened his tie. 'One of those cold, hot, cold, hot days,' he said. 'Because the buzzer on your gate doesn't work I came straight up. I hope you don't mind.'

'Ah. Come in.'

He followed Bella to the table where the animals were sitting patiently. 'Does this mean that Deidre's owner—' she pointed at the dog '—is not home yet?'

He took his phone out of his pocket and read a message out loud. *'Please tell Bella that Will is staying in overnight. Hopefully he will be home tomorrow but will need bed rest. He has asked if she will look after Deidre until he is home. And then can she take her for walks until he is on his feet again. Please buy a collar and lead on your way there.'* Jorge looked up. 'That last bit was for me — it's in the car.'

'Of course! I've just acquired two cats without trying. A dog won't make much difference. They've already lived together at Will's so they've just all moved house temporarily.

Can you text her back?' Bella poured herself a glass of water. 'Would you like one?'

'No, thank you — I have to go back to work, but wait.' He scrolled down the screen. 'Here is another message . . . *I have told Will I will do his shopping and keep an eye on him until he is better. What a wonderful man. I've never been drawn to a hippie like him before. Where has he been all my life . . . ?*' Jorge put his hand over his mouth. 'I do apologise.' He tried not to laugh. 'My aunt was recently divorced and has been on many unsuccessful dates. And sometimes she says — or texts — things before she thinks.'

Bella grinned. 'Maybe this is the start of something wonderful.'

'Maybe.' Jorge smiled. 'I will get you the collar and lead and I bought some dog food.'

'Oh, thank goodness. I was going to give her some cat food but I suspect there may have been a fight.'

He walked down the steps to the car and Bella followed him out.

'Here you are.' He handed her a plastic bag. 'I wonder. Would you like to go out for a bite to eat tomorrow night in Lagos? Strictly professional, don't worry. I thought you may like to talk about the property market and there is a live band in town we can enjoy too.'

Strictly professional, mused Bella, thinking that getting some unbiased advice would be helpful. 'That's kind of you. Yes, thank you.'

'Excellent.' He smiled again. Bella noticed attractive boy-ish dimples on his cheeks. 'I will come straight from work. Is it OK if we meet in town?'

'Yes, that's fine.'

'About seven? By the carousel?'

'I'll be there.'

He took a card out of his wallet. 'Here is my number in case there is a problem.' Then he climbed in the car. '*Ciao. Até logo.* Until later.' He switched the engine on and drove away.

Deidre and the cats were sitting on the patio. 'More information is always welcome, especially from an expert guide.'

The animals didn't respond so she went back into the house. She checked her ever-growing list on the computer.

Things to do:
Find out what's in the outbuilding — do an inventory.
Decide whether I need a skip. Where do I find a skip?
Find out what's planted in the land around the house.
List any vegetables, fruits (useful to know for information
for selling — may improve the value of the property. And
in case I need to get it looked after if long-term rental is the
best thing currently)

She glanced around the room again to see if there were any geckos, picked up a broom, her notepad and pen, and strode purposefully to the outbuilding, with Deidre trotting after her.

Pulling the door open slightly she peered inside. 'There's a lot of stuff, Deidre,' she muttered. 'Basically, my worst nightmare.' She opened the door wide and fastened it to the hook on the wall, reasoning that at least when she'd cleared the place she could put it on the 'made it better' list. Which would make her feel better too.

Edging inside, Bella was overwhelmed by the smell of old furniture, leaves and other unidentifiable aromas. 'Eau de musty,' she explained to the dog, who was sniffing a green-and-yellow chest of drawers. 'Please don't find anything in there that's worth smelling, Deidre.'

Clearing her throat, she scribbled on the pad:

1 x green-and-yellow chest of drawers

But the pen made a hole in the paper, so she put it on top of the chest of drawers, wrote it again, then felt something run over her left foot.

It was a very large spider, followed by several more scurrying out from under the furniture. 'Oh, oh!' She jumped away, knocked into the door and two geckos darted along the ceiling. Something else scuttled across the floor, which looked a little bit like a cockroach.

'No. Nope. No.' She turned and walked back outside. 'I did not ask for this. I am a capable, successful career woman with a nice, plush office and people who work for me and a nice, clean flat in a nice, clean part of London. I do not want to deal with unidentifiable bugs or lizards or whatever, Auntie Flo.' She pulled the door shut, leaned on it and sank onto the ground, staring at a stork hovering in the air in the distance. Deidre sat next to her and licked her face.

'Thank you.' She patted the dog's head, stood up and went back into the house, realising she'd left her pad and paper on top of the chest of drawers, and opened her laptop. She added to her 'Things to do' list:

Find out how much it costs to get someone to help sort out the outbuilding.

She picked up the phone and called her mother.

'Hi, Mum. How is everything today?'

There was a pause. 'Your father is having a bad day, darling. Aches and pains and just very, very low. His mobility isn't good.' She was trying to sound upbeat, but Bella noticed the weariness in her voice.

'Oh. Do you want me to speak to him?' A familiar anxious knot curled its way into her stomach.

'He's asleep. Frustrated because he can't write anything when he's like this. Or get into the garden.'

'Shall I chase up the builders about a quote for modifying downstairs again?'

'I don't want you to have to pay for that, darling. We could just move to a bungalow. Or a maisonette.'

'You love that house, Mum. You love that garden. You have wonderful neighbours. I want to help you stay there.' She realised she sounded sharper than she meant to. 'I'm sorry. I can pay for it. It's important.'

'What's the weather like over in Portugal?' Her mother was forcing herself to sound cheerful.

'It's mostly warm. Occasionally wet. Sometimes windy. Sunny. Lovely. I wish you could come over to visit before I come home.'

'I'd love to. When your dad's improved a bit. He always does.'

'Hopefully he'll improve soon.'

Deidre began to run around, barking.

'Is that a dog?'

'Yes. My neighbour's. I'm dog-sitting for the night.'

'Ah . . . how lovely. Flo was always looking after other people's animals. And other people.' The doorbell rang in the background. 'I've got to go. I'm doing a few hours at the shop and Miranda's giving me a lift. Bye, darling.'

'Bye, Mum.' Bella ended the call and watched Deidre. A memory of her parents dancing around Flo's garden with umbrella-filled cocktails in their hands, laughing, flitted into her mind.

Thank goodness we didn't know then what was going to happen to us when we got home, she thought. Then she made herself write a mental list of what to get on with next.

* * *

Bella spent the afternoon measuring the swimming pool, climbing down into the leaves and other things that had gathered at the bottom, then looked at the land at the back of the house. Having realised that using the tape measure she'd found would be very challenging, she decided to take some photographs of it instead and search the web for '*best way to estimate the size of some land*'.

A loud bell chimed four in the distance. Bella picked up her phone and absent-mindedly called Lil.

'You're still in Portugal, aren't you?' Lil sounded confused.

'Yes.'

'So why are you calling? You're on a sort of holiday.'

'Oh God!' Bella giggled. 'It's four o'clock and I always check in with the team when I'm working from home.'

'But you're not at work.'

Bella paused for a moment. 'How are things without me?'

'It's been less than two weeks.' Lil sounded like she was walking into a coffee shop.

'Are you in Berger's?'

'Yes. Worked from eight today.'

'How did the report go down?'

'Bella!' Lil said sternly. 'You'll be back at work soon enough.'

Bella didn't say anything.

'It was highly praised, if you must know. Now go and have a glass of wine or flirt with someone. Or—' her voice rose over the chatter in the café '—even better, find a lovely attractive man and have a fling. Sleep with him. Have some fun. You know what that is? Fun!'

The noise in the café stopped suddenly. 'You said that loudly, didn't you?' Bella bit her lip and tried not to laugh.

'I'm going to have to get my coffee from somewhere else,' hissed Lil to the sound of the door being pushed open. 'And it's your fault. For turning into a workaholic who forgets she's on leave.'

'You do have a point.' Bella shook her head. 'Pathetic.'

'Quite. Now. Go on. Enjoy yourself. I've got to go — I'm going to a pole dancing lesson tonight. I'll have a core of steel in about five years.'

'Bye.'

'And I don't want to speak to you for at least two more weeks. I mean that kindly.'

'I appreciate it.'

'Now go away. Love you.' Lil ended the call.

Bella stepped onto the decking, lay down and curled into an embarrassed ball. 'I am an idiot,' she muttered.

Then, realising that Deidre probably needed some exercise, she uncurled herself, managed to put a lead on the dog's collar, and began her first dog walk in her entire life.

As Bella walked out through the gates onto the lane, a car pulled up next to her.

'*Olá.*' An elderly man with black hair flecked with grey rolled down the window.

'*Olá.*' Bella stopped walking.

'I see you've walked down from the old house — the Nest, is that what it's called?'

'That's right. Can I help you?'

'I wondered if you know whether anyone is living there. I heard it's been empty for a while.'

'I'm living there at the moment.'

'Ah, I see. I live at the other end of the Algarve and have business in Lagos. I haven't been here for a long time so I thought I'd just take a detour for old times' sake. And I found myself here.'

'Old times' sake?' Deidre was getting restless and trying to walk away. 'Sorry — this isn't my dog. I haven't stolen her — that sounds bad — I'm walking her for a neighbour.'

He smiled. 'I won't delay you any longer. It's good to see that tree is still here.' He looked up at the jacaranda, which had sprouted more purple blossom.

Bella nodded. 'Yes, it's beautiful.'

The man turned the engine back on. 'Enjoy your day. Goodbye.' He rolled up the window and drove off.

Bella watched, wondering what 'old times' sake' was, but Deidre pulled so hard on the lead she nearly fell over, so she gave in and allowed the dog to take her for a walk.

Deidre headed down the lane to the beach. The sun was hanging low over the sea, casting a gold translucent light over the waves, seagulls calling to one another over the roar of the ocean. As she walked along the shore, she thought about the ever-growing list of things to think about before she even did anything. She thought of her parents, and how much it would cost to alter their house so her father could live downstairs and have some kind of quality of life. And then she thought of work. She had to start working again in a few weeks. And she had to 'make Flo's house better' before she could do anything with it. How was she supposed to do all of that if she didn't know what it meant?

She began to cry, suddenly overwhelmed, and for the third time that day, sank to the ground. 'I must stop it.' She gritted her teeth, wiping tears out of her eyes. 'I am a strong and capable career woman.'

Deidre slobbered over her face.

'I'm just tired. I am strong and I am capable.' A large fly buzzed around and got tangled in her hair. Bella pulled at it, as it buzzed into her ear. 'Get away! Just—'

The dog sat down and began to whine.

'Oh, no. No — don't do that. Please—' Her shoulders began to shake with laughter, and sobs, and she put her head in her hands.

'Oh dear,' said a familiar voice gently. 'This is a sorry scene.'

Bella opened her eyes. Hugo was crouching down next to her, smiling kindly.

'I've got geckos in the house and in that outbuilding. And massive spiders. And now a fly has moved into my hair. And I don't know how big the land is. And what is "make it better"? I mean, what is that?' Then she realised what she'd said and stopped. 'Please ignore that.' She wiped her face. 'I'm very capable, you know. I have a good job and responsibilities and I GET STUFF DONE.' She almost shouted the last three words.

'One or two geckos in the house are fine — they eat the bugs. I give mine names.' He sat down next to her. 'I popped round your house to give you an update on Will, and you weren't there, so I thought I'd see if I could locate you on this massive beach.'

'Oh. Thank you. How is he?' She sniffed.

'Out of action for a few days. Home tomorrow. Being guarded by Elena.'

'Oh yes. Jorge told me.'

'Jorge?' He looked surprised.

'Her nephew.'

'I know. I didn't know you knew him.' He rubbed Deidre's ears.

'Elena sent him round with a lead for the dog and to ask me to look after her tonight. And assume dog-walking duties.'

'Ah. Elena has taken a shine to Will.' He smiled and stood up, holding out his hand to help her.

'I suppose I'd better get back to my pet geckos.' Bella took his hand and stood up, and as she did, saw a small white bird with a black beak hovering over the sea in front of them. It turned upside down and spun towards the water like a screwdriver, diving into the waves, then sweeping out again into the air.

'Did you see that?' Bella prodded Hugo's arm.

'I don't think it was successful in catching its dinner on this occasion.' He laughed. 'There is always something to see. It is like a huge cinema screen.'

They walked back to the dunes, Deidre ambling happily next to them.

'All of this is a lot for you all of a sudden,' said Hugo.

'I organise and analyse things every day for my job. I'm on top of things usually.'

'Still. An old house in a new country and all you have to learn.'

Bella glanced at him, admiring his long, black eyelashes, and attractive stubble, fighting the urge to touch his face to find out what it felt like.

'This small meltdown . . .' She didn't want him to think she was weak or vulnerable.

85

'I won't tell a soul.' He smiled at her, but she looked away, unable to meet his gaze.

Someone had pinned a flyer onto a tree close to the path next to Hugo's café. 'What's this?' He took it down. 'Ah, again.' He showed it to her.

It was the same flyer that Will had found. 'This is what caused Will's accident,' she said.

Hugo's expression changed. 'Money, money, money. These people aren't ethical, I know it.'

Bella thought about her parents again. 'It may make a big difference to someone.'

'There are other ways.' His voice was low. He looked at her as if he was about to say something else, but Deidre pulled on the lead.

'I'd better go in and speak to my restaurant manager. A day off is never really a day off.' He nodded and walked away.

Bella turned away too, allowing Deidre to pull her home.

When she got there, she itemised everything she needed to do in her diary day by day, including yoga classes, an hour here and there for rest and relaxation and leaving gaps for dog walking. 'There you go,' she said to Yin and Yang, who were following her up the stairs. 'Back in control.' Placing the diary on the bedside table, she double-checked tomorrow's tasks.

7.30 a.m. — get up
8 a.m. — walk the dog
9 a.m. — message Will about his leg
9.30 a.m. — research how to clean swimming pool
10.30 a.m. — go for coffee at Hugo's café and ask about what's on that patch of land
Midday — shop for food
1 p.m. to 3 p.m. — inventory of bedroom 3. Leave bedroom 4 for later — there's a lot in it.
3 p.m. to 4 p.m. — research charity shops and projects for possible donations
4 p.m. to 5 p.m. — start to clean bedroom 2

5 p.m. — walk the dog
6 p.m. — get ready for meal out
6.30 p.m. — drive into town to meet Jorge

'God . . . not much actual house stuff,' she muttered. She turned the page to the following day.

8 a.m. — walk the dog
9 a.m. — check in with Will about his leg
10.30 a.m. — yoga at The House on the Hill
11.45 to 2.30 p.m. — visit estate agents to gather information
3 p.m. to 4 p.m. — input information
4 p.m. to 5 p.m. — do inventory of bedroom 2
5 p.m. — walk the dog
6 p.m. onwards — RELAX

'That's better.' She sighed, turned out the light, switched on the ambient rainforest noise and drifted into a listless sleep.

CHAPTER 7

Can I see her? I'm missing her.

Will's text had arrived before Bella had messaged him. She checked the time. It was just past 7 a.m.

I'll bring her round after her walk. What time suits you?

As soon as possible. Elena and Jorge moved a bed from my spare room into the living room, so I've been watching rubbish tv since 5.30 a.m.!

I'll be there around 8.

She climbed out of bed and nearly tripped over Deidre who was sleeping in the doorway to her bedroom. Yin and Yang were basking in the sun on the landing, stretching slowly as they heard her move.

'We're on, Deidre,' Bella whispered. The dog's tail started to wag, and she clambered to her feet, following Bella down the stairs to the kitchen. She fed the animals, went back upstairs to the shower, got dressed, ate some fruit outside on the patio, had a drink of water, and put the lead on Deidre. She was on lesson five on the app — *O Restaurant*.

'I have a reservation. *Eu tenho uma reserva.* Repeat.'

'*Eu tenho uma reserva,*' she said, but as she stepped outside, decided to listen to the waves and birdsong instead.

The early-morning air was laced with the scent of orange blossom and sea, a riot of colourful wildflowers bursting out of the verges at the side of the road. Bella walked hurriedly down to the beach. 'Just a quick bit of exercise before you see Will,' she told Deidre.

The dog barked and pulled on the lead just as Bella got to the top of one of the dunes. Hugo was standing on one leg near the shore in what she assumed was a tree pose. She paused for a moment, with one leg pointing towards him, the other almost at a right angle ready to take her the other way.

She checked her watch and decided that as a chat with him was on her to-do list for tomorrow, she'd walk away along the lagoon instead of the beach. He put his leg down and stretched his arms up above his head, before beginning another sun salutation. Bella's head told her to move, but her feet remained firmly rooted to the spot, until Deidre pulled her again. 'Sorry,' she muttered, allowing the dog to take her in the opposite direction.

'I need to be disciplined,' she explained to the dog, who had begun to sniff under a bush. 'The out-of-office is on for now, but I'm still very much at work as far as the house is concerned.'

Deidre sat down and looked up at her.

'So, I've drifted enough. Back to being organised. And that also means listening to my Portuguese lessons instead of birds.'

The dog barked. 'Glad you understand. Come on.' Bella strode off, away from the dunes, determined to stick to her timetable for the day.

Deidre whined excitedly as Bella rang the bell at the gate to Will's house.

'I've got a dog that's really pleased to see you,' she told the intercom. The gate clicked open, and she took off the lead and watched her bound over to the house.

'The front door's open,' shouted Will from inside as Deidre disappeared from view.

Bella walked up the pathway to the little white cottage, its windowsills decorated with terracotta pots bursting with deep red and orange flowers dotted along the covered terrace.

'What a lovely home you have.' She stepped inside.

Will was sitting up in a bed that had been placed in the middle of the living room, with a small table next to it that had a bottle of water, a glass and a packet of biscuits on it.

Deidre was licking his face. Will was laughing. 'Ha. Lovely to have you home, my girl.' He rubbed the dog's ears. 'Thanks for looking after her. I was surprised how much I missed her last night.'

'She's very good company. How are you today?'

'Well, dosed up to the eyeballs with painkillers, so quite happy at the moment.'

'Do you need me to get you anything from the kitchen?' Deidre ran around the room excitedly.

'I'm all right, thank you. Elena is coming round later apparently. She feels very responsible. Even though I was already in the ditch when she drove past.' He laughed again.

'Do you want me to take Deidre, or leave her here?'

'Can you leave her here? There's dog food in the cupboard. Can you put some out for her? And I don't want to impose, but can you pop round and take her for a walk later?'

'It's no imposition.' Bella went into the kitchen and spooned the dog food into a dish.

'We have only just met though.'

'Ah, you were a friend of Flo's so . . .'

Deidre ate her second breakfast of the day.

'I hope I'm not laid up for too long. I rely on those airport pick-ups to top up my pension. And I can't do any odd jobs for a while either. Another income stream suspended.' He closed his eyes.

'I'm sure you'll be better in no time.' Bella put her upbeat voice on.

'Hello! Hello!' Elena strode into the house carrying a bag of shopping. 'Hello, Bella. And hello, Will. How is my patient today?'

'I'm not really your patient, Elena.' Will smiled. 'You really don't have to keep popping in.'

'Oh but I do.' She took the bag into the kitchen. 'I rescheduled my appointment with Hugo and he lives so close I thought I'd come round and make sure you're comfortable.' She smoothed her pleated yellow skirt down self-consciously. 'I bought this yesterday. It's not too informal for an accountancy meeting, is it?' she asked Bella.

'No. It's lovely. Very bright.' Bella checked her watch. 'I'd better go.' She backed out of the room. 'I'll be back around five to take Deidre for her walk.'

She turned and walked down the drive, just as Elena laughed loudly and slightly skittishly. 'Right.' She checked the calendar on her phone so she could feel a sense of achievement at completing the dog-walking task that was on there.

* * *

Bella focused on cleaning and clearing the house for the rest of the day, took Deidre for her second walk and, by the time she arrived in the centre of Lagos that evening, she was feeling quite satisfied with her progress.

Jorge waved at her as she approached the carousel opposite the river, children squealing happily as it turned. Stalls were set up next to the shops and a band was playing 'I've Got a Feeling' on trumpets and drums next to the statue.

'Hello. There's a festival this evening, so everywhere is busy.' Jorge put his phone in his pocket and smiled.

'It looks like fun. Flo's house is very quiet at night.'

'Well, Lagos is anything but quiet when things like this are going on.' The band began to play 'Uptown Funk', and Bella's step lightened as she walked next to him along the cobbles.

91

He leaned towards her. 'I hope you like fish, because I've booked a nice, relaxed restaurant that specialises in *cataplana* — fish stew. You don't have to have it, but it's good.'

'I do like fish.'

'Good. But I just have to pop into this shop for a new mobile phone case. It will only take a moment. Is that OK?'

'Absolutely fine.' Bella lingered near the toy section at the front. A clockwork crab was inching sideways along the floor, and a flower peeping out of a flowerpot was repeating what a little girl was saying to it.

'*Olá*,' squealed the girl.

'*Olá*,' said the flower after a moment.

'*Chamo-me Justina*,' giggled the girl.

'*Chamo-me Justina*,' the flower repeated.

Bella stood in front of a stork with a pink head. '*Olá*,' she said quietly.

'*Olá*,' replied the stork. The little girl chuckled at her, and Bella beamed back.

'This shop is so full of silly rubbish, isn't it?' Jorge muttered under his breath. 'But it is good for other things like umbrellas and phone cases, you know, practical things.' He checked his watch as they walked out. 'I've made us late. So sorry. It's not far.'

Bella almost had to break into a trot to keep up with Jorge's long strides. They turned left at the green-tiled building then right into a narrow street flanked with shops on one side and restaurants on the other, the tables on the pavement full of diners chatting and laughing, the low buzz of conversation accompanied by a woman playing 'Simply the Best' on a violin outside an ice cream shop.

A family was ambling slowly in front of them, and lingered at the corner, where a living statue of John Travolta had begun to move to 'Night Fever'. Bella briefly lost sight of Jorge and spun around trying to find him.

'Bella,' said the statue.

She looked up, confused.

'It's me — Duarte da Silva.' He gyrated to the music as she tried to remember who he was.

'Ah,' she said eventually.

'It's me, the Duarte you met at Hugo's restaurant.'

'Of course. You really are a living statue?'

'Today I am. I like the challenge. I decided to be John Travolta this time.' The music stopped and some children put a few coins in a hat he'd placed on the floor. 'You're the one that I want.' He stated. 'No . . . wrong film . . . *Look Who's Talking.*' He frowned, frustrated. 'What does he say in *Saturday Night Fever*?'

'I don't know.' Bella shook her head, giggling. 'I don't think living statues say anything.'

'Oh.' He shook his hips. 'I am trying to give it more depth.'

'I'll check.' She took her phone out of her bag and scrolled through *Saturday Night Fever* quotes. 'Um.' She looked up at him. 'I think the content is a bit too adult for a living statue. Maybe if you had a late-night living statue event you could use some quotes. But—' she put the phone away 'living statues in my experience don't say anything.'

'Bella!' She heard her voice again. Jorge was waving from the other side of the street.

Duarte raised his eyebrow. 'That's my Tony Curtis impression. The raised eyebrow, I mean. So, you have started seeing Jorge?'

'No. This is a business dinner. He's telling me about the property market and what I need to do.'

'Aha. Remember the heat and sun here plays havoc with people's judgement.' The music stopped and he got off the plinth. He touched the side of his nose. 'Business meeting.' Then he winked and picked up the hat. 'I think I'm going to have to find a better patch.'

'I'd better go.' Bella touched his arm. 'That was surprising. A new experience for me. I've never spoken to a living statue before. Bye now.' She pushed her way gently through the crowd towards Jorge.

* * *

93

'So, there's a place in Cascais where the cataplana is cooked in wine and cream. It's very high-end.' Jorge was spooning some potatoes from a copper pot onto his plate. 'This is more rustic. Just as nice. But—' he picked up his knife and fork '—my dream is to live by the sea in Cascais and to eat rich cataplana whenever I want.'

'Cascais?' Bella smiled as his face became animated.

'I would also have a weekday flat in Lisbon. That's where I'm from originally. On the outskirts. I'd live in Lapa perhaps. In that part of Lisbon there is a lot of money.'

'I'll have to visit sometime. So, your ambition is to . . . ?'

'Be rich!' He laughed. 'I am very ambitious. I feel you are the same. It's a good thing isn't it. How are you finding the cataplana?'

Bella spooned some more onto her plate. 'It's delicious. I love the way it's cooked. It has a real sense of occasion.'

'I expect your great-aunt has a cataplana pot in the kitchen. You can try to cook it yourself.'

Bella shook her head. 'Oh, no. Cooking is not my best subject. I keep it simple. I don't really have much time, to be honest. You know how it is. Work takes up a lot of my time.'

'Mine too.' He leaned forward. 'I have dreams of a better life and I have to just get my head down and make it happen.'

'I feel like that too.' Bella took a bite of some fish. 'Mmmm, lovely.'

'So, I have many contacts I can introduce you to. The market is good whether you want to sell or rent. Or the land itself — there's enough there for several houses or just one very big one.'

'The land for redevelopment thing?' Bella paused. 'I'm not sure about that. I think that selling the house is probably the way to go. Although, if renting for a while is more cost effective that might have to happen. But there's a cost to my time that I have to factor in, so it's a last and temporary resort really.'

Jorge beamed at her. 'Wow. You are really doing this properly.'

'It's part of my job. Gathering information in order to make a rational and well-thought-out decision.'

'Exactly the right person to deal with Florence's house.' He spooned some more fish stew onto his plate.

'The "make it better" clause in the will is a bit difficult to measure.'

Jorge looked back up at her. 'Surely that's just clean it and mend things?'

Bella's stomach fluttered uncomfortably. 'I can't work with that kind of vagueness. I hate to say it, given I'm all about facts and figures — I just have a sense there's more to it.'

'You'll know when it's better.' He smiled again.

Bella smiled back, recognising something in him that reminded her of Gino when he was at his best. 'It sounds an odd thing to say at a sort of business meeting, I know,' she said.

'Well business meetings are a way of airing all sorts of information. I have gathered a lot of—' he laughed '—facts — let's get back to facts — and have put them together for you.' He reached into his briefcase, pulled out a file and handed it to her. 'I've also put the contact details of people who may be interested in buying the house without going through an estate agent — developers, you know.'

'OK, thank you.' Bella took the file and glanced inside. 'I do enjoy research.'

Two men strode into the restaurant and began talking to one of the waiters.

'Well!' Jorge stood up and waved at them. 'This is fortunate. Lenny and Martim. They are builders. They are always looking for new plots to develop.'

Bella stood up too as the men walked towards the table. '*Olá, boa tarde!*' Jorge shook their hands enthusiastically. 'I'd like to introduce you to Bella Creswell. She is the new owner of Florence Creswell's house.'

'Ah.' The older of the two men bowed. 'It is very good to meet you. That is in a very nice place. If you are ever thinking of selling the plot, please let us know. We are looking for spaces to build housing.'

'This area needs it,' the younger man said. 'We are happy to talk with no pressure at any time.'

'Thank you.' Bella smiled at them, mentally adding them to her list of things to research.

'It must be very quiet out there without her menagerie,' the younger man said.

'Well, her cats have moved back in temporarily, and yesterday I looked after my neighbour's dog, but that's as far as my menagerie will go. I had a visit from some birdwatchers recently too, but they won't come back. The less I have to worry about the better.'

'It's much easier to make the right decisions without emotional attachments to people or animals.' Jorge fleetingly brushed his hand across hers. 'We very much are kindred spirits.'

The older man shook her hand. 'We won't interrupt your evening any longer.' He turned to Jorge, and Bella observed them briefly, remembering her first encounter with Gino — his ambition and drive and humour and how he'd somehow understood her as soon as they'd met.

But Gino was now in San Francisco. And she couldn't remember where or when his sense of humour had gone.

Jorge brushed her hand again, and they sat down. 'They are good people to know.'

Lenny and Martim joined another man at a table in a corner of the restaurant. He was wearing an expensive shirt. His thick black hair was flecked with grey and he was staring at Bella intently.

'Who's their friend?' She nodded towards him. 'He looks familiar.'

'I believe his name is Francisco Lopes? Another builder.' Jorge spooned some more food onto his plate as the man, Martim and Lenny had a short discussion then left the restaurant together.

Bella glanced at the man again, then remembered who he was. 'The man in the car who was there for old times' sake.'

'Did you say something?' Jorge was dipping some bread in the sauce.

'No. No . . . just thinking out loud.'

CHAPTER 8

Bella fell into a deep sleep, accompanied by her rainforest noise, because getting used to the 'sound of the silence', as she referred to it when talking to her parents, wasn't as easy as she'd hoped.

She woke slowly to the sound of the cats skittering loudly on the tile floors, then running up and down the stairs over and over again. It sounded like they were doing cat parkour, or a feline fun run. Then there was silence until they launched themselves on the bed, meowing in unison.

'What . . . ?' Bella sleepily checked the clock. It was 6.45 a.m. 'I was hoping for a lie-in, you two. Don't need to walk Deidre till nine.'

The cats jumped off the bed and stood next to the door onto the balcony.

'Why don't you go out of the cat flap? Why am I talking to my cats — no, *the* cats — as if they can understand me?'

She lay flat on her back for a moment, attempting to wake up enough to get out of bed.

And then she heard it — a fast, loud clicking noise coming from somewhere above her. Her mind raced, trying to identify what it could be before she had to go out and see for herself.

The sound of wings flapping startled Bella even more. She'd never heard wings make that much noise before. If they *were* wings, they were very big wings.

Jumping down to the floor, she pulled on her wrap and walked slowly over to the balcony door, wanting to know what was outside, but not sure what she would find.

She opened the blinds. A large stork was standing on the balcony holding a twig in its beak.

Bella stared for a moment. The stork remained completely still.

'Oh my goodness. You beautiful thing,' she murmured.

It flew upward and over the house out of sight. She stepped outside and looked around. The twig landed on the floor in front of her.

She looked up and gasped.

The stork was gliding slowly onto the roof of the outbuilding, perching next to another stork, which was waiting elegantly next to a half-built nest hanging on the chimney stack, their long-limbed silhouettes illuminated in the early-morning sun.

'What does this mean?' She glanced at the cats, who were now both sitting at her feet in silence. 'Are these Aunt Flo's storks? Are they moving back in?'

Bella couldn't move, captivated as the birds worked, wishing she had brought her phone so she could take a photograph, but unwilling to move in case she missed any of what she was watching.

One of them flapped its wings, launching itself effortlessly into the air, followed by the second, and she stared at them flying into the distance, gliding over the treetops until they disappeared from view.

Bella ran into the bedroom and picked up the phone, wanting to share the news, but unsure who to tell. So, she wrote, *The storks are back*, found Hugo's number and sent it.

Going downstairs in a kind of daze, she made herself a cup of tea, then noticed the picture again.

The amble by its very definition does not have to have an actual firm destination, often fizzling out in a café, on a beach, or in a shop en route. Although it isn't really en route as you are not actually going anywhere. You are ambling.

'Still don't know what that means. But I am going somewhere, though,' she told it. 'I'm making this place better. Whatever *that* means. And those big birds, beautiful though they may be, must not be a distraction.' She took the drink outside and sat on a chair on the patio, listening to the waves crash in the distance and wondering where the storks should go on the spreadsheet. Were they an issue to solve before she sold the house, or were they just there? And should they really be described as an issue? Because how could anything that wonderful be an issue?

And what would happen to them once someone else owned the house?

Bella shivered. Then took a sip of her tea.

* * *

Elena answered the intercom. '*Olá*, Bella. Come in. Do you want some breakfast? I have made Will some.'

'Oh, hello. I mean—' she searched her brain for the right Portuguese phrase '—*bom dia. Como está?*'

The door clicked open. '*Tudo bem, Bella*,' replied Elena.

'*Obrigada*,' murmured Bella, feeling pleased with herself, then walked up the path to the front door.

Paul Anka singing 'Put Your Head on My Shoulder' drifted outside onto the patio along with the smell of pancakes.

'The door's open,' shouted Elena.

Bella walked in.

Elena was wearing a pink floral pinny over a light green sundress and was standing next to Will holding a plate stacked with pancakes. He was sitting in a chair with a table in front of him, set with a teapot and cup, orange juice and a vase with one pink rose on it. It looked like a scene from a 1950s film.

Deidre was gazing longingly at the food.

Will looked confused.

'He needs to rest.' Elena put the plate down. 'He can't walk very well at the moment, and I feel responsible so am making sure he eats properly.'

'I'm fine.' Will shook his head. 'I eat out most of the time. Bread and crackers is all right by me when I'm home.' He picked up his knife and fork.

'Oh, Will.' Elena giggled girlishly. 'Bread and crackers...'

'The storks are back.' Bella hadn't meant to say that first. She'd planned on asking how Will was and then checking if now was the right time to take Deidre for a walk.

His face cracked into a wide smile. 'Brilliant,' he said. 'On the outbuilding roof?'

'Yes. What do I do? Are they safe? I mean, what do I do?' Bella looked from one to the other.

'Nothing,' said Will.

'Nothing,' said Elena.

'Oh. I couldn't find anything on the internet about it either.'

'Just enjoy it.' Will began to eat.

'Will there be babies, do you think? Is that why they're back?'

'Maybe. Or perhaps they've just been displaced by some building work somewhere. Or they could just have wanted to come home.'

'So, they are living with me now?'

'Looks like it,' said Will. 'Beautiful creatures.'

Elena watched him, then poured him some tea.

'What about . . .' Bella searched to find the right words. 'Bird mess?'

'No more than any other bird.' Elena looked thoughtful and turned to Will.

'Although they are very, very big birds.' He smiled at her.

'Right. OK.' Bella sighed. 'I'll take Deidre for her walk then.' At the word 'walk' the dog jumped up and trotted to the door.

Bella put the lead on, took a breath and inwardly repeated, *I am a capable woman who can deal with this. I get things done. I get things done.*

The dog dragged her down the path and onto the lane.

'Beach?' she asked, then put on her language app and tried to focus on that rather than her ever-growing family of wildlife.

* * *

After dropping Deidre back at Will's, she headed to the house, ringing her parents as she did. Her father answered the phone.

'And how is my only daughter enjoying her Portuguese adventure?'

'I wouldn't call it an adventure, Dad. It does feel a bit disorganised, to be honest, rather than an adventure.'

'Oh. My. God!' He guffawed then began to cough. 'That will never do. You haven't been disorganised since you were a toddler.'

'I'm not disorganised, Dad.' Her face broke into a grin. 'It's everything else. Random cats, a dog, and now storks. They've all moved in.'

'Make sure you get some human company too. You know what you're like. Solitary.'

'I'm not solitary. Am I?'

'You just work too hard.'

'No I don't.' Her voice began to rise petulantly, a reminder of her teenage self.

'Yes you do.'

'No I don't.'

'Wish I could come and visit.' His voice got quieter.

'You can. We've got nearly six months before I can actually sell it. Or rent it.'

'I'm not sure I'll be able to travel again, Bella. I'm just being realistic.'

'Plenty of people with mobility issues travel, Dad.'

'I've got to get back to the computer,' he said abruptly. 'I've got a deadline. Send some photos.'

He rang off. Tears pricked her eyes. 'I'll get the money to adapt the house and build that extension. And then everything will be better,' she told the phone.

She went through her bag and found the card the builders had given her the night before and called the number. It went straight to voicemail. 'Hi. This is Bella Creswell. We met yesterday evening when I was with Jorge. I'm interested in finding out more about what you do. Are you able to come over to the house in the next few days? Many thanks. Bye.'

Then she went home, opened the laptop and added: *Appointment made with developers re info on sale price and other information.*

* * *

She sat down at a table in the café, took a notebook and pen out of her bag and looked for Hugo. He was talking to a young couple at another table, so she waved at Quiet Julian and said slowly, '*Olá. Um galão se faz favor.*'

'A *galão*? Yes?'

'Yes.' Bella nodded, rather pleased with herself for remembering the words without relistening to her app.

'Where is Deidre?' Hugo walked past with a tray.

And hello to you, thought Bella. *How are you?* But instead she said, 'Will was missing her so I'm back to simply dog-walking duties.'

'Ah. One less animal to look after.'

'Actually. I've got storks. I sent you a message. I thought I should tell you. I thought you should know. I don't know why . . .'

'Storks?' He put the tray down.

'I've made it sound like I've got some kind of uncomfortable condition like—' She was trying not to say piles, but that was all she could summon up, so she stopped speaking and took a breath. 'They arrived this morning. They've moved

103

into a nest on the roof of the outbuilding and have now flown off somewhere.'

'Probably to Ikea. There's one not far away.' He smiled, his eyes crinkling attractively again. 'Making it nice and homely, you know.'

Bella giggled as Quiet Julian put her drink down on the table. 'But what do I do?'

'Nothing. They are just coming home. Their nest would have been there even when they weren't. No one went on the outbuilding roof to check after Flo died, to be honest.'

'So they are just there? That's what Will and Elena said.'

'Yes. Aren't you excited? They are beautiful.'

Bella picked up the *galão*. 'I'm just a bit surprised, that's all. There were a few pigeons around the flat in London but they are very much smaller than storks.'

Hugo sat down opposite her. 'Flo called them Harry and Sally. She loved the film.'

'Harry and Sally, Yin and Yang, Deidre — though I'm only walking Deidre.' She took a sip of the coffee and put it back on the table. 'I haven't even got a goldfish at home.'

'Bella.' Hugo leaned forward and Bella experienced the full force of his dark-chocolate eyes and rare smile. 'You haven't got them. They have got you.'

'No. They live with me. Temporarily. They haven't *got* me.' Bella picked up the drink again and took another sip. 'They are quite difficult to place in the spreadsheet though.'

Hugo stared at her for a moment. 'Why would you put them on a spreadsheet? You can't quantify them.'

'I have to.' She shrugged. 'Apparently I have to "make it better" according to the will, so how will that be established if I don't quantify things?'

He smiled and leaned back. 'We live in different worlds, Bella. I live in one where you can measure some things and some things are instinctive.'

'Yes, some things are instinctive, but the contents of a will are not.' She put her drink down. 'Talking of the house and wills and making things better — do you have any idea what's planted on that land behind the house?'

'That's very specific.'

Bella wondered if he was making fun of her or if he was just making a statement of fact.

'That's because I want to sell the house, but I may have to get a tenant in for a while if the market isn't right. So if I keep the house and keep the land as it is I'll have to employ someone to — what's the word — tend it — or I could just put grass and flowers on it. And I need to know how much all that would cost to help me make my decision.'

'You are very thorough.' He stood up. 'I have to get back to work. I do have some information somewhere — my parents advised Flo on what to plant when she first bought the house. I know she's got some root vegetables and strawberries as I used to help her sometimes. I'll look for it.'

'And if I kept it like it is, what would I do with the crop? Is there a crop?' But Hugo was already walking to another table, and Bella was beginning to wonder if there was just too much information to collect to help her make her decision and if she could magically find her instinct somewhere. And if she did, whether she would believe it anyway.

'Oh Geno . . .' The Dexys Midnight Runners song suddenly ran through her mind. She cleared her throat and picked up her *galão*. Instinct? She almost laughed. She had followed her first instinct with Gino. And look what happened there.

CHAPTER 9

'I Feel Good' blasted out of the yoga studio so loudly that Bella could hear it as soon as she stepped out of her car. She almost danced up the steps into The House on the Hill and grinned at Ignacio, who was rushing out of the office after Elena, who was strutting down the steps.

'*Olá*, Bella!' she shouted. 'I feel great after my meditation. Enjoy!' She climbed into her car.

'Great motivator.' Bella grinned at Ignacio.

He stood in the doorway shaking his head. 'She took the remote control to the sound system and turned it on once the last meditation class left. She waved it at me when she walked out.' He moved a couple of plants on one of the tables next to the door. 'I saw her put something here . . . Aha!' He picked up a remote control and held it aloft triumphantly. 'I had "What a Wonderful World" by Louis Armstrong ready to greet my students to set the right tone.' He switched the music off. 'I really don't know what's got into her.'

'I do!' shouted Minnie from the office.

Bella followed Ignacio into the studio.

'I think there's a man.' Minnie came in behind them.

Ignacio unfolded his yoga mat. 'What man?'

'I don't know. She won't confirm it is a man. She says she's just on a new HRT patch.'

'If there is a man, wouldn't she just tell you instead of using a kind of musical code?' sighed Ignacio, sounding slightly exasperated.

'Well it could be someone we know and she doesn't want any feedback.' Minnie bit her lip. She looked like she was enjoying herself. 'She's kissed a huge number of frogs in her pursuit of perfect love since her divorce, she's always looking for feedback.'

'If she says it is Hormone Replacement Therapy, Minnie, then it must be.' Ignacio switched on a diffuser, which began to puff scent into the air.

'She's my best friend and it isn't.' Minnie turned to Bella. 'Do you have any idea? She said there was an incident near your house the other day. And—' she lowered her voice '—I noticed a rolled-up floral pinny in her bag. She's never worn a pinny in her life. She hasn't had any contact with a saucepan for years. She's Elena, the queen of the microwave.'

Bella shook her head. 'I don't have any idea.' Which was true, as all she had seen was Elena cooking pancakes for Will. And she had also witnessed her wearing a pink dress and floral pinny. And the day before that, a yellow pleated skirt. Which could be what she normally wore. She didn't think it was but was not prepared to speculate.

'I'm not sure I believe you either.' Minnie smiled.

'Bella is a paying customer, Minnie.' Ignacio took her hand and led her towards the door. 'You can't insult her like that.'

'You're part of the family though, Bella, because of Flo.'

'That doesn't mean you can ask questions like that.' Ignacio shook his head.

'I can. Elena is my friend. And before we met, she was very much interested in my private life. So, it's payback time.' Minnie laughed. 'I just think Bella's not prepared to say anything as she doesn't know us well enough yet, do you? But you will.' She waved at Bella as Ignacio closed the door behind her.

'I can't apologise enough.' Ignacio went through his iPhone to select the background music. 'But do you know anything? Is there a man? I'm not sure I can cope, tracking the progress of whatever this is through her choice of music.'

'Honestly I've only met Elena once or twice, so . . .'

'She was recently divorced when I met Minnie. And if I may say so, a little bit vulnerable.' He touched his nose. 'Don't tell her I said that. And she made a few not-very-good choices. Minnie would tell her what she thought. She didn't like it.'

Bella heard the door open behind her as another student came in.

'Well, I . . .' Bella was searching for the right words.

'Now she's into birdwatching and keeps trying to persuade us to go. I mean a bird is a bird, isn't it? I can see them any time of day almost anywhere. Oh, talking of which—' he broke into a smile again '—I hear the storks are back. That is wonderful.'

'Ah, yes, they are. How did you know?'

He switched the music on as some more students came into the room. 'I don't know actually. Word gets around. Now, I'd better start the class.'

Bella took a mat from the cupboard, put it on the floor and lay down, while working out some useful wording just in case anyone else asked her about Elena, a bit like the PR department at work would write a statement in a press release.

* * *

'Is that one of the houses near the east end of the boardwalk?' The estate agent was looking at a map on her computer.

'It's a bit further on, a few hundred metres back from the café, there. ' Bella pointed at a dot by the sea.

'Yes. Lovely spot. I don't think anything has come up for sale in that area for a very long time. It's so idyllic no one wants to move. It just means any valuation will be a bit broader than if we had something similar to compare it to.'

'Do you have information on what needs to be done legally if I want to sell? Are there any taxes that need to be paid, for example?' Bella opened her pad and wrote *Costs of selling* on it.

'I've got a leaflet here.' The estate agent took a glossy pamphlet out of her drawer and gave it to Bella. She closed her notepad and put the pen away.

'Is the market buoyant?'

'Oh yes. Properties are being snapped up. Demand is definitely outstripping supply. Would you like me to arrange for someone to come round for a look?'

'Yes please. I'm also considering keeping the house and renting it out.'

The estate agent took another pamphlet from the drawer and gave it to Bella. 'We can give you an idea of what you can get for rental when we come round.'

'Yes please, but selling is my preference.'

The agent opened the calendar on her computer. 'How about next Monday at 11 a.m.?'

Bella checked the calendar on her phone before she remembered there was nothing in it next week apart from every day — *Walk Deidre TBC.*

'Absolutely fine with me.' Bella typed the information into her calendar and felt a satisfying sense of achievement, then walked into two more agents and made more appointments for the same day.

Deciding to treat herself to a celebratory salad, she found a table at a café in a tiny square where a jacaranda tree was in full bloom. The sound of Frank Sinatra singing 'The Thought of You' oozed from inside and she looked up into the branches of the tree, at the purple blossom and deep green leaves, and wondered how long the tree outside the gate would blossom for, and the one opposite the house in her garden. She had begun to enjoy sitting underneath its pink glow drinking tea in the afternoon. Her mind drifted to her flat in London and the view of the cherry trees lining the street, a blanket of pink when they burst into bloom. She realised she was going to miss it this year and felt a little sad.

Since when did I get emotional about trees? she thought.

The waitress came over. '*Olá, bom dia.* What would you like?'

Bella scanned the menu and tried to order it in Portuguese. '*Quero . . .*' she said slowly, looking at the waitress for encouragement, who was smiling and nodding.

'*Um galão, um . . . pequena garrafa?* Bottle? Yes . . . *sim? de água com gás.*' She said the last four words quickly in case she got confused mid-sentence.

'Right, a *galão* and a small bottle of sparkling water. *É tudo?*'

Bella rifled through her memory, but she couldn't work out what '*é tudo*' meant.

'Is that all, is what I mean.' The waitress smiled kindly.

'Ah, no, actually.' Bella ran her finger down the menu. '*Uma salada de atum . . . por favor? Faz favor . . .* please?'

'A tuna salad, of course. And any of those are fine for saying please.'

'Thank you.' Bella leaned back in her chair, relaxing a bit, happy she'd achieved two things this morning — organising the valuations of the house and ordering food and drink in very basic Portuguese.

Frank Sinatra began singing 'I've Got You Under My Skin' and she logged onto her emails, scrolling down to the most recent one from work sent to her private account.

From: Lulu Maclaine, HR
SUBJECT: Application to work remotely from Portugal
Hi Bella,

I hope this finds you well.

We just need another document from you so we can approve your request to work from Portugal. Can you send a copy of your passport? It has to be a hard copy verified by a legal representative in Portugal. Unfortunately, the digital copy you sent isn't acceptable.

Everything else is in place, so once we've got that it should go through very quickly and you'll be able to return to work on 1 May as we'd hoped. We have also fast-tracked your digital passport so you can legally work in Portugal, and that has arrived too.

I have also attached the last form you need to fill in so you can now work for three days a week instead of five due to your family circumstances. When you wish to go back to full-time, we will need to fill in more forms.

I've attached all the correct HR wording and protocol on another document.

I look forward to hearing from you soon.

Kind Regards,

Lulu MacLaine

HEAD OF HR VERONWY ENTERPRISES

Back to work very soon if all goes to plan — her inner work voice sounded like it was staring at her coffee and water and judging her for relaxing. 'Better get on with the house then,' she muttered, finishing her meal quickly and hurrying back to the car. 'Better ring the solicitors to get the documents printed and annotated before I do anything else.'

She turned on the radio and pulled out into the road, thinking about two days' less money per week. 'Money Too Tight to Mention' by Simply Red filled the car. She switched it off, knowing how important it was to make as much money out of the house as possible.

As Bella turned towards the lane that led to the track to the house, she noticed two men walking around and taking photos next to her gate. As she got closer she realised it was Lenny and Martim.

Pulling up next to them, she rolled the car window down. 'Hello, are you here to see me?'

'Yes.' Martim leaned down to speak to her. 'We were hoping we'd catch you after you left the message.'

'Ah, OK. I assumed you'd arrange an appointment so I could make sure I was here.' Bella almost said, 'Because I've got rather a full diary.' But she realised she was still in 'Bella at work in the UK' mode, and actually she didn't have a full diary at all.

'Is it convenient to come and look?' Lenny took a photograph of the lane.

'Um . . . yes, why not? It's a bit of a mess, to be honest.'

'We are assessing the plot and the land so how the house looks is no problem.' Lenny smiled.

'Of course.' Bella laughed.

That's because they will want to knock your house down, Bella. There was that sensible work voice again. She stopped laughing, suddenly feeling slightly uncomfortable.

'Are you in your car? I'll leave the gate open.' She drove on towards the house. *Research, research, research,* she thought to herself, *which allows me to make a rational and sensible decision. Remember that: information, research and rational.*

The cats were sitting on the patio, stretched out together in a sliver of sunlight, the storks standing elegantly on the roof of the outbuilding as another flitted across the skyline. Tiny, velvet-red bougainvillea flowers were trickling out of the window boxes, given a new lease of life by Bella's half-hearted attention.

'Rational!' she said out loud, before parking the car and climbing out.

Lenny joined her as Martim reversed their truck and turned the engine off. 'This is a good stretch of land.' He spun around slowly. 'As far as I know, the boundary is far enough from the coast to build on, but we will need to check. And—' he noticed the storks '—Storks. Well. This may not be cut and dried but there are ways and means.'

One of the birds stretched its wings, stepped out of the nest and flew to the ground nearby.

'Ways and means?' she asked. 'Things have to be done properly.'

Lenny winked at her. 'Of course they do.'

Martim walked towards them and took out his phone. 'I'll get on with taking some photos.'

'This is a great patch.' Lenny looked at the tree. 'It won't take long to take that down.'

A bird sat on a branch high above them. Bella cleared her throat. 'I didn't think you'd want to just clear everything.'

'Oh yes. It's easier.'

Martim walked around the house. 'It won't take long to level this,' he shouted. 'Or the outbuilding.'

Bella's heart began to pound. 'You couldn't build around them?' She already knew what they were going to say.

'Oh no. We build high-spec villas. Even if it were apartments, these old run-down buildings wouldn't be in keeping.'

'I never thought of Aunt Flo's home as run-down.' Her voice was quiet.

'You'd rather call it "rustic", I expect.' Lenny laughed.

Bella looked at him. 'Are you making fun of me?'

'Oh no.' He put his hands up. 'I'm sorry. Sometimes my sense of humour gets the better of me. I've been in this business so long I forget people have feelings.'

The stork picked up a twig and flew back onto the roof.

'There's about half an acre of land at the back too.' Martim reappeared from behind the house.

'You're sitting on a goldmine, Bella.' Lenny tried to look friendly, but Bella decided his face wasn't quite made for it. 'I can call you Bella, can't I? I feel as you know Jorge we are friends already.'

Bella nodded, but she just wanted them to go. 'So, thank you for coming.'

'We appreciate you allowing us to look round at such short notice.' Martim shook her hand. 'We'll be in touch with a quote and then we can take it from there.'

'I'm considering a range of options. I'd welcome the quote, but I have to weigh everything up before I make a decision.'

'Of course.' Lenny tried to smile again. 'We look forward to speaking to you soon.'

They both climbed in the car, and Bella watched them drive off, the tight grin plastered on her face masking the sick feeling in her stomach at the realisation of what selling the land would mean.

The car turned out onto the lane and Bella looked back at the house. 'I'm so sorry. I'm not letting you get knocked down. Absolutely not.' She hurried inside, opened her laptop, logged onto the spreadsheet and deleted the section headed '*Selling the land*'.

'I can only apologise, Auntie Flo.' She spoke to a wall. 'Sometimes you just have to check, and this isn't instinct, this is rational — I didn't like them, and I don't do business with people I don't like.'

CHAPTER 10

Bella waved at the builder as he got into his car. Will had recommended him as 'a good and reliable guy. He'll give an honest opinion. Honestly.'

Bella had been quite worried about hearing his honest opinion about repainting the outside of the house and out-house, given the tuts and sharp intakes of breath he'd been emitting as he walked round inspecting the property.

He sat on one of the patio chairs and Bella handed him a glass of lemonade. He checked his pad and moved his fingers down what he'd written, muttering to himself.

'I knew Flo,' he said eventually, looking up. 'So, I'm not going to beat around the bush . . .'

Bella steeled herself, her heart beating a little faster.

'You may as well just give it a good clean and get new tiles made to put where the other ones were. You can get larger azulejos made that are bigger than the old ones and they'll cover up the damage to the wall.'

'Oh.' Bella sighed, relieved. 'I thought it was going to be worse than that.'

'No.' He allowed himself a smile. 'I painted it all a year before Flo passed away and, if I say so myself, I did a very good job.'

Bella looked at the empty spaces where the tiles had been. 'Can you recommend anywhere I can get new ones made, or can I just buy some from a shop?'

'You can buy some from a shop ready-made, virtually anywhere.' He slowly touched the wall and ran his hand down it. 'But if you want it to be in keeping with what your aunt left, you can go to Silves to the man who made the originals. There's a bit of a story to them I think.'

'Oh, what's that?'

He checked his watch. 'I can't remember. But it's a good one. I'll text you the name of the shop. Got to be off.' He handed her back the empty glass. 'Nice to meet you. Do you need any help with that swimming pool? If you do, let me know.'

'I'm not sure whether it's worth doing anything to it at the moment. I'm selling up.'

'I heard you couldn't get rid of it for six months.' He walked over to his van.

'No. I've got to make it better too. I suppose a nice swimming pool would count towards that.' Bella attempted to calculate the potential cost and time it would take.

'Come high summer, you'll be glad of it. Starting your day with a lovely cool swim.'

Bella remembered her family running out on their first day at Auntie Flo's house and jumping in the pool, screaming. She could feel the cold water around her and the warmth of the sun as she'd floated back to the surface.

'Can you send me a quote?' she asked. 'I can't commit yet, but the more information I have, the better.'

'Of course. Nice to meet you, Bella.'

'Nice to meet you too.'

He got into his car and started the engine, and Bella snapped photos of the old tiles so she could take them to the shop in Silves.

* * *

116

Deidre bounded up the track, followed by Elena and Will, who was using a walking stick. 'Hello, lovely.' She knelt down and fussed the dog, then walked towards the others as they were making slow progress. 'You're up quite early today.'

'I'm trying to get him interested in birdwatching.' Elena held up her binoculars. 'He's not quite ready for dancing yet, with his knees in the state they are.'

'I'm not sure I'll ever be ready for dancing, Elena.' He kissed her on the cheek, and she giggled quietly. 'But I'll give it a try if it keeps you happy.'

'Is there a rare bird here again? I had a visit from some bird-watchers a few weeks ago.' Bella laughed. 'Early in the morning. Very early.'

'No, no.' Elena shook her head. 'We're giving Deidre a run before I take Will over towards Cape St Vincent. We're having a day out. There's lots to see.'

'It'll be good to get out of the house. I've been going mad the past week or so being cooped up.'

Elena squeezed his hand. 'To the wide-open spaces of the west we go.'

Deidre stopped dancing around the cats and ran back over to them. 'Do you want me to keep her for today so she's not on her own?' Bella asked. 'I've got to do some clearing up before all the estate agents arrive tomorrow to do their valuations, so the company would be nice.'

'Are you sure?' Will looked relieved. 'I don't like leaving her for too long. She's not used to it.'

'Of course I'm sure. Shall I bribe her with a doggy treat?' Bella began to walk into the house. 'Quick . . . I'll distract her while you go.'

'Treats!' she shouted at the dog, who followed her inside, as did the cats, getting in on the action too.

As she got the packet out of the cupboard Bella looked at the animals staring expectantly at her, who only one month ago she had never met and now couldn't imagine being without.

She stopped, confused. 'No, no, no!' she told herself firmly. 'I'm temporary. No attachments.'

She opened her laptop and attempted to focus on her spreadsheet to remind herself what she was there to do. The '*Miscellaneous*' section was very long, so she closed it, took a bin bag out of the cupboard and went round the back of the house to make a start on sweeping up the mountain of dead leaves and vegetation that had amassed over the past year.

* * *

Later that day Bella allowed herself a trip into town, reasoning that buying some tiles from a shop and sticking them on the wall would be an easy fix and stop her feeling like she was falling down a rabbit hole of things to do and facts to find out.

Deidre followed her obediently as they made their way along the street, then sat at her feet when she treated herself to a tall glass of iced tea at a café, where she sat for a while watching people amble past until another dog began to bark nearby.

Bella paid for the drink and undid Deidre's lead from the chair, taking her to a shop opposite, where she browsed the shelves for azulejos that looked similar to the ones that had fallen off the house. Holding up a vibrant blue, white and yellow tile that was almost perfect, she looked at it, then the photograph of the originals, then it, then the photograph of the originals until they merged into one. She put it down and turned around.

Hugo was carrying an empty box out of the café. '*Olá!*' He waved, then walked over towards her. He'd shaved, Bella noticed, wondering if he was more or less attractive without the stubble, then realised she was doing the same to him as she was doing to the tiles.

'I'm trying to buy replacement tiles to put on the house. Apparently it's cheaper and easier than getting the walls repaired and repainted. But—' she sighed '—I can't find anything right.'

'That's because you need to get them replaced authentically, by the man who made the originals.'

'The builder did suggest that. He said there was a story behind them.'

'Yes there is. But also, the house deserves them.' He leaned in closer. 'And they don't cost that much, you know.'

Deidre pulled on the lead. 'I've got to go. Where is this place?'

'In Silves. Have you been?'

'No. I'd like to go, but I start work next week and haven't got time for a day out.'

'I have to go for a meeting there soon. I will let you know when and if it works for you I can give you a lift there. But not back, I'll then need to go on for some family business in Monchique.'

'That's very kind. Thank you.'

'I've just got to go into the shop here.' He pointed at the same one Bella had popped into with Jorge. 'I've got to buy a present for a cousin's daughter. They also do tiles if you want to look.'

'I may as well, just as a comparison.' Deidre was already following Hugo, so she didn't really have any choice.

He was standing in front of the toy stork that Bella had spoken to when she was waiting for Jorge.

'*Olá*,' he said. '*Como está?*' The stork moved its head and replied slowly. Hugo laughed. 'She will love this.'

'She will love this,' said the stork after a moment.

Bella grinned. 'My name is Bella.'

'My name is Bella,' replied the stork.

'This is such a silly shop. I love it.' Hugo grinned, picking up a box with a stork painted on the side. 'This is definitely the one.'

'The one,' said the stork.

The clockwork crab bumped into Bella's foot, then careered off again, and Deidre followed it.

'Time to go. I'm not sure what'll happen if this dog manages to catch that toy.' Bella smiled at Hugo.

'I mean it about the lift to Silves.' He walked towards the cash desk. '*Adeus. Até a próxima.*'

'*Até a próxima.* Bye.' Bella managed to pull a reluctant Deidre out of the shop and walked towards the river.

She felt a satisfying calmness. She had one fewer tiny thing to think about.

She checked her calendar on the phone. That afternoon was earmarked for going through the knick-knacks in the chest of drawers in the living room, and then hiding all the others in the house in cupboards before the estate agents came the following day. She added '*walk the dog*' to the list, then scrolled through to the following day. It started with yoga — 8.30 a.m., then the first estate agent visit was at ten thirty, with the last at four.

'Progress,' she said to the dog. 'Excellent.'

* * *

Switching off the ambient rainforest soundtrack that kept resetting itself throughout the night now, Bella woke before the alarm, pinpricks of light dotting the floor towards the bed. Rolling over, she smiled at the two cats who were sitting quietly, staring at her.

'Hungry?' She climbed out of bed and opened the shutters, then stepped onto the balcony. The storks were already awake, preening their feathers as a flock of birds swooped out towards the mountains behind them. Trying to put a name to the sound of the sea, she said a few words out loud. 'Roaring . . . No, sometimes it's roars — today it's not. Lapping . . . No, sounds like a lake. Today it's calm and—'

The alarm on her phone began to buzz.

'Maybe,' she said to the cats, 'I'll just call it the sound of the sea. Right.' She walked back inside. 'It's a big day today, so I have to start it properly. Food anyone?'

She padded down the stairs, followed by the cats, who were by now chattering, emitting squeaks, chirps and the occasional meow, then got ready for her visit to the House on the Hill. She drove there with the windows down, the breeze in her hair, grateful for feeling in control finally after all these weeks.

Elena was hurrying down the steps of the House on the Hill when she arrived, dressed for work and smiling widely.

Bella locked her car. 'How was Cape St Vincent?'

'Cape St Vincent?' Elena looked confused.

'Yes. I didn't have time to ask Will yesterday when he collected Deidre. Looked like it did him good.'

'Oh, yes, um, no.' Elena got into her car. 'We didn't actually make it that far to be honest.'

'Oh, well, anywhere nice? I don't know the area, so you could say anywhere!' She laughed.

'We got as far as Burgau, then had to turn back as he'd left his wallet at home. And then, well . . .' Elena closed the door and rolled down the window. 'We didn't really leave the house.' She rolled the window up, started the car and drove out of the car park, leaving Bella feeling she'd been given a bit too much information.

As she walked up the steps, 'Loving You' by Minnie Riperton was blasting through the speakers and Ignacio was walking across the hall.

'I've told you to hide the remote control.' Minnie was in the office, laughing.

'I have my lessons planned and the music is a part of it. She is being very disruptive and she has hidden the remote. Again.'

Minnie saw Bella walk past and ran in front of her. 'Who is it? I know it's a man, isn't it? She won't tell me. Well, she is telling me through the medium of music. She is deliberately winding me up!'

'Who are you talking about?' Bella tried to go into the yoga room.

'It's Will, isn't it?' Minnie was smiling now. 'She won't tell me because he's a bit of a nomad, hippie, alternative culture kind of man and she thinks I won't approve.'

'I think you should ask her.' Bella held up her yoga mat assertively.

'Stop harassing our students, Auntie Min.' Layla was walking down the stairs. 'I've got the spare remote here, Ignacio.' She handed it to him and he turned the music off.

'There. Now.' He followed Bella into the yoga room. 'Is it Will? I think it is. He's a lovely fellow. Much more reliable than he used to be, apparently. Always a different woman on the scene for a while.' He turned the music on again. 'Bill Withers, 'Lovely Day',' he whispered. 'That's how I wanted your entrance to start.'

'That's very atmospheric.' Bella unrolled her mat. 'And I'm sure Elena is happy. She seems like a sensible woman. I mean, she's an accountant.'

She thought she heard Ignacio snort under his breath, so lay down on her mat and began to stretch.

* * *

Bella sat at the laptop after the last estate agent had gone, inputting their verbal valuations for selling and letting with *TBC* on all of them until she'd got it all in writing.

A small pile of leaflets was next to her, ready to be read through so she could also input relevant facts. She'd put some music on in the background, the cats were sprawled on the table next to her, and she was enjoying herself putting everything in order. But as she typed she began to wonder if she was collecting a little too much information. Although, usually, she could never have too much information. Her working life was all about collecting information and making recommendations, after all.

Sitting back after an hour or so, she looked at the tabs she'd added on the spreadsheet. Then she revisited the '*Miscellaneous*' section. The cats were on it, the storks were on it, the land was on it with a question about vegetables, and the outhouse was on it. She closed the tab, got up and poured herself a glass of wine, feeling confused, then sat down and opened another document. That one was for her parents and their house, with details on money spent on therapy and counselling for her father over the years, small adaptations to the house, and money paid into the bank account she'd set up to save for the future in case her father's condition became even worse. She had also written a miscellaneous section on that. She opened it. It said: *My parents love their house. It is their sanctuary and their protection. They never want to leave. They may have to one day.*

She closed the tab, then made herself feel worse by opening the file of information that had been gathered from the date of her father's car accident to now, which she had subtly and incrementally taken over from her mother as she became an adult. She stared at the date — 8 February — then scrolled to the email folder entitled '*Flo's house correspondence*' and opened the letter from the Portuguese solicitors informing her that she had inherited her great-aunt's house. She stared at the date. 8 February. It was the same date, just twenty-three years apart.

'My mother would say that was a sign,' Bella said to Yin and Yang. 'I say it's just a coincidence.' She took another sip of wine and calculated the number of months before the accident that the family had been in Flo's house — six months. Bella was eight when she was in the Nest first, and nine when her father hadn't returned home from work on a dark, cold February evening. She turned the music up to try to drown out the memory of the phone ringing at 7.30 p.m. and how in what seemed like an instant, her mother's face had changed for ever.

She suddenly felt very sick.

A knock at the door made her jump. 'It's me. Hugo.' He was outside shouting. 'Can you hear me? The music is very loud.'

Bella turned off the song — Maroon 5's 'Must Get Out' — and opened the door.

He was standing on the patio, smiling nervously. 'I was passing and thought instead of ringing you I would stop by

123

and tell you I'm going to Silves tomorrow if you would like a lift. Your buzzer at your gate still isn't working.'

'Oh.' Bella was trying to force herself back from the past.

'Are you OK? You look a bit pale. I thought it was easier than sending a message. The signal is a bit random out here.'

'Ah. Oh. Yes.'

One of the storks flew down from its nest and began to strut gracefully behind the outbuilding.

'Sorry,' she said. 'I've been knee deep in estate agents today and I appear to have got a bit overwhelmed.' She stood aside. 'Do you want to come in for a moment?'

Hugo's face lit up. Bella's heart flip-flopped, and she turned away quickly, hoping that whatever emotion that had caused that wouldn't be reflected in her expression.

'I have wine.' She picked up the bottle.

'Thank you. But not today. I have to go to an open event at a local school to talk about environmental matters. A company will be there who may be interested in getting on board with sponsorship for the charity.' He looked around the room. 'Coming over here over the past few weeks again has sort of reminded me what I wanted to do. It's full of Flo's positive energy. You seem to have brought it back. So I made a few phone calls and this is the result.'

'That sounds very exciting.'

The cats jumped off the table and purred around Hugo's feet.

'Well, they are pleased to see you.' That wasn't quite what she'd meant. 'I mean, I don't mean I'm *not* pleased to see you. Um, that doesn't sound right either.'

Hugo smiled again. 'I think you've had a lot of information today. Maybe you have brain overload.'

'But my job is to collect information, interpret it and write reports recommending a range of possible actions.' She sighed. 'You can never have too much information, can you?'

'May I make an observation?' He picked up Yin or Yang and stroked their head absent-mindedly. 'When you write reports you have a timescale and a specific question?'

'Yes.' Bella tried not to look at his dark, chocolate-coloured eyes.

'Whereas with a place like this that you have inherited you can ask many, many, many questions and keep asking more and more. And of course, there is the emotional connection.'

'I haven't got an emotional connection to the house.'

'It is your great-aunt Flo's house. Even I have an emotional connection to it.'

The cat jumped out of his arms and onto the floor.

'Have you managed to do any tangible things? Get rid of things, for example?'

'A few. But I keep getting distracted. It's difficult getting rid of knick-knacks when they are so lovely. So then I need to find somewhere to take them. And then I've got to find the best place — a second-hand shop, a charity, an auction . . .'

'I think you have spreadsheet fatigue.'

Bella shook her head, smiling. 'I've never heard of that before.'

'It's a fairly new phenomenon. It's brought on by instant access to laptops and an internet connection that allows the sufferer to research absolutely everything within seconds, gaining access to information they never knew they needed and don't know what to do with.'

'Ah . . . yes.' Bella felt the need for another glass of wine. 'On this occasion there is a lot to think about. Although at least I've got rid of the option to sell the land and house to a developer.'

'You have?' Hugo looked relieved. 'That's good news. I wasn't sure. I had two men come to the café earlier trying to persuade me that selling my land was a good idea. Again. They implied that you were very keen to do so yourself.'

'I'm not. I ruled it out. They were talking about knocking down the trees and, well—'

'So, no emotional connection then?'

Bella laughed. 'I believe that, rationally speaking, not doing that is the best option.'

Hugo took his car key out of his pocket. 'I'd best be off. Maybe if you got the new tiles ordered that would make you feel better. Doing something tangible. Then putting them on the wall, that would be another tangible thing. And you could tick them both off your spreadsheet list of things to do?' He smiled again.

'I think that is a good idea.' Bella could feel her stress ebb away a smidgen. 'I've got to start work again next week and I think that maybe that is making me a bit tense too.'

'Of course. You are only human.'

'Nah.' Bella laughed. 'Career machine, me.'

Hugo shook his head. 'No one is a machine. Right. I will meet you at the end of your track at nine thirty tomorrow morning. *Até logo.* See you later.'

He closed the door behind him and Bella shut the laptop. He was right — she needed to give herself a rest. 'No more information for tonight, chaps,' she told the cats. 'Fancy a treat?'

She went to the kitchen and gave them some nibbles, then took her glass of wine onto the patio and sat for a while, listening to the sea and the breeze and the birds.

CHAPTER 11

Hugo waved as he pulled the car up next to Bella at the end of the track. '*Olá! Bom dia!*' He rolled down the window. 'Your lift to Silves is here!'

'*Bom dia.*' Bella got in the car next to him. '*Como está?*'

'Ah, excellent. Portuguese phrases so early in the morning! *Tudo bem, obrigado.* That's "all good, thanks".'

'Yes.' Bella nodded. 'I know that. But I've run out of greetings in Portuguese now, so are you OK with English?'

He laughed. 'Of course.'

'How did your event go last night?' She did up her seat belt and he drove up the lane.

'Very well, thank you. I spoke to some people. One or two sounded very interested. I handed out my card.' He pulled out onto the main road towards Silves. 'I can show you the stork hotel if you like?'

'The what? There's a hotel for storks?' Bella laughed. 'A building? A sanctuary?'

'No.' He shook his head. 'That's what we call it. It's just on the other side of Odiáxere. Keep looking to the right after the Cactus restaurant.'

'I didn't realise storks were so prevalent here.' Bella gazed out of the window at the low, colourful buildings of

127

the village, passers-by ambling slowly along its cobbled streets in the morning sun.

'For protected birds there are a lot of them, yes. Are you OK if I put some music on?'

'Go ahead.' Bella resisted the urge to touch his arm as he pushed his hand through his wavy black hair. 'Surprise me.'

'Oh.' He grinned. 'I was just going to put the radio on. So it will be pot luck.' He raised his hand dramatically. 'Are you ready for whatever this will be?'

Bella nodded. 'Of course. I love a surprise.'

He pressed a button on the dashboard with a flourish halfway through 'Daylight' by Harry Styles.

'Oh, this is a win then.' Bella leaned back. 'This reminds me of summer.'

'You're in the right place for that.' Hugo pointed to the right. 'Keep looking . . . keep looking . . . keep . . . LOOK!'

Bella peered out of the window. All she could see was a field. 'I'm not . . . Oh . . . oh!' Tree stumps were dotted along the grass as far as the eye could see, and standing on every one of them were storks. 'Oh.' Her eyes widened. 'I—'

'It's quite a sight, isn't it?' Hugo switched on the indicator. 'But brief as I have to take this other road.'

'Is that a natural phenomenon or has someone cut all their trees down for the storks?'

'A bit of both I think.' They turned northwards. 'But you'll see more as we go, on the tall chimney stacks along the road, and supermarket signs. They live on the sign above The Pingo Doce near the marina too.'

'I'll have to look next time.' Bella leaned back. 'This means my two storks are nothing to get excited about.'

'Well, yes they are.'

'I've only got two. And maybe some chicks coming soon. This field has about fifty.'

'They are special because they have chosen to live with you.'

Bella laughed. 'It's because I am near trees for twigs and insects and other things I'd rather not know about.'

She could feel Hugo's eyes on her. She carried on staring out of the window.

'You may have a point. But I prefer to look on the more magical side of things.'

'Ahhhh, magic.' Bella sighed. 'Where would that go on my spreadsheet?'

He laughed. 'You haven't been here long enough — yet.'

'Mmmmm.'

'Mmmmm.' Hugo moved the dial on the radio. 'Pot luck and what shall we find? Maybe a song about spreadsheets.'

Bella giggled.

'"Me and You and a Spreadsheet named Boo", "Spreadsheets Too Tight to Mention", "It's a Kind of Spreadsheet".'

'I'm afraid you are quite bad at this.'

'I'm offended.' He turned the volume on. 'And I give up.'

'One Day Like This' poured out of the speakers.

'But I'd say as this is pot luck we've struck gold,' he went on. 'This song feels like a film to me.'

'When I hear it, I imagine myself opening the windows in the morning and waving at everyone as they go past.'

'You can wave at people if you want now. Although — there are not many people, no pavements.'

'No.'

'No.'

'I'm sorry I can't give you a lift back.' Hugo turned left again. 'I have to go to Monchique after I've been to the Camara for another business meeting.'

'It's all right. I'm happy to get a taxi back. It's kind of you to give me a lift.'

'I'm glad of the company. Now, shall we play music station lottery again?' He pressed the button on the dashboard. 'Ahh, bossa nova.' Hugo moved his shoulders. 'If I could dance I would. But I have to drive.'

'Are we there yet?' Bella asked, deadpan. 'Are we nearly there yet? Please are we there yet?'

'Shall we just listen to the music and you can enjoy the view?' Hugo glanced at her.

'No dancing?'

'No dancing.'

Bella leaned back in the seat. 'OK. But we won't be long will we? I've got to clear out one of the bedrooms when I get back.'

* * *

Hugo parked the car next to the river and opened the door. 'I'll show you where the tile shop is. It's just past the council building.'

Bella picked up her bag and got out. A wave of heat wrapped itself around her as though she was standing in front of a fan heater. 'Wow. It's not even midday.'

'There's plenty of shade on the way up.' Hugo locked the car and began to walk.

Bella paused for a moment. Bright white buildings with red-tiled roofs hugged the hill, huddling together as they snaked towards the summit. 'It looks like a kind of wedding cake.' She got her phone out of her bag and took a photograph so she could send it to her parents.

'I've never heard it described like that before.' Hugo waited for her at the zebra crossing. 'Follow me.'

They made their way along the quiet, narrow cobbled streets, slowly climbing upwards until they came to a square flanked by lush green trees casting a canopy of shade away from the glare of the sun. 'There's the Camara — the town hall.' Hugo pointed at an imposing building in front of them.

Bella spun slowly around. 'It's so quiet,' she whispered. 'I thought where I'm living is quiet, but compared to this it's a real cacophony, what with the sea and the birds and . . . why is it so quiet here?'

'I've never really thought about it.' Hugo closed his eyes for a moment. 'Yes—' he opened them '—you're right. It's silent. That sea and those birds really are very noisy after all.' He smiled at Bella. 'You're not sure if I'm joking or not, are you?'

'No . . .'

He pointed to a gap between two buildings. 'The tile place is just here.' He guided her down another narrow lane and stopped outside a shop window decorated with vibrantly patterned azulejos.

'How gorgeous.' Bella peered inside. 'I'm sure I can get what I need here. But it looks a bit dark.'

Hugo tried to open the door. 'Oh. Ah. This note on the window says there's someone here from eleven thirty until 1 p.m. today. And then from three till seven.'

'I'll come back, it's fine. I've not got much time. I've got too much to do to hang around. Starting work next week again. But I'm here now.' She was talking very quickly, and she tried to slow herself down again. 'But—' she took a breath '—Yes. I am here now. I'll look at the castle. Can you point me in the right direction?'

Hugo shook his head kindly. 'Would you like me to come over and help you with some clearing out before you start work? I'm sure once you've tackled the outbuilding, you will get a tremendous amount of satisfaction. And—' Bella wasn't sure if he winked at her or not '—you can tick it off your spreadsheet, and perhaps enjoy some of the delights the Algarve has to offer without feeling you need to use a stopwatch.'

'Are you sure? That would help a lot. That particular building feels like it has some kind of radioactive glow around it that's stopping me going in. I'm sure it's not really radioactive. I think it's probably the spiders, geckos and potentially maybe cockroaches.'

'I'll check my diary and message you with the date I can do it.'

'Thank you.'

He smiled and began to walk back towards the Camara. 'So, it's just here to the right and carry on up the hill.'

'That easy?' Bella followed him.

'Yes, just up. Keep going up. But remember—' he looked at the clock on the municipal building '—it's ten thirty now

— make sure you're back in time for the shop to open or at least before it closes for lunch or you'll waste your day. I mean it's not a waste, but given you've got to add clearing out another room to the "done" section of your spreadsheet . . .'

'I wish I'd never told you that.' Bella walked away. 'Thank you for the lift. Don't be late for your appointment.'

He smiled. '*Até a próxima*. Until the next time.' He waved and climbed the steps to the Camara.

Bella took the bottle of water out of her bag and walked slowly along the winding streets to the top of the hill. There was a small queue outside the castle walls at the ticket office. After she paid, she was greeted by a riot of purple blossom hanging from the jacaranda trees.

Climbing the steps to the top of the castle walls, she took in the view of the hills in the distance and the sea to the south, the river meandering its way through the valley towards Portimão. Bella followed the gaze of a couple and their little boy, who were filming something below the castle walls. A stork was feeding its young in a nest on a chimney on one of the houses, and on the rooftop behind it another stork was guarding its chicks in its own nest. In the sky another stork swooped towards another nest on another building.

The little boy shrieked happily, pointing at more storks on more nests, and Bella giggled with him, lifted by his excitement. *That was me*, she thought. *That was me watching the storks on the roof with Aunt Flo. So many years ago.*

Is that what it felt like? Enjoying the moment?

She glanced at the boy again, pulling his father's hand and waving at the birds. And she wanted to, too. So she did, waving at them with the little boy, while his parents laughed.

The family moved on, but Bella stayed where she was, mesmerised by the birds flying to and fro from the rooftops to the distant woodlands and meadows and back, set on feeding their young. Looking after their babies. Somewhere at the back of her mind a memory tried to force its way to the front, so she breathed slowly to shut it down.

Her phone buzzed in her bag and brought her back to the present. She took it out, absent-mindedly. It was a reminder for a regular work meeting that she had forgotten. Telling herself that this time next week she would be in attendance, albeit remotely, Bella noticed the time. It was five past twelve.

'Oh, bloody hell. Where's the time gone?' She shoved the phone away and hurried down the steps, out of the calm oasis of the castle and onto the cobbled streets, following the signs to the Camara. She tried to work out what had happened, given that she had arrived at eleven and it was now twelve. Had she been staring at birds all that time?

The art of the amble, whispered her inner voice.

Bella ignored it and opened the door of the tile shop, which tinkled as she stepped inside.

'*Bom dia!*' an elderly man with thinning grey hair stood behind a counter.

'*Bom dia.*' Bella took her phone out in case she needed to attempt to translate what she wanted to say into Portuguese. '*Fala inglês?*'

'Yes, I do speak English.' The man smiled. 'How can I help you?'

'I have to get some decorative tiles replaced that were on the front of my aunt's house. Apparently it's cheaper to do that than get the whole thing replastered or whatever it's called.'

'Do you have a design in mind?'

'Ah, actually. I've photographs of the tiles. They fell off the wall and broke but I've put them together like a jigsaw really so you can see.'

She opened the photographs and showed them to him.

'Ah. Dona Florence?' He shook his head. 'So sad to have lost her.'

'I'm her great-niece. Bella.' She smiled at him. 'She left me the house.'

'The Nest is yours? How marvellous. What a wonderful, unique place.'

133

'Yes, yes it is. I need to get it back up to scratch. It was empty for a while.'

'These were very special designs. Done by Francisco Lopes for her when she first moved in. They were involved for a while.'

'Oh?' Bella's heart raced a little. 'I have no idea of her personal life. It's nice to know a bit.'

'His family lived next door. His great-nephew Hugo owns the place now, doesn't he?'

'Hugo? He lives next door, yes. He didn't mention his uncle had painted the tiles.'

'There is bad blood, I think, so maybe that's why he hasn't told you. It was very sad. It didn't work out. I think Francisco wanted to move in and develop the land around the house. It was very desirable even then. But she wouldn't let him. It was not a pleasant break-up. He is a very rich man now. Builds high-end houses.' He shook his head sadly. 'He was a talented artist and designer.' He pointed at the photographs of the tiles. 'You can see it here.'

Bella studied the photographs. 'Maybe I should get new designs if these were from something sad?'

'She kept them on the wall? They only fell off after she died?'

Bella nodded.

'Well, maybe she wanted them there to remind her of the happy times she had with him. He was very angry — she rejected him apparently.' The man took a ledger from a shelf behind him. 'Greed, I suppose. Maybe it got the better of him.'

The door opened and another customer walked in.

'If you leave me your details I can ring you with an estimate?'

'Thank you.' Bella handed him her card. 'Don't worry about the estimate. I'm happy to go ahead.' Hundreds of questions careered around her mind. She glanced at the person standing behind her and decided the questions would have to wait. 'Thank you for your help. *Obrigada. Adeus.*'

'You're welcome. I will be in touch.' He read the card. 'Bella Creswell. I hope you are enjoying Portugal.'

The town clock chimed in the distance and Bella remembered the time.

'Yes, I am.' She opened the door. 'A bit too much actually,' she muttered, walking down the hill to find a taxi.

Her phone rang in her bag and she took it out. 'Hello, Lil. Is everything OK?'

'How's Portugal?' She sounded like she was in a lift.

'It's lovely. Although I keep getting distracted and can't keep to my timetable. It's very strange and not like me at all. How's England?'

'It's all fine. All good. Very Englandy. Very May. We've had hail, rain, wind and now it's twenty-five degrees and sunny. And it's only just lunchtime.'

'Ah, a lot of weather . . . Is everything all right?'

'Yes of course. Look.' She lowered her voice. 'I know we're not supposed to contact you about work stuff until you're back at work but some changes are in the offing and I thought you needed to know so it's not a surprise.'

'Changes? I haven't even been gone for a month.'

'It has been quick. Changes in the department. New manager coming in, talks of a takeover.'

'So Marnie Dubois has left?'

'Moved to another department this morning.'

'But she was the one who made sure I could work part-time. I hope it sticks.'

'It's all been agreed with HR, so yes. And they allowed you to do that because you're so very, very excellent at your job.'

Bella found herself standing next to a taxi rank.

'I'd better go,' Lil said. 'Nothing to worry about. I know how much you value information.'

Bella climbed into the taxi. 'Yes, you're right. I do.'

'Speak next week in a work capacity then.'

'Thanks, Lil.'

'Bye.' Lil rang off and Bella rubbed her temple. Unsettling news from work was the last thing she needed at the moment.

'Where to?' asked the taxi driver.

'Lagos, *se faz favor.*' Bella showed him the address on the phone.

As she leaned back, she wondered why Hugo hadn't mentioned his uncle and the tiles to her, and more importantly, his relationship with Flo.

CHAPTER 12

Bella was sitting outside on the patio drinking a cup of tea, cocooned in the heat of the morning sun when she realised something was different.

One of the storks seemed busier than usual, flying back and forth to the nest over and over again. Bella watched for a while then decided to go up to the roof terrace to check everything was all right.

Standing on the sun-baked roof, she looked over at the nest guarded by Harry or Sally, and she could make out four tiny grey, furry heads peeping out over the top, their beaks open wide.

Bella stared, wanting to jump up and down and clap. Harry and Sally had babies now. She didn't just have two storks on her roof, she had six. For a few moments her mind raced off, wondering what she could call the newborns, names almost falling from the sky — Fleur, Keanu, Meg, Colin, Juan, Lola, Grace. Then she tried to find names more fitting for southern Europe — Cristina, Pedro, Tomás, Gino.

Gino. Bella tried to stop thinking. She didn't want the name to be there, but once it was, she couldn't stop the thoughts.

They wrapped themselves around her, repeatedly pushing the top of her head like a button. On, off, on, off.

'I think we should try for a baby, Bella.' Gino looked up from his computer. *'We are the right age, we have the right income. It's the correct next step.'*

Bella put a plate of nibbles on the table in front of them. 'Is it the right time? Just because all of our friends are having children? Shouldn't we wait until it's the right time for us?'

'When is the right time for us? This focus on work we both have? What's it for, really?'

Bella looked at him. 'You're right. You're right.' She put her arms around him. 'Let's be parents. It's in our plan, I suppose. We can just bring it forward.'

Bella couldn't breathe properly. She sat on a chair and closed her eyes. But the thoughts wouldn't stop.

She put her head in her hands, trying to drag her mind back from the past, pulling it away from the darkness, back to the light on the roof of Aunt Flo's house. But the thoughts wouldn't stop.

'We've been trying for six months, Bella. Why aren't we pregnant?' Gino had a pregnancy website open. *'Are you eating properly? Resting? You're working too hard. That's what it is.'*

'It doesn't happen overnight, Gino. Just because we want it to. I'll make an appointment to see the doctor. Give me some dates you're free.'

'Why do I need to come?' He closed the page. She noticed the one open behind it was a recruitment page for a company in America. *'We need to move forward. You don't want to be too old to have a baby. You need to reprioritise your work/life balance.'*

Bella remembered struggling to formulate the words. 'Are you blaming me?'

He turned round and touched her arm, softly. 'No, no. It's me. I'm getting frustrated. You know how it is. I have a plan and I work towards it and it always comes to fruition.'

'Well, let's both go and see the doctor and we can see if we can both do something to help.'

'You book the appointment and I'll try to get there. But it's your body. You need to be less stressed and work less hard.'

He closed the laptop and walked out of the room. He didn't hear Bella say, 'But it could be you? It may not be me.'

The storks flapped their wings, chattering loudly at their chicks, and Bella opened her eyes, tears streaming down her face. Her breathing started to ease and the pressure on her head lifted. She looked up, imagining the memories dissipating into the air.

'Bella?' Hugo's voice shouted from the garden. 'Bella?'

Wiping her cheeks with her sleeve she stood and fixed a smile on her face.

'I'm on the roof!' she called, leaning on the wall.

Hugo looked up at her and for a second no words would come out of her mouth.

'I've just been tidying up. I'll be with you in a moment.' She went slowly down the stairs, pausing to check her reflection in the bathroom mirror, pulled a brush through her hair and walked out of the door, feeling somehow lighter than when she'd walked in.

Hugo was standing next to the tree, the shade dappling his arms with leaf-shape spots.

Bella smiled, relieved that he was there.

'Right.' He looked at her. 'Are you ready? Who knows what opening these doors may release?'

Bella stepped back onto the grass. 'You may think it's funny, but I'm urban. A city-dweller. All this nature and lizards and insects business is not really my bag. So I'm getting out of the way.'

'It will be fine.' He shook his head, smiling. 'There is nothing to be afraid of.' He opened the doors dramatically. 'You see.' He pointed at the floor. 'Nothing is running out from under anything.'

Bella took a deep breath as Hugo moved further inside. 'You're right. I'm being a bit of a lightweight.'

As she approached the door, Hugo shrieked.

'Get off me!'

'Hugo?' She ran into the outhouse to see what had happened.

Hugo was standing next to the wall with a large cobweb draped over his shoulder, grinning.

'What?' For a moment Bella couldn't work out what was happening.

And then he started laughing. 'I'm sorry, I couldn't resist it.'

'You are a very bad person,' she managed to say, before she laughed too. 'You frightened the life out of me.'

He caught her eye. 'I wouldn't let any harm come to you,' he said seriously.

They stood for a moment, staring at each other until the sound of a stork chattering broke the silence.

'I think you have baby storks now?'

'It appears I do. I noticed them earlier in the nest and it's very lovely. Anyway, as you are giving me your time, shall we start?' She forced herself to sound businesslike, even as Hugo took his T-shirt off and draped it over a chest of drawers. 'Yes, right.' She addressed a light switch on the wall behind him. 'Where shall we start?'

'I will take this corner for now as it has what looks like the most rubbish in it. Why don't you start at the section near the door?' He picked up a bin bag from a roll that was on the floor. 'We have rubbish in the skip, a pile of things to keep and a pile of things to either recycle or give away.'

'It's hot already isn't it?' murmured Bella.

'This is why we need to start now and drink lots of water.' He smiled. 'Shall we begin?'

'Yes, let's begin.' Bella opened a wardrobe to see what was inside, and they spent the rest of the afternoon working quietly together, Bella reminding herself periodically that they were definitely doing something to 'make it better'.

* * *

140

'I have some food and drink in the house if you'd like to come over.' Hugo put his T-shirt back on.

Bella stopped looking at his left foot and was able to meet his gaze once he'd done that. 'I should really be feeding you after helping me clear this out.' She looked at the separate piles of rubbish, furniture and knick-knacks that had been sorted into piles to throw out, to donate and to sell. There was also a small pile of things to keep that Bella had been unable to part with, which she'd sort out in a week or so. She wasn't ready to let them go yet.

'The restaurant manager offered to drop a selection of food off for us at my house. So, it would be rude not to come.'

Bella wanted to go and lie down in a darkened room but was also very hungry. And she wanted to be with Hugo. Somewhere at the back of her mind she was frightened that if he went, she'd be alone with her thoughts again. 'It would be rude not to,' she said, turning towards the track.

'No, we won't go the formal way. We'll climb over the fence behind the orange trees.' Hugo walked along the path that took them through the orange grove.

Bella followed him wearily as they moved through the field, the cicadas screaming at them as they went. She sighed. 'Got to get this sorted too. I suppose it comes under the remit of making it better. And as I've said, in the unlikely event that I rented the place out for a while before I sold it, I'd need to get someone to look after it.'

'I could look after it — I could pay you for the fruit and vegetables,' replied Hugo.

'I suppose you could.' She climbed over the fence into his garden. The donkey brayed in welcome. 'Afternoon!' she said, stroking its head, as Hugo went into the house.

'Just sit wherever you want to,' he shouted. 'I'll get the food.'

'What's the donkey's name?' Bella tickled its ears.

'Mateus.' Hugo had brought out some glasses and put them on the table on the terrace.

'Oh, what a day.' Bella stretched and sat down. 'I honestly am so grateful for your help.'

Hugo smiled at her. 'I won't say it was my pleasure because it was very hard work. But I'm glad I could help in a small way.'

'There weren't as many — things — crawling around as I expected.' She winced. 'I'm rather embarrassed about the screaming.'

He laughed. 'I think that perhaps that is what drove some of them away.'

'Maybe I should market myself as a kind of holistic pest control service.'

Yin and Yang jumped over the fence next to the olive tree and padded over to her. 'I've never had pets, but aren't these cats sort of behaving like dogs?' Bella stroked them as they climbed up next to her.

'Everything connected to Flo is very much whatever it wants to be.' Hugo picked up his guitar. 'I should have taken this in earlier. All this heat won't do it any good at all. I'll get us a drink. What would you like with your food? Wine, beer, water, tea?'

Bella tried to get up, but the swinging seat moved backwards and forwards, so she couldn't quite get her feet on the floor. 'I'm trying to help. I'm sorry. First you spend the afternoon clearing the outbuilding, and now you are feeding me because I haven't got any food worth mentioning in my own house.'

'Well, I didn't cook it. I think I'll bring you wine.'

Bella glanced at the guitar. 'Can I have a go? I tried learning when I was a teenager but never had the time to practise.'

He handed it to her. 'Of course. It's a great stress release.'

She looked at it for a moment, then ran her hands along the neck and strummed the strings tunelessly. 'In my head I'm Audrey Hepburn sitting at a window in *Breakfast at Tiffany's* singing "Moon River",' she shouted. 'In reality . . .' She laughed. 'Anything but.'

A small plane buzzed over the beach in the late-afternoon sun, trailing a banner advertising something. The noise was strangely comforting. Bella stretched again and lay down next to the cats, still holding the guitar and closed her eyes. 'Just for a moment,' she murmured.

'Bella . . . Bella . . .' A hand gently brushed her arm. 'The feast is here.' Hugo's voice was gentle, but it sounded like he was trying not to laugh.

She opened her eyes. 'Oh. How long have I been asleep? How embarrassing.'

Hugo was crouching down next to her. 'I've been inside for just over five minutes, so really not long. I'm impressed how well you've looked after the guitar.'

Her arms were clutching it to her as if it was a very large teddy bear. 'Oh.' She giggled and tried to sit up.

Hugo took her hand. 'Here.'

She looked up at him. His dark-chocolate eyes held her gaze for a moment and they moved closer, and closer, until their lips were so close she could feel his breath. Then Yin or Yang jumped off the seat, making it rock slightly and at the same time Hugo's phone buzzed on the table.

They both looked away, the moment gone.

'Just a group message from the café. The manager's onto it.' He put it down and pointed at a table on the patio. 'Your feast awaits.'

The table was set with a red-and-white-checked tablecloth, a basket of bread, cold meats, cheese and a salad, with a large bottle of water in the middle, a bottle of wine and a tiny vase with a yellow carnation in it.

Bella looked up at him, pretending that what had just nearly happened hadn't nearly happened. 'I've been asleep for longer than five minutes, haven't I?'

He pulled a chair out for her. 'In this part of the world time is an abstract construct. Your table awaits, madam.'

Bella lay the guitar on the swing seat and sat at the table. It was the most romantic thing anyone had ever done for her.

Something unfamiliar fluttered in her chest. Her rational voice was trying to be rational. *It's the sun. It's the sky. It's a hot country. He can cook. He can play the guitar. He grows vegetables. But . . . but . . . He's gorgeous. I mean, those eyes.*

'Wine?' Hugo held the bottle over her glass.

She nodded then picked up a piece of bread.

That face. Those legs, continued the rational part of her brain. *That chest. His hair curls at the nape of his neck. That tattoo of the yacht. Of course you want to fall into bed with him. I mean, of course. But . . .*

'Thank you.' Bella picked up the glass and took a very long gulp.

She waited for something from her rational voice after the 'but'.

You don't live here, said the voice eventually. *And if it's just a fling and it goes wrong, that's another bad memory of Aunt Flo's house to carry around.*

She sighed. It was a bit lame, but rationally, absolutely correct.

And then he picked up the guitar.

Oh bugger, the rational voice said.

The fluttering sensation returned.

'So, you want to sing "Moon River"?' he asked, playing the first few chords.

'Yes. I'd love to.'

'Right, as you can see, the chords are very simple. And you just sing the words slowly, using the guitar as a kind of accent.'

He sang the first few lines then beamed. 'I haven't sung in front of anyone for so long. The band split up years ago. As you have provided an audience of one, I couldn't help myself.'

'Well, no one has given me an exclusive concert before. I mean—' she struggled to find the words '—it's very intense, isn't it?' She took another gulp of wine. 'Rubbish way of describing it,' she muttered.

'Do you want to try?' He walked over to her. 'It'll be easier if we sit next to each other so I can show you the chords.'

'Right.' Bella took the guitar.

'Did you manage to learn anything when you tried it when you were young?'

Bella held her left hand over the neck, then wiggled her fingers over the strings but didn't put them anywhere. 'As it happens, no.'

'OK. So . . .' Hugo moved slightly closer. Bella kept looking at the guitar. 'If you put this finger here—' he pointed at a string '—then this finger here . . .'

Bella followed his instructions.

'This one here, and finally this one over here.'

Bella stretched her hand to reach the right string but couldn't quite manage so Hugo gently took her hand and helped her.

'Thank you.' She looked up into his eyes. He was so close she could feel his breath on her neck.

She looked away and played the note.

'Good,' he said quietly. 'Now, move to this one.' He took her hand and moved it gently over the right strings.

Bella forced herself not to look up and played again. 'It's not easy to get the right pressure, the tips of my fingers are hurting already.' She played the two chords one after the other.

'You get used to it.'

One of the cats jumped up between them and sat on her lap.

'Looks like Yin or Yang wants to learn too.' She heard the smile in his voice and looked up again. He was gazing towards the rocks of Ponte de Piedade glowing gold in the distance, the setting sun throwing a silver triangle onto the sea. 'Sunsets,' he said softly. 'When I'm not working I just sit here and watch them.'

Bella gazed at him, trying to think of something to say. 'I would too,' was all she could manage.

His phone buzzed again, and again. He picked it up. 'Even on my day off.' He shook his head. 'I'm sorry. There's an issue with one of the staff. They've had to leave because of a family emergency and they can't get anyone to replace her at such notice. So . . .'

Their eyes locked again. Bella felt like she was going to fall into them.

No, shouted her rational inner voice. *Remember Gino. Throwing caution to the wind. The instant attraction, that soulmate rubbish . . . and look what happened there.*

'Oh well.' She looked away, then stood up.

'Please, let's eat the food before I go. I won't get a chance to have anything myself once I'm working.'

They sat down and ate quickly and in silence, until Hugo said, 'So, what are your hobbies when you are at home, Bella? Apart from not playing the guitar?'

'Hobbies?' Bella thought for a moment. 'I . . . go to the gym . . . yoga . . . I — I don't really have time to be honest.'

'It must be nice to have friends around, and to go out for meals.' He shook his head. 'My social life revolves around the café these days. That's where my friends come to see me.'

Bella didn't say anything. There was Lil, but Lil was her work friend. They didn't really socialise. Her friendships these days were done mostly by messaging apps, arranging and rearranging and eventually cancelling meet-ups.

Hugo stood. 'I'd best head off, then.'

'Can I help tidy up?' Bella stood too.

'No.' He shook his head. 'It will only take me a few minutes. I think you need to go home and relax.'

* * *

Bella spent the next few days in a frenzy of tidying up, sifting through Flo's old things and putting them into piles in the same way she'd dealt with everything in the outhouse. Unfortunately, all of it was then 'filed' in the outhouse, and not much was getting thrown away. She had ordered a skip, but the company kept changing the delivery date, so on the day before her first day back at work, when she looked in the fourth bedroom, cluttered with furniture and boxes, she paused. It felt like a portal to another dimension. 'A furniture dimension,' she told the cats as they sat behind her on the landing.

She decided to call a ceasefire with Auntie Flo's 'stuff'. Although, she reasoned, she was not stopping, simply reorganising her priorities. 'Because,' she closed the door and announced to the house, 'in my world, dealing with a lot of old furniture and moving it on is "making it better". And since I don't know what you meant by that phrase—' she was now talking to Great-Aunt Flo as she walked down the stairs '—in this instance, I'm deciding.'

In the living room, something darted behind the chest of drawers out of the corner of her eye, and she wearily wondered what else could be in the fourth bedroom apart from furniture.

She made a cup of tea, took her laptop outside and sat in the shade, trying to find things on her list to write '*DONE*' in bold, dark letters next to. When she ran out of things to do that to, she made another section entitled '*Outhouse temporary storing station*', and subheadings with '*Furniture*', '*Ornaments*', '*Clothes*', '*Definitely Rubbish*', '*Bags to put out for the binmen*'. She added the last one as it was an easy fix, and she contemplated adding '*Binmen have taken*' to it as another way of feeling she was making progress.

Her phone rang, but she didn't recognise the number so waited to see if anyone left a voicemail, which they did. It was Ignacio.

'*Olá*, Bella. *Bom dia*. This is Ignacio. Duarte and I are at the end of your track but don't want to drive up without letting you know we are here. And the buzzer is not working, so we can't ring it.'

Bella rolled her eyes, irritated she kept forgetting to fix the buzzer. She was supposed to be organised and she couldn't work out why that kept falling off her list of things to make better.

She rang him back. 'Hi, Ignacio. Of course you can come in. But just one thing. Where is the buzzer? People keep mentioning it, but I haven't located it yet.'

'*Excelente!* We have a small favour to ask. And the buzzer is behind the bushes.'

'Right, thanks. See you in a moment.'

She took her laptop inside and waited for them on the patio. They drove up in Duarte's electric Porsche.

'*Olá*, Bella!' Duarte got out. 'It is so very nice to see you again. Isn't it, Ignacio?'

'It certainly is.' Ignacio got out and shook her hand warmly.

'What a lovely surprise.' She tried not to stare but there was something strange in the way they were dressed.

'Ha!' Duarte beamed. 'We are dressed as Laurel and Hardy. We have been practising our living statue performance and are going to a local nursery school where there is a little festival of dance.'

'Although—' Ignacio moved his bow-tie slightly '—we are living statues so won't actually be dancing.'

'I must say, I am enjoying semi-retirement a great deal.' Duarte fussed over the cats.

Ignacio laughed. 'Do you remember the last time we were here dressed like this?'

Duarte thought for a moment. 'Three years ago? Was it for Hugo's birthday? That fancy dress party.' He shook his head and smiled. 'She loved having people here, you know.'

'It left a big gap in our lives when she left us.' Ignacio looked at the floor and cleared his throat. 'We are promoting movement and mindfulness and are going to hand out flyers for the House on the Hill at the event. Hopefully some parents might be interested.'

Duarte picked up Yin or Yang. 'And Layla is thinking of putting on a fundraising event for the charity Hugo is planning on setting up. Your aunt first suggested it but we just couldn't even think about doing it after she passed. But now we all feel reenergised.'

'What a brilliant idea.' Bella wondered what her aunt would think of Laurel and Hardy reappearing in the garden and suppressed a giggle. 'Would you like something to drink?'

'Well, this is presumptuous.' Duarte put down the cat. 'But we were at Hugo's café yesterday and he mentioned you were going through Flo's belongings and there were quite a few old clothes.'

'So, we wondered if we could look through them before you get rid of them.' Ignacio sounded excited.

'I am, as part of my film producer role, beginning acting classes for free at a local college as part of my community engagement, and think there may be some clothes we could put in what I like to call—' Duarte put his fingers in the air to indicate inverted commas '—our "dressing-up box".'

'Of course you can. Would you like to do it now?'

'Actually, no time, but we will arrange it soon. We will check with you first.'

'Yes, no problem.'

Ignacio took out his wallet and handed her a card. 'Here is the name of the electrician we use at The House. He can fix the buzzer for you.'

'Ah, one less thing to worry about.' Bella read it and looked up as they got back in the car.

'*Adeus, até a próxima*,' shouted Duarte.

They headed off down the track, and Bella wondered in what world she ever thought she'd see Laurel and Hardy driving an open-topped electric Porsche.

CHAPTER 13

Bella logged on to her work account for the first time in four weeks. The cats sat either side of the computer, on top of the pad and diary she had laid out on the table. Taking a deep breath, she scanned her emails, then closed her eyes when she saw she had 3,600 unread messages despite her out-of-office message. 'No, it's fine.' She looked at Yin and Yang. 'Once they'd seen that they would have contacted the right person. So it's fine. I just have to go through and delete.'

She checked the time — 7 a.m. She had two hours before anyone else would be logged on, and three hours before their first Zoom meeting, so she began to trawl through the messages, sipping tea and trying to un-fuzz her brain, which didn't feel as razor sharp as it had a month ago when she'd arrived in Lagos.

Having read through one particularly long message three times before realising it had been sent to her in error, Bella decided she had been enjoying far too much sun and relaxation, so put the radio on in the background to try to help motivate her through the emails. Because, she reasoned, once she'd done that she could hit the ground running and get on with this part-time thing before she could go back to full-time and life would return to normal.

She heard something skitter along the wall behind her and glanced back. It had gone, and she felt surprisingly relaxed about it. It was completely normal at Flo's house, but definitely not in her modern fourth-floor flat in London. Apart from the mice she'd found a few years before.

Making her second cup of tea at 8 a.m., she was interrupted by a knock on the door.

'Is that you, Deidre?'

Bella opened the door to find Elena dressed in a sleek green jumpsuit and white-and-yellow trainers.

'She's run off again, and I thought she might be here.' Elena was breathing heavily and had broken into a little bit of a sweat.

'No, no, she isn't.' Bella smiled. 'I like your outfit.'

Elena twirled around. 'It's a bit dressy for dog walking but I feel the need to always look my best when I see Will. Although, this outfit is not good for chasing dogs.'

'Well, it's lovely. I'm sorry, I'm working, or I'd offer you a tea or something.'

'Tea?' Elena looked confused. 'Oh, yes, I forgot, you're British.' She smoothed her trousers. 'This isn't really my kind of thing, but, you know, anyway, if you see her, here's my number.' Elena handed her a card. 'I will leave you to it then. Deidre's certainly keeping me on my toes.' She turned to walk down the track, then began to trot. 'There you are!' she shouted. 'You naughty dog! Deidre! Deidre . . .'

Bella went inside and settled back down with her drink, her heart thumping nervously the closer she got to ten.

'Hello, Bella.' Lil was smiling at her from her computer screen. 'Well, this is exciting in your new Portuguese home.'

'Temporarily.' Bella smiled back. 'But yes, it's quite a nice set-up.'

'It looks very calm and serene.'

'Oh yes. It's so quiet here. Not like when I'm working at home in the UK with all that traffic noise and people walking along the street. I hardly see anyone.'

'I'm not sure how you're managing with that given you like to be in the middle of everything.' Lil laughed. 'Now, I think our new head of department will be organising a catch-up with you, but she's only just started so we'll just carry on as is, shall we?'

Everyone on the call nodded and murmured their agreement.

'I thought I just saw something run along the wall behind you, Bella,' someone said.

'Oh.' Bella decided it was easiest not to explain the geckos.

'There it is — I saw it too!' said someone else.

Bella glanced back and pretended to examine the wall. 'I can't see anything, but I'll have a look around after work.'

'Maybe it's the internet connection,' said Lil.

'Probably is. Right, I'm ready to get on, shall we start?'

* * *

'This is nice.' Bella got out of the car and Deidre bounded out behind her.

'Yes, dogs aren't allowed on some beaches in the summer, or even all year round, so I thought this would be a good change.' Jorge walked towards her, then kissed her on both cheeks.

'Will has a check-up today so asked if I'd take this one for a walk.' Deidre was rolling around on her back in the grass. 'I'm always happy to. She's lovely.'

'I'm glad you said yes to meeting up. It was rather spontaneous on my part.'

'Your message arrived at just the right time. I've started working again so needed a de-stress somewhere different.'

'You have a lot on.' Jorge began to walk. 'How did all the visits go from the estate agents?'

'Very useful. I want to make sure that when I get it valued I choose the right ones.'

'I like to have information — you know, pros and cons, positives and negatives — so I can weigh them up and make the right decisions.' Jorge picked up a stick and threw it for

Deidre. 'Of course, with business there is always a little bit of instinct.' He took his baseball hat off to push his fringe out of his eyes, then put it back on again. 'But I believe that also comes from knowledge.'

Deidre collected the stick and dropped it in front of them, wagging her tail.

'I agree. Though maybe it's not instinct but confidence in what you know.' Bella glanced at him, wondering whether she found him attractive or not. She knew he *was* attractive. It was a fact. Whereas Hugo was definitely attractive and she could feel it. But Hugo wasn't her type. She swept the image of him practising yoga on the beach in a wetsuit away firmly, along with the near-kiss. She hadn't seen him since then. Was it her avoiding him, or him avoiding her, she wondered.

'And you also get advice from lots of people, don't you? Mostly with the best of intentions.' He picked up the stick. 'Shall we get a drink? There's a café over there under the trees.'

'Oh, yes please.' Bella nodded. 'I could do with a nice cold drink before I get back to some work.'

'It's Sunday.' Jorge shook his head. 'I thought you were working part-time?'

They found a table and sat down. 'I am. But it's my first week back and I'm trying to get on top of things so it's taking a bit more time than normal. Although, to be honest, my job has never really been nine to five, more like eight until I've finished.' Bella felt an unexpected knot in her stomach. 'Due to a restructure, the department has a new boss so things will change a bit, I expect.'

'Ah, I understand.' Jorge waved at the waitress to get her attention. 'Unfortunate timing though.'

'Yes indeed.' Bella stroked Deidre's ears absent-mindedly. The knot in her stomach began to unravel. 'Hopefully it will be OK.'

'I think that I may be so keen on working and making money because my mother works so hard. She is alone and I want to make life easier for her.'

Bella glanced at him. 'I understand. My father had an accident when I was a child and life has been challenging for my parents ever since. I want them to be happy, so I try to take the financial pressure from them.'

'I knew we were similar.' Jorge smiled and leaned forward, catching her gaze and holding it for a moment.

'*Olá, bom dia.*' the waitress brought over a bowl of water for the dog and put it in front of her, then smiled at Jorge and Bella expectantly.

'*Uma bica e . . .*' Jorge smiled at Bella.

'*Um . . .*' Bella rifled through her Portuguese words in her head. '*Sumol de laranjana natural . . . se faz . . . favor?*'

'*Muito bem!*' Jorge shook her hand. 'Well done. Keep at it.'

'Fresh orange juice?' asked the waitress.

'Yes please.' Bella wondered if she'd ever get to the day when someone didn't need to check what she'd said.

'One day you will look and sound so confident that no one will check what you've said in Portuguese after you've said it.'

'I was wondering that.' Bella looked at him again, her gaze now hidden under her sunglasses, reflecting that he appeared to be able to read her mind.

The drinks arrived. Jorge picked up his cup and took a sip of the coffee. 'So, I hear that Hugo is taking forward his plans for the charity he and your aunt were planning to launch.'

'Is he?' Bella picked up the glass. It felt cool and refreshing, so she held it for a second before taking a drink. 'I knew he was talking to people about it but didn't know it was that far forward. Did he tell you?'

'Oh, no.' He shook his head. 'We don't really talk. I have only met him a couple of times through my aunt and the people at the House on the Hill. I heard it through the grapevine.'

'Ah, the grapevine.' Bella added it to her list of things to ask even more questions about.

'I wonder how he's going to get the right access. Has he spoken to you about using some of your land? I believe the track to his house is too narrow but borders your orchard?'

'He hasn't mentioned it.' Bella took another long sip of her drink. 'I've only been here since April. We don't know each other that well. He seems to be a very honest man, so I'm sure he would talk to me about it if he needed to.'

'Of course.' Jorge leaned back in his seat. 'I have a friend who he hurt very badly. She doesn't like him very much. Now, anyway.'

'None of my business,' Bella said quickly. 'I'm only passing through, as you know. So, he is just my neighbour.'

'Just your neighbour, of course. Gossip . . . I sometimes forget myself. And when my friend and he split up, there was sadness and anger on both sides. And I just hear her side.'

'Absolutely.' Bella didn't want to hear any more about Hugo's love life. But she did want to hear about the road access. From him, not third or fourth hand from Jorge. She looked at her watch. 'I'd better go. The sooner I get this report finished the sooner I can move onto more work on the house.'

'Are you going into town tonight? My aunt tells me that Ignacio and Duarte will be a double act of living statues.' He laughed. 'I love their *joie de vivre* and sense of fun.'

'I may pop in for a walk around later.' She checked her phone, thinking about how much work she had left to catch up with. 'I can't wait to see them if I do. Where will they be?'

'I'm not sure. My aunt was quite vague. She's been like that since she met Will.' He put his cup down and paid for the drinks.

'I'll pay my share.' Bella took her purse out of her bag.

'No.' He put his hand on hers. 'Next time it's your turn.'

'Yes. I'll make sure it is.' Bella stood up to go.

'Did you speak to Lenny and Martim in the end?'

'Ah, yes I did.' Deidre clambered to her feet and barked at Bella excitedly. 'Thank you for passing me their contact details.'

'Of course, they will know all about the access issues with Hugo's place. Your aunt and one of his relatives had a big falling out about it many years ago. His—' he thought for a moment '—uncle . . . great-uncle . . . anyway, a long time ago.'

'I'm still weighing everything up property-wise.' Bella held her hand out to shake his, but he leaned in and kissed her on both cheeks. 'We are in Portugal, Bella.'

'Well, off I go!' She put the lead on Deidre.

'*Até a próxima.*' He smiled.

'Until next time.' She waved at him as she climbed in the car.

'Such a lot of information, Deidre,' she said to the dog. 'I'm not sure I wanted all of it.'

* * *

As Bella arrived at Will's to drop Deidre off, Lenny and Martim were sitting in a truck talking to him from their window.

'That was a very useful chat,' she heard Martim say. 'If you need any more information just let us know.' He wound the window up and started the engine, waving at Bella as they drove off.

Will was standing in the doorway looking drained.

'Is everything all right?' Bella got out of her car followed by the dog, who bounded up to Will and bounced around him excitedly.

He broke into a smile. 'Yes. Just . . .' He rubbed his face. 'I'm not going to be able to get back to work for a few weeks, and I'm finding not being able to walk properly frustrating.'

Bella nodded, thinking about her father on one of his good days hobbling around the house on his sticks, and then on a bad day when he couldn't get out of a chair without her mother helping him. Whatever kind of day it was, his expression was determined, but exhausted.

'And the money . . . well . . . I rely on my earnings to top up my pension.'

'Is that what Lenny and Martim were here about? Money for your house?'

'They just arrived. I didn't ask them to come.' He sounded defensive. 'They've heard from somewhere about my accident and have been attempting to make me an offer they think I can't refuse.'

'I know it's none of my business, but I didn't realise the money issue was that bad.' Bella got Deidre's lead out of the car and handed it to Will.

He sighed. 'Early days. But I don't know how they knew about me. And they seemed to think you were considering selling your land.'

'I decided against it,' Bella said. 'It didn't seem right to knock the place down and bulldoze over all the love Great-Aunt Flo put into it.'

'Ah.' He smiled weakly. 'You are getting drawn in, aren't you? When you arrived, it was one of your options. You've fallen in love with it.'

'No, I haven't.' Bella could feel herself bristle. 'I'm making a rational decision based on extensive research. That's what I do.'

'Whatever you say. They are quite persistent though, those two. They said they were working for a third party.'

'Did they? Who?'

'A third party who wishes to remain anonymous apparently.'

'Right.' Bella glanced at her watch. 'I'd better go. I've got work to finish, then house stuff.'

'Elena is bringing around a meat loaf or something, so I'd better make the table.' His eyes widened. 'What's happening to me! I didn't own a tablecloth till last week.' He laughed. 'It was a gift. From Elena.'

'Enjoy.' Bella got back into the car. 'Anytime you want me to look after Deidre just ask.'

'Thanks.' He waved at her as she drove off, and when she got to the end of his drive she paused. 'Right or left? Home or Hugo's café?'

She decided to see if Hugo was at work to check if the rumour Jorge had heard was true, and she could have a snack

157

at the same time to save her cooking lunch at home. 'Yes, that is an effective use of my time,' she announced to the road.

The café was busy, so she settled at a corner table, enjoying the buzz of conversation around her, and ordered a *galão* from Quiet Julian. 'Is Hugo here?' she asked.

Julian nodded.

'Can you tell him Bella's here and I need to ask him something.'

A family were playing football on the beach close by, and a man was walking along selling donuts, ringing a bell, shouting '*Bolinhas!*' A woman walked over to him to buy one. Bella just watched, her mind beginning to calm down.

She thought of ambling and having no firm destination and smiled. When she'd left the house that morning, it was to meet Jorge and then go home and work. But she'd come here instead. *Although*, muttered her inner voice, *you do have a final destination, and that is home. This is just a detour to gather information. Not an amble.*

'Bella.' Hugo sat down in front of her, wiping his hands on his apron. 'Busy day.' He smiled, but tiredly.

'I'll only keep you a second.'

'No—' he held his hand up '—I didn't mean it like that. I always have time for my neighbours.'

'It's about that actually.' Her heart began to race. 'You know your idea of the educational establishment on your land? The charity you and my aunt were going to set up?'

'Yes.' He was looking at the door.

Bella followed his gaze. A woman was standing at the entrance talking on her phone. She was wearing a long, expensive-looking red dress, and her dark brown hair was cut in a sleek bob.

'Sorry. There's a lot going on.' Hugo's smile had faded a little.

'Well, I heard that you may need some of my land for road access. Is that right?'

'Where did you hear that?' He looked confused.

'Jorge.'

Hugo glanced at the woman again. 'I have only met Jorge a couple of times. Why would he say that?'

'He heard it on the grapevine, I think . . .' Bella was beginning to feel uncomfortable. 'I just have to ask, that's all.'

'For the spreadsheet?' Hugo stood up. His smile had disappeared.

'I need to know anything that may impact the house.'

'No, you don't. You don't need to know all the things you are finding out about.' He watched the woman walk down the steps and into the car park. 'You're leaving anyway. You need to understand the market but you are making it very complicated.' He stared at her, frowning. 'Why is that, Bella?'

Bella looked down, confused. 'Why are you so . . . ?' She looked up at him again, searching for the words. 'So . . . like this?'

He shook his head. 'I'm sorry. I've got to go.'

Bella took her purse out and placed money on the table for her drink, then left without finishing it, wondering what had happened. He was rude, dismissive and he hadn't even answered the question.

Walking down the steps she noticed the woman Hugo had been watching sitting in her car. She was still on her phone. 'It was a bit of a surprise,' the woman was saying. 'It didn't go very well. I will have to try again. *Adeus*, Martim.'

Bella turned on the engine. Her mind wasn't calm anymore, trying to make sense of the last few minutes, persuading herself that Martim was a very common name and she was making something out of nothing.

She put the radio on, turned the volume up, and allowed the Rolling Stones singing 'Angry' to power her home.

CHAPTER 14

Bella woke early the following morning and lingered in bed for a while listening to the storks chatting outside, enjoying the clicks of their beaks and swishing of their wings. Rolling over, she examined the pinpricks of light dotting the floor, deciding they looked like diamonds glowing in the early-morning sun, then mentally went through her day. Department Zoom meeting at nine thirty, then individual chats with project leaders, then planning, after which she tried to remember the contents of her fridge so she could work out what she needed to buy at the supermarket that evening.

But none of it worked. The questions she was trying not to think about still managed to force their way to the forefront of her mind. Why had Hugo been so rude to her yesterday? And, just as importantly, why was she so upset?

You could go and ask him, answered her inner voice reasonably. *And as for the second question, that is obvious.*

Deciding to ignore that, she went downstairs, fed the cats, made herself a cup of tea and opened the door. The morning glow flooded in, so she stepped outside, feeling as if she was in a bath of sunlight. Sitting down, she looked at the tangled red bougainvillea that was beginning to thrive in the window boxes and some orange and white flowers she couldn't identify that seemed to have bloomed overnight. The storks continued to bustle, and the sea roared calmly in the distance.

Glancing up at the gaps the fallen tiles had left, she decided to ring the man in the shop in Silves she'd ordered the new ones from to check their progress. Then she got up, pushing everything out of her mind except for her workday ahead.

* * *

'It has taken a bit of getting used to.' Bella adjusted the screen so she could see everyone. 'It is so quiet here.'

'Yes, very different from central London, I should think,' Bella's new head of department, Jules, said. 'But it must be lovely not to have car horns and all that traffic noise.'

'During the day, yes. But as I told everyone at our last meeting, at night I've resorted to a rainforest soundtrack on Alexa to mask the silence.' Bella laughed at her own joke again.

'Shouldn't you have one with police sirens on it and drunks shouting for kebabs?' Lil giggled.

'I don't think they do one of those. Perhaps there's an opening for an entrepreneurial type — ambient city noise.'

The cats walked inside and ambled over to her.

'Well.' Jules uploaded a document. 'Here are the stats for the last quarter. As you can see, they are very healthy, but we still need to increase our output.'

'Right.'

The cats jumped onto the table and sat down either side of the computer, purring loudly.

'What's that? I can hear some interference?' one of Bella's colleagues said.

'Oh, I think it's the cats.' Bella moved the screen so they could all see them.

Everyone emitted a collective 'ahhh'.

'I thought you were only there for six months maximum?' Jules took her glasses off and cleaned them. 'Cats seem a bit permanent.'

'No. They used to belong to my aunt, and when I moved in, so did they. They'll go back to my neighbours when I leave.'

Lil sighed. 'Sooooo cute.'

'Shall we get on? Cats and dogs are just a part of hybrid working these days. Lola here—' Jules picked up a rabbit and put it on the table '—is a house-trained rabbit. The kids love her. She poos everywhere and chews through wires.' She smoothed the rabbit's ears. 'She really is a pest. But we all love her.' The rabbit jumped off the table. 'Right. As I was saying, can I hear clicking?'

'Is it interference on the computer?' Bella's colleagues started to press buttons and fiddle with their headphones.

'I think it's the storks.' Bella went to the door to check. One of them was standing in the garden with a twig in its mouth, while the other was on the nest chattering and clicking.

She closed the door and sat at the computer again. 'Sorry about that. They are a bit noisy today.'

'Did you say storks?' Jules asked, eyes wide.

'Yes. They live on the roof of the outbuilding.'

'How wonderful.' One of her colleagues clapped her hands gleefully.

'Aren't they a bit messy?' asked someone else.

'Um . . . I suppose so. No more than any other birds. There are a lot around here . . . bit of a birdwatcher's paradise. I found a large group in my garden not so long ago.'

'What, storks?' asked her friend.

'No, birdwatchers.'

'Right.' Her boss cleared her throat. 'Let's get on. Hopefully there won't be any more interruptions.'

'I've closed the front door now. I only leave it open in case Deidre wanders over.' Bella wished she hadn't said anything, wondering where her businesslike brain had gone. She always kept her input to a minimum so she could get on with her work as soon as possible, and certainly never, ever indulged in informal chit-chat.

'Oh, it's nice you've made some friends already,' Lil said.

'Ha, well, Deidre's a dog who lives next door.' Bella was about to explain why Deidre was prone to make unexpected visits but managed to stop herself. 'It's a long story,' she muttered. 'So, how are we going to increase our output? Are some of our tasks being reassigned?' She moved a pad in front of her and picked up a pen to make sure she looked like she was fully engaged.

'We have reorganised some of the workload as you have temporarily rearranged your working week to three days,' Jules explained, uploading another document. 'This is where we are now — as per the email sent out two weeks ago. So, I'm looking for ideas on how to streamline some of our work and operations—'

A dog started barking outside very loudly. Bella attempted to ignore it. Everyone looked up and tried to work out where it was coming from. Bella knew. It was Deidre. She smiled serenely, hoping the dog would get bored and lie down outside until the meeting finished and she could let her in.

Deidre continued to bark. Then she began to whine, and the cats meowed. Bella got up and let the dog in, then sat down. 'Sorry about that.' She cleared her throat and ignored the dog running around excitedly, her paws pattering noisily on the tiles. 'She'll calm down in a minute.'

'The joys of working from home,' someone said and everyone murmured in agreement.

The storks started up their clattering noise again. Bella resisted the urge to put her head in her hands. *This is not who I am*, she thought. *I am not chaos. I am not—*

'Deidre! Deidre! There you are!' Elena almost galloped into the house. 'Oh, Bella — she ran off.'

'This is Elena.' Bella's voice sounded slightly strained.

Deidre wagged her tail and darted around, avoiding Elena's attempts to catch her.

'Deidre, come back!'

The six faces on the Zoom call displayed various expressions ranging from laughing out loud to mild irritation.

'I'm on a work call, Elena.' Bella stood up. 'I'll be back in a second. I've got some treats in the kitchen.'

'I can only apologise,' she heard Elena say. 'I rescued Bella's neighbour from a ditch nearby a few weeks ago, then hurt his back when I got him into my car. So I have been trying to make amends since then.'

Bella opened a cupboard and picked out some dog treats.

'Ah, yes, Bella mentioned something about that,' Lil was saying.

'I've never had any pets and I thought it would be helpful to offer to take his dog for walks when he wasn't up to it. Bella has been helping out too. And—' Elena's voice lowered '—if I'm honest, I'm trying to impress him. I'm a very well-established accountant with my own business, and he is an old hippie who's lived on his own for a long time, but I confess that I am rather smitten.'

Bella tried not to picture her boss's face as she hurried back into the room and put a treat on the floor in front of the dog.

'Here we are, Elena.' Bella picked up the lead and handed it over.

'Oh, thank you. And sorry, Bella.' She waved at the screen. 'Sorry, everyone, to disturb your meeting. Bye. Come on, Deidre, let's get you back to Will.'

Bella sat down as she walked out and closed the door behind her.

'That's a very busy place for somewhere that's supposed to be so quiet.' Lil laughed.

'Do you get many interruptions like that?' Jules asked.

Bella shook her head. 'No. Absolutely not. The house is at the end of a track off a narrow lane.'

'Good. Good news.' Jules uploaded another document. 'Now, let's get on with our ideas, shall we?'

Bella's stomach churned. *Mustn't undo all these years of hard work with all of — this.* Her inner voice sounded slightly stressed. *Whatever this is.*

164

At the end of the meeting, Lil said, 'Hey, Bella, can you stay on for a moment when everyone's signed off? I've got a question about some stats I need to run by you.'

'No problem.' Bella watched the faces of her colleagues leave the meeting, then smiled at Lil.

'So, things seem interesting over there.'

Bella laughed thinly. 'A bit more than I was expecting, to be honest.'

'How's the hunky neighbour?'

'Not sure.' Bella didn't want to say any more.

'What about the lovely finance man? Jorge?'

Bella's mind flew back to their coffee, remembering how he'd been talking to her and staring directly into her eyes. 'Um, very helpful.' She glanced at the clock. 'So, what is it that you want to run by me?'

'Why have you decided to temporarily relocate to Portugal? I didn't think about it when you went as it was done in such a hurry but . . .' She shook her head. 'You could have taken a holiday, visited, worked out what's best, paid someone to sort it out for you, and popped over when needed.'

'I needed to see it so I can be sure I'm getting the right price when I sell.'

'I don't think you need to be there for six months to do that. You've made your life difficult with work, and it's for less money because you've gone part-time.'

'I have to make it better.' Bella couldn't quite formulate the words to explain why she'd decided to disrupt her life like this. Possibly because she didn't really know.

'You could pay someone to do that. I mean, how much information do you need to make the decision?'

Bella rifled through her mind, trying to pinpoint the reason that had pushed her to Portugal so quickly. 'Someone else asked me that too.'

'Well? I'm your friend. Your work set-up is clearly not quite right at the moment there.'

Yin or Yang nuzzled Bella's hand. 'It seems so silly . . . so irrational . . . but the letter arrived from the solicitor on the same date my dad had his car accident. It was years before. He was only forty. Everything changed for him on that date. For my mum. For me.'

'Oh, Bella. How old were you?'

'I was nine. I was eight when we came here. That was such a magical holiday. And it was sort of our only holiday.'

'Your dad does work though? And your mum?'

Bella didn't want to talk about it, but somehow the words poured out and she couldn't stop them. 'He was a PE teacher. Then suddenly he couldn't walk properly. Lost that. So, now he marks exams. And writes sports reports for newspapers and websites. But his mobility is getting worse, and then there's the depression. And my mum is his carer and works when she can, and I want their life to be better than that.'

'So you support them, don't you?'

'Yes. As much as I can financially.'

'Oh, Bella.' Lil reached her hand towards her camera. 'I wish I could give you a hug.'

'They need the house to be adapted so he can live downstairs now. They love that house. My mum loves the garden. If I sell this, it could pay for the adaptation. If I rent it out, I could provide them with a regular income.'

'But that doesn't explain why you're over there now?'

'But you know — in the will it said I had to make it better. This place — I don't know — it just triggered me, because I've been trying to make things better for my mum and dad since I was nine. And Gino had gone. Gosh!' Bella took a breath, then found herself smiling at Lil. 'I hadn't really thought about it, which is unlike me, Miss "I must have information!" This seems to be entirely based on instinct. Oh.' Bella widened her eyes.

'Indeed.' Lil smiled again. 'I'm as surprised as you are!' A buzzer went in the background. 'I've got another meeting, got to go.'

'Me too. Thanks, Lil.'

'What for?'

'For making me think.'

* * *

Bella decided to lose herself in the holiday crowds in the centre of Lagos that evening. Her day at work and the trip to the supermarket hadn't filled up enough of her day or her thoughts to stop the chatter that was crowding in on her.

Why did you come and stay? Why did you upend your life and your job? What were you thinking?

For once, obviously nothing.

You are usually on top of everything. You can't blame a date on a solicitor's letter for almost catapulting yourself over here.

I wouldn't use the word catapult.

A man in a bowler hat and a bow-tie was riding a unicycle and juggling in the square, making the children squeal and their parents laugh. Bella lingered for a while, trying to concentrate on what he was doing so she couldn't think.

It is a bit more complicated with the house than I expected, she told herself. *Didn't expect the land it's on to be so popular. Didn't expect it all to be so lovely. Didn't expect to feel so very responsible for doing the right thing for Great-Aunt Flo.*

'Oh,' she said out loud. 'If I hadn't have come over it would have been so much easier.'

A woman standing next to her laughed. 'It's worth the trip though, isn't it? It may be easier not to make the effort but look what you get when you're here.' She gave her child a coin. 'There you are. Wait till he's finished with the juggling and give him this.'

'Yes, food for thought.' Bella nodded, then drifted off. She wandered along the avenida towards the fort, the distant lights of Meia Praia and Alvor twinkling around the bay. A man stood by the river fishing as a boat crowded with people coasted past on its way back to the marina, blasting out 'Wake

Me Up Before You Go Go' to wild cheers and singing from its passengers. Bella watched them, waiting for the music to get quieter as they got further away, then walked onto the town beach, taking her sandals off and wiggling her toes in the cool, soothing sand. The moon cast a triangle of light onto the black sea, and she walked towards it, allowing the water to lap gently over her ankles, concentrating on its quiet rhythm as if she was counting, the chatter in her head slowly drifting away.

She padded back up to the path, put on her sandals, and made her way back to the noise and bustle of the town. She bought herself a chocolate-chip ice cream and meandered along a side street, pausing at a jewellery stall selling silver rings and bracelets, then turned and walked past a man singing 'Nessun Dorma', finding herself in the square in front of the lime-green building again. Sitting on a wall, she finished her ice cream, gazing absent-mindedly at the passers-by.

Under one of the jacaranda trees on the opposite side, Bella noticed a man and a woman having an animated discussion. Standing up, she checked her bag for her car keys, then looked at the couple again. It was Hugo and the woman who had been at the café. He was shaking his head as she walked away towards a side street. Hugo watched the woman go, looked at the floor and walked off in the opposite direction.

Bella wasn't sure what she had seen, but Hugo didn't seem very happy. She decided to follow him from a distance to check that he was all right, skirting around the crowds so she wouldn't lose sight of him.

As he disappeared along a crowded, narrow street, Bella tried to keep up but her progress was slowed by the café tables dotting the pavement and the people happily ambling past, chatting, or pausing in front of shop windows. Someone began to play 'La Vie en Rose' on an accordion and a group of diners roared with laughter at a joke a waiter had made.

She caught sight of Hugo's red T-shirt as he disappeared around another corner. He moved quickly, frustrating Bella as she weaved around the tide of people she felt were walking towards her. She hurried onto the road Hugo had turned onto. He was leaning against his car, staring at a shop window.

Bella waited for a moment, then walked up to him tentatively. 'Hi.' She waved. 'What a surprise. Fancy seeing you here.' She glanced into the window. It was full of pots and pans. 'Are you researching new kitchen equipment?'

He looked at her blankly, then seemed to come to. 'Kitchen equipment?'

Bella nodded at the window. 'You seemed to be very interested in the contents of that shop.'

'Oh.' He shook his head and attempted a smile. 'No. I was trying to clear my head.'

'Can I help?' Bella decided not to mention she'd been following him. Especially because of that night. That evening. That near-miss when he'd helped her clear the outbuilding. She tried to suppress what she knew was a tiny trickle of jealousy.

'You know when someone from your past that you loved — really loved — that all-consuming love that you thought would never end?' Hugo seemed to be addressing the shop window.

Bella took a small step back. *Don't be jealous*, she told herself. *You're only passing through.*

'But one day you realise that they've stopped loving you. And they don't even like you. And one of the reasons you know is because they take the things that make you who you are and twist them into bad things.'

The accordion player began to play 'I've Got You Under My Skin', the notes drifting quietly along the darkened street.

'My ex asked to meet me for a drink. I haven't heard from her for over a year. She turned up at the café earlier asking questions about my house and my land again, so I decided we needed to talk about it, just to clear the air. And then she . . .' He turned away from the window and looked at Bella. 'She accused me of sitting on land that could be used for housing for local people. I want to grow food. I use it usefully. She said

I was selfish. But I'm not!' He shook his head. 'And I know she's working for a company that builds expensive villas. I know who she works for.'

Bella moved forward and touched his hand. 'I'm sorry, that doesn't feel fair.'

'No. She met me to try to persuade me to sell. Again. And when I said no, again, she twisted everything. Again. I think she enjoyed it.'

'You must still care about her?' The words came out of Bella's mouth before she could stop them.

'No. No!' he almost shouted. 'I couldn't, could I? I shouldn't . . .' He leaned back against his car. 'I was thinking back on my way here. When we met she wasn't like this. It was after eighteen months or so she started to try to persuade me to sell. And I wouldn't. And after a while she left and got a job working for a development company, but, well, that's imma-terial. Now I wonder if it was me or my house she wanted all along.'

'Maybe you're thinking that because you're angry? Maybe she just changed.' Bella was clutching at straws. He was upset, and it was upsetting her. Which was making her confused.

He didn't say anything, then seemed to try to make him-self move. 'I've had too much to drink. I can't drive home.'

'I've brought my car. I'll take you. Is it OK to leave your car here?'

He sighed, his body almost hunched. 'Yes. And that's kind . . . are you sure? I'm embarrassed I've drunk too much.'

'Of course I'm sure.' Bella put her bright-and-friendly-yet-assertive voice on. 'I'm planning on a morning coffee at the café. Can't have the owner stuck in town and unhappy. And hungover.'

'Oh, yes,' he muttered. 'I've got an early delivery. No rest for the wicked.' He looked up at Bella and tried to laugh. 'Because that's what I am — wicked — for not selling my land that I use to grow things on and want also to use to educate — to her.'

170

'My car is on the avenida.' Bella began to walk. 'Let's get you home. I'm sure you'll feel better when you're there.'

They walked silently through the busy streets to Bella's car and got in.

Hugo turned to her. 'Thank you.' His voice was shaky. 'Is it OK if I close my eyes? I feel . . . I feel . . . not too well.'

Bella touched his arm. 'Whatever's best. I'll give you a nudge when we get you home.'

She pulled out into the traffic and began to drive away from the lights and people, and onto the quiet road behind Meia Praia. Hugo seemed to be asleep, and she thought about what he had said about his ex.

'My ex, Gino, said he loved me because I was so ambitious and strong and committed to my career.' Saying the words out loud felt better than the phrases rattling around in her head with nowhere to go, and she couldn't stop. 'He said we were the same in that way. And he was right — I loved the fact he was so driven and forward-thinking and had a plan. We both had a plan . . . but now I know my plan was just trying to keep things the same really.'

She glanced over. Hugo's breathing was steady and calm.

'Then we decided to try for a baby. And it didn't happen. And he left me. By text. He said I was working too hard and if I had done things differently then I would have got pregnant just like that.' She stopped talking for a moment. Hugo's eyes were still closed.

'I know now he was frustrated and projecting it on to me. Didn't help then though.'

'And. And—' she took a breath '—the massive irony of this is that I'd just done a pregnancy test. I didn't tell him as I didn't want to get his hopes up just in case. Guess what — I was pregnant . . .'

She wiped the tears that were running down her face.

'I decided not to tell him until I had to. I knew when he sent that text I never wanted to see him again unless it was absolutely necessary. And six weeks later I wasn't pregnant anymore. I lost the baby. I know it happens. It happens more than you think until it happens to you. That early in a first pregnancy.'

She stopped the car at the gate to Hugo's house. 'So, because I couldn't do what he wanted me to, he turned everything about me that he'd loved into something he hated.'

Bella looked at Hugo again and touched him gently on the shoulder. 'We are home. Can you open the gate? Hugo? Hugo . . .'

He opened his eyes slowly. 'Home?' He took a key fob out of his pocket and pointed it at the gate. They watched as it opened slowly. Then Bella drove him up to the house and made sure he got inside.

* * *

The alarm went off at 7.15 a.m. the following morning so Bella could keep up to date with her work before the working day officially began, reasoning that once she was in the flow of her temporarily part-time role, she wouldn't start early, she would just finish late as usual.

Her mind drifted back to last night. To Hugo. To his vulnerability, his sadness. And she wondered why confiding in a person who was fast asleep and couldn't hear had been so freeing.

She switched off the ambient rainforest track and listened to the storks outside. Yin and Yang padded into the room and jumped onto the bed, purring and chirping. A donkey brayed outside.

'Mateus sounds close today.' She looked at the cats, who were too busy pawing the bedcover to care, reasoning it must be the breeze carrying the noise.

The donkey brayed again. Bella stretched out of bed and walked downstairs. The cats followed, pattering behind her, brushing against her ankles while she filled the kettle. After spooning their food into their bowls, she made a cup of tea and took it to the front door so she could drink it on the patio.

Mateus was standing on the doorstep. He snorted loudly. Bella stared for a moment.

'Hello?' She looked around to see if Hugo was there. 'This a nice surprise.'

The donkey brayed, then turned away.

'Are you trying to tell me something?'

The donkey snorted again.

For a moment, Bella felt like she was in one of those television programmes where animals try to communicate with humans.

'Hugo?' she shouted, walking out into the garden. 'Are you there?'

Mateus began to bray repeatedly. Bella felt uneasy so rushed back inside, got dressed quickly, and patted the donkey. 'Did you come via the road? No, you didn't, did you?'

She walked across the vegetable patch, then through the grove, the donkey following her, the scent of oranges heavy in the air, then stopped when she got to the fence. 'You couldn't have climbed over, could you?'

Mateus trotted over to the corner, then through a tiny gap in the bushes. 'Oh, ah, good.' Bella followed and hurried to the house, her heart pounding.

She knocked on the door, the donkey standing placidly behind her. 'It's fine. I'm sure it's fine. I think.' She lowered her voice. 'It may be a hangover after last night.'

'Hugo? Hugo?' Bella knocked again and shook her head apologetically at the donkey. 'He's not usually like this, is he? I mean, I got the impression he's very reliable.'

The donkey snorted.

'Is that a yes or a no? That ex of his really must have hurt him.' Bella felt a little flutter in her chest. 'Oh.' She put her hand on it, considering a visit to the doctor as it had started to happen a lot.

She knocked on the door again. 'Your donkey escaped,' she called. 'He turned up at my house. I'm worried.'

Something crashed to the floor inside.

'Oh no.' Hugo's voice was low and a little cracked.

'What's going on? Hugo. Hugo?' Bella pushed the door in case it was unlocked. It was.

Hugo was sitting on the floor, leaning against the sofa. The shattered remnants of a broken glass were scattered in front of him. 'I rolled off the sofa and knocked it over.' His voice was quiet, his hair matted on his head and his T-shirt stained from, Bella decided, whatever he'd been drinking after she'd left the previous night.

'I thought you were turning in after I dropped you off?' she asked, opening the shutters and then the windows. 'Needs a bit of freshening up in here.'

'Mateus.' Hugo tried to get up. 'Why are you in the house?'

The donkey was standing behind Bella, as if it was trying to look stern.

'I found him on my patio first thing this morning. He'd got out of the gate at the end of your drive I think. It was unlocked when I arrived.'

Hugo put his hand on his forehand and rubbed it. 'I thought I'd locked it. I — Oh, I'm sorry. Thank you for bringing him back. He used to go over to your aunt's sometimes when he was hungry and I was a bit late feeding him.'

'Would you like a cup of tea?' Bella didn't know what else to do so utilised her mother's generic remedy.

'I don't have tea in the house. I'm Portuguese.'

'Coffee then.'

Hugo put his hand over his mouth. 'No.' He shook his head.

'Water then.' Bella walked into the kitchen and poured him a glass, then rooted around for some bread.

'Here.' She handed them both to him. 'Little and often.' She glanced at her watch. 'I've got to prepare for a work meeting later. Will you be OK?'

Hugo nodded and took a sip of the water. He looked up at her, his chocolate-brown eyes baleful and vulnerable.

There was that flutter in her chest again.

'Are you working at the restaurant today?' She decided being practical would stop whatever surge of pity she was feeling, as what Hugo was experiencing was entirely self-inflicted.

'Ahhh.' He closed his eyes. 'What's the time?'

'7.45 a.m.' Bella's voice was louder than she meant it to be.

'I've got a delivery at 8.15. Julian's not in till nine thirty.' He tried to get up but sank back towards the sofa.

'How long will it take?' The words leaped out of Bella's mouth before she had time to think.

'Fifteen minutes.' He tried to get up again.

'I'll do it. Do you have the keys?'

He looked up at her, his eyes wide with gratitude. 'Thank you. I will message him but he rolls out of bed only half an hour before the shift. He has a key. I'll try my manager, but she lives forty minutes away.'

'You'll have to open late. I can't do that. I've no time and I've no clue.'

'I am grateful that you can meet the delivery guy. Just tell the driver to put everything in the kitchen and Julian can put it all away. And me. Once I have recovered.' He rubbed his forehead again. 'And given myself a stern talking to.'

Bella picked up his phone from the table and handed it to him. 'I've got to run.'

'The keys are hanging by the door. And the security code is on a card there on the table. I keep it there in case someone needs it. I've got a few. Just take it.'

'OK.' Bella edged past the donkey. 'I think you owe Mateus an apology and thanks. He was clearly worried about you.' She sighed. 'I can't believe I just said that.'

'Thank you, Mateus.' Hugo sounded genuinely grateful.

Bella laughed. 'Right. I'll message when I've done it.' She turned around and wiggled her finger at him. 'And you owe me. I'm having to rearrange my schedule. And I've no idea what I'm doing.'

'Thank you.' Hugo put his hand on his chest earnestly.

Bella tried to look angry but couldn't manage it and hurried towards the door.

'Bella,' Hugo called after her. 'I'm sorry you had that experience with your ex. I'm sorry about the baby.'

She froze, unable to turn around and look at him.

'I . . . I thought you were asleep.' Her voice was quiet.

'Not quite.'

'What you said, about taking the things you are and turning them against you . . . it just triggered me. It's nothing.'

'It's not nothing, Bella.'

She still couldn't turn round.

'I hope you had the right support after it happened. All of it . . . the miscarriage. The break-up.'

'I didn't tell anyone about the miscarriage. I didn't tell anyone. I didn't want to worry anyone. I didn't want to upset my parents.'

'Oh, Bella.'

She felt the need to run. And so she did.

* * *

Bella put her Portuguese language app on and stuck her headphones in, attempting to drown out the noise in her head. She decided to pretend the conversation hadn't happened. It was easier. Gino was the past. It was just something to do with Flo's house and the memories and the storks. That was all. Something that had to be felt and cleared. And that's what was happening now. She forced herself not to think of Hugo and his words. 'Oh, Bella.'

Diving back into work mode she mentally planned the day, rearranging her tasks for before work actually began so she could get some control, and pretending that repeating the Portuguese phrases in her headphones would be useful just in case the delivery man didn't speak English. At least the words she had mastered would be beautifully pronounced even if they weren't the right ones, she decided, her brain

176

slowly calming as she dragged herself back to her comfort zone. Which was pushing her emotions away.

A few people were walking along the beach, moving through the glistening swathes of moisture left by the tide on the sand, the sun illuminating the white crests of the waves as they broke gently on the shore. Bella allowed herself to watch for a moment, trying to commit it to memory, for those dark winter days when she would look out of the window of her flat over the grey London skyline.

The sound of a truck moving closer made her turn around, and she took the keys out of her bag, punched in the code and opened the front door, hurrying back into the kitchens to find the back door.

Taking her headphones out, she took a few deep breaths to compose herself then went outside, smiling, as the truck parked and the driver got out.

'*Bom dia!*' she said brightly.

'*Tudo bem?*'

Bella rifled through her Portuguese language files in her mind until she realised that '*Tudo bem*' was a good enough reply.

The man scratched his beard and smiled. 'Is English better for you?'

'Oh yes, please. I'm just doing this as a favour at the last minute, so I haven't had time to rehearse the right words.'

'Ah, well.' The man opened the back of the truck. 'At least you tried. Thank you. *Obrigado.*' He unloaded crates of beer. 'In the kitchen as usual?'

'Yes, please.' Bella held the door open as he brought the crates in then gave her a receipt to sign.

'Where's Hugo?' he asked as he was leaving. 'He's usually here on a Thursday.'

'Urgent appointment. He'll be along soon.' Bella waved at him and let the door slowly close behind him. '*Obrigada. Até logo,*' she said, feeling pleased with her command of the Portuguese language, then put the receipt on a worktop,

177

locked the kitchen door and went out into the café, checking her watch. 'Better get a wiggle on,' she muttered.

Outside she bumped into Ignacio and Duarte.

'*Olá*, Bella!' Ignacio beamed. 'Hugo sent a rather garbled message just now asking for some assistance, and as we had just finished our morning beach yoga, I thought I'd check in to see how things are.'

'It's all OK. I've just taken in the delivery. So, I'm off.'

'Good, good.' Duarte glanced around. 'As I'm here, I wouldn't mind a coffee.'

'But it's closed.' Bella was locking the door.

'Hugo won't mind. I'll leave the money next to the till.'

'Um, but . . .' One of Bella's feet was trying to walk down the steps, while the other was rooted to the spot. 'I've got the key, and I don't think I should just leave it with you. He trusted me with it, and it doesn't feel right.'

'Of course.' Ignacio took her hand. 'I completely understand. So, we'll make you a coffee too. I used to work with my brother in our restaurant.'

'I have to get back for work.' Bella looked at the sea shining in the distance, then thought of the day ahead, alone in the Nest with her thoughts. She checked her watch.

'Just a fifteen-minute pause before your workday.' Duarte smiled at her. 'You are in Portugal. And look.' He waved his hand expansively at the view. 'This will set you up nicely.'

'I've got forty-five minutes, I suppose.' She sighed. 'Why not.'

'Excellent, good. Good!' Ignacio clapped his hands. 'This will be fun. I haven't made a coffee in a café for about two years or so.'

Duarte followed him in. 'Can you show me? I'd like to have a go. Add it to my list.' He turned to Bella. 'We had a strenuous yoga session this morning. I am trying to improve my core strength in order to increase the length of time I am able to stand completely still when I am performing my living statue routine. Ignacio is early days, statue-wise but he is really

178

getting into it. But, of course, as a yoga instructor he has a core of steel.' Duarte looked like he was going to thump Ignacio in the stomach to demonstrate, but Ignacio stepped out of the way and walked to the counter.

Duarte was about to follow him over but hesitated and looked at Bella. 'Sit down and relax.' He patted one of the sofas inside that faced the sea. 'You have done a good deed already today and this is your reward.'

Bella gave in and sank down. She checked her watch again, calculating that a brisk fifteen-minute walk back home would get her in front of her computer in plenty of time.

'I think you are someone who starts work early and finishes late?'

'Isn't everyone?'

'For a while, a lot of people are. But allow yourself to start on time today. You deserve to be more than just work, work, work. Now — what would you like to drink? Ignacio can make you yours. My first attempt may take a while.'

'A *galão*, please.'

'For you, my dear, it is our pleasure. Now, rest.'

Bella nodded and leaned back as the coffee machine steamed into life and the two men bickered about who was going to do what. She watched a cargo boat chug slowly eastwards across the sea and imagined what it was carrying. Spices, car parts, furniture, toys, or maybe guitars.

'Here you are.' Ignacio placed the glass on the table in front of her. 'I must get back to make sure Duarte doesn't break anything.'

Bella took her first sip of the coffee as Deidre ran in through the door that no one had remembered to close and barked. 'Hello, my darling.' Bella stroked her ears. 'Where's Will? Or is it Elena walking you today?'

'You're open early!' Will was limping up the steps.

'We're not actually open.' Bella ushered him in. 'It's a long story but Hugo's not here yet.'

'Oh my — is Ignacio revisiting his barista roots?' He put his stick down and sat next to Bella.

'I think he's enjoying himself.' Bella took another sip of the drink.

'Ah, Will.' Duarte waved at him. 'Can I practise on you? What would you like?'

'I'll make it easy. A *bica*.' He turned back to Bella. 'A black coffee,' he explained. 'Like an espresso.'

'I'll remember that.' Bella noticed some walkers standing on the boardwalk nearby pointing at the café, so stood up. 'Better close the door in case we get customers.' Deidre noticed their dog and bounded outside, past the dog, then onto the beach.

'Oh. I've got to get her to the vets at nine thirty. If she's in one of those moods, I won't get her back till she's been running around for hours. And dogs aren't allowed on the beach at this time.' Will tried to pull himself to his feet.

'I'll get her.' Bella patted his arm.

'Thank you.' He handed her the lead. 'Good luck!'

Bella hurried out onto the decking and shut the door behind her, checking the closed sign was clearly visible, then trotted after Deidre, who was now almost cantering towards the sea.

'Deidre!' she called. 'Deidre!'

The dog carried on running. Bella carried on trotting.

'Looks like you need a lasso!' shouted a surfer from the shallows.

'Have you got one?'

'Not on me.' He laughed as she finally got the dog's attention.

'Deidre!' she squealed. 'Come on, lovely.' The dog padded over to her, her tail wagging. 'I don't need any more exercise after that.'

Bella put the lead on her and walked her back towards the café. 'You got further than I was expecting,' she muttered, glancing at her watch. 'I'm going to be late.'

She hurried up the steps, opened the door, gently pushed Deidre inside, and shouted, 'Can you stay here till Julian arrives with the keys? Got to run. I'm late.' Then she ran back up the road towards the house.

* * *

By the time she managed to switch on the computer and connect to the internet, she'd developed a stitch.

'Ah, Bella. Better late than never.' Jules the boss wasn't smiling.

'I've had a slight emergency. I can only apologise.'

'Oh no, what happened?' Lil asked. 'Your face is bright red.'

'Long story involving a donkey and a dog.'

'The dog that joined the meeting the other week?' Jules carried on going through some paperwork.

'Yes,' Bella replied slowly. 'But she's not here. She's in a café at the moment. Not having a drink. Well, she might be. Someone may have given her some water. But not coffee. She's not on her own.'

She noticed Jules checking her phone. 'I've got another meeting in half an hour, so can we get on? We're late enough as it is.'

Bella checked her watch. 'I'm only three minutes late.'

Her boss ignored her. 'So, just a few words before we begin, given we've got that deadline tomorrow afternoon.'

Bella sighed inwardly. *I've got to make this work*, she thought. *Can't go back after this with a reputation for unreliability after all the years I've worked so hard.*

A strand of her unbrushed hair fell over her eyes. She pushed it behind her ear, hoping her image was so small on the screen that no one would notice, and, working out when she could have a quick break for a shower, she tried to concentrate on what her colleagues were saying.

181

CHAPTER 15

I hear there was some drama with Hugo yesterday morning.
I hope that hasn't impacted on you?

Bella read Jorge's text message and decided to ignore the question, wondering how he knew about Hugo, then realised that everyone seemed to know everything about everyone anyway, so shrugged it off.

She pulled the tape from the cardboard box, reassuring herself he didn't mean her conversation with Hugo. Her stomach churned uncomfortably so she took control, not wanting to talk about Hugo and his ex at all. She looked at the phone.

I'm popping into town this evening. I hear there is a food
festival near the town walls. Care to join me? Jorge

Reasoning she could talk to him about Lenny and Martim to see if he knew why they were so keen on buying the land around Flo's house, she decided she would probably accept his invitation, and pulled out the tiles which were enclosed in bubble wrap.

Putting them on the table, Bella ran her hands over the smooth cream background, slowly tracing the outline of the blue patterns, which were exactly the same as the old, shattered tiles. She clapped her hands happily. Once this was done it could be ticked off her to-do list.

She collected from the outbuilding the adhesive she had bought to fit the tiles onto the walls, admiring the space, now almost clear thanks to the help Hugo had given her.

'Hello?' Hugo was shouting from the gate at the end of the track.

Bella felt her heart flip nervously.

'I come in peace. To apologise.'

'Come in!' yelled Bella, taking a breath to remind herself not to look directly into his chocolate-brown eyes.

He walked up the track, holding a bottle of champagne and a bunch of sunflowers in front of him as if they were a shield. 'I'm so very, very sorry,' he said. 'I'm very embarrassed, and I should have come round yesterday, but I don't drink often and after managing a day at work on that hangover I just crawled home. Mateus wasn't at all happy with me. He started braying at 6 a.m. this morning as punishment.'

Bella tried to speak, but his unshaven face looked sexy and vulnerable and handsome and she wanted to run her hands through his untidy, tousled hair and stroke his face gently, tracing the outlines with the tips of her fingers. She couldn't seem to get any words out.

One of the storks strode to the edge of the roof and took flight. Bella watched its long legs stretch out behind it like a ballerina and regained the power of speech.

'Thank you for the apology.' She searched for something else to say. Nothing came.

'Haven't got the buzzer on the front gate sorted out yet then?' He handed her the flowers.

'It's on my long list of things to do,' Bella said flatly. 'I've got the number of an electrician from Ignacio, so it'll be done soon.'

'And another thing to apologise for.' He looked sheepish. 'The words just came out of my mouth.' Hugo noticed the tiles. 'Ah, they have arrived. They look exactly the same as the others.' He looked up and grinned. 'But not broken.'

Bella managed to drag her gaze to the house. 'I'm about to put them up actually.'

'Can I do it for you? I'm keen to make amends as much as possible.'

Bella shook her head. 'Thank you, but I think I should do this. Aunt Flo would have after all. And even I can stick something onto something.'

'Of course. I shall pass you the tiles? Then you will have both hands free for the task.' He put the champagne and flowers on the patio table and followed Bella to the wall.

She attached the adhesive, then Hugo handed her the first tile and she stuck it on the wall, covering up the grey gap it had left, then repeated it with the others.

She stepped back. 'Oh!' The wall looked complete again. She felt a satisfying warmth as she surveyed her work. Taking another step backwards, she almost knocked into Hugo.

'Beautiful,' he said, as she turned around.

'Sorry. Wasn't looking where I was going.'

Their eyes locked again, his breath so close she could feel it on her neck. 'I . . . um . . .'

'You have some of the adhesive on your face.' He touched her cheek and brushed it gently.

Bella moved closer to him, hypnotised.

Something fell to the ground next to them. They both looked up. A stork looked down.

'That very large twig is supposed to go into the nest, Harry or Sally.' Bella picked it up. Whatever was pulling her towards him had gone. And a part of her was relieved. *Too complicated*, she thought. But another part was quietly whispering about missed opportunities.

'I think—' Hugo was now standing under the tree, looking at the wall '—you have definitely made it better. That part of the wall, anyway.'

Bella edged slowly backwards, keeping the wall in sight as she did, examining the tiles and how they looked, until she was under the tree next to him. 'Yes,' she beamed. 'I have, haven't I?'

He picked up the sunflowers and champagne again. 'You can tick it off the spreadsheet now, can't you, and celebrate with these.'

Bella took them. 'Would you like a glass of champagne? I can fast-track it by putting it in the freezer?'

Hugo winced and shook his head. 'No alcohol for me today. And don't put sparkling wines in freezers. They may explode.'

'Ah, that'd be a waste. A cup of tea then?'

'I have to go. I have boring administration to do at home. And—' he beamed excitedly '—I have a meeting to prepare for about the charity. I have so many plans all of a sudden. I can spend less time at the café, get someone to help me with planting and tending the land and . . . I just need to secure some investment.'

'That's wonderful news.' Bella pointed at the house. 'My next task is to get someone to power-wash the outside walls. Another simple thing I can tick off the list.'

They looked at each other again, this time a little awkwardly.

'So, I had better go.'

'Thank you for the presents as well as the apology.'

Hugo leaned in and kissed her on the cheek, then walked back along the track like a man with somewhere very important to go.

He stopped and glanced back. 'Your aunt told me about what happened to your family. She said your parents are lovely. You don't need to shield them from everything. You should value yourself.'

Bella froze again, her thoughts stuck.

'Oh . . .' he added. 'Those builders Lenny and Martim have been to see me again. After my land. Said you were considering selling yours to them. I told them you weren't . . . you haven't changed your mind, have you?'

'No!' Bella shook her head. 'You're not wanting to build an access road on my land, are you? I know you said no, but—'

'No!' Hugo looked surprised. 'No! That would . . . no!' He turned again and walked down the track.

The atmosphere had changed so suddenly, Bella didn't know what to do, so she hurried after him.

He turned back and they stared at each other in silence. Bella's mind was racing but she couldn't seem to make the words into a comprehensible sentence.

'No. Enjoy the rest of your day,' she managed to say. Then it was Bella's turn to walk away, and as she did, she saw the new tiles where they belonged on the wall of the house and felt a surge of pride. And out of nowhere, the pride was suddenly mixed with anger.

'No one's going to knock you down,' she muttered. 'Not now I've done that and cleared the outbuilding.'

* * *

Jorge was sitting on a bench in Praca Infante Dom Henrique, the sky over the bay beyond glowing a dusky pink as the sun set. He was scrolling through his phone, his forehead creased with concentration and had taken his tie off, holding it scrunched in one hand. Behind him children jumped on two giant trampolines and food trucks crowded the pathway while roadies set up equipment on a stage set in front of them.

'*Olá*, hello.' Bella sat down next to him. 'I'm not late, am I?'

'Not at all. I finished work a few minutes early.' He smiled at her. 'You have caught the sun, Bella. Living here suits you.'

'I'm not living here, technically, to be honest.'

'Perhaps you will decide to stay?'

'No. My work and my family are in the UK, and my flat, so lovely though this is, I'm still just passing through.'

He stood. 'Shall we?' They walked towards the food trucks. 'Do you have any particular food in mind?'

Meat and fish sizzled on barbecues, the smell of spices and smoke drifting from the trucks hanging deliciously in the air. Bella's mouth began to water. 'There's so much to choose from. I have no idea.' She laughed. 'Any recommendations?'

'My friend has a taco truck over here.' He waved at a young man with cropped hair.

The man waved back and held up some food. 'Do you want to try some?'

'It smells very nice.' Bella nodded. 'Yes, please.'

They watched as he plated up the food. 'I've got something to ask you about Lenny and Martim.' Bella glanced at Jorge's face to gauge his reaction.

'I only know them in a professional capacity.' He took the taco, his expression friendly and open. 'But ask away.'

'They've been to see Will and Hugo recently asking them about selling the land. As well as me — well, I asked them — but I'm getting a bit anxious about it.'

'Shall we sit opposite the fountains?' Jorge nodded over at a free bench. 'Call me a child but I do enjoy it when they make them turn pink and blue!'

'Me too. Small pleasures.' Bella followed him over and they sat down.

'So — before I take a bite out of this delicious taco — I would say that Lenny and Martim are just businessmen who are looking for an opportunity. Nothing to be worried about.'

'What if one of the others says yes?' An anxious knot twisted in her stomach as soon as the words came out of her mouth.

'Do you think one of them might?' He was still looking at the taco.

'No . . . I don't know . . . but—'

'Would that be a bad thing?'

'Actually, I think it might be.' Bella took a bite out her food and realised what she'd said. 'I like it how it is.'

'Does that mean you aren't selling your land?'

'I've decided not to in the end. The idea of redeveloping it has made me uncomfortable.'

'What if you sell the house and then whoever buys it decides to knock it down and redevelop it or sell it to Martim and Lenny?' He smiled at her. 'I'm just playing devil's advocate, Bella. People like us need to have all the information before us, and potential outcomes, before we make any big decision like this.'

'Yes, we do.' Bella felt herself relax a little. 'It's good you understand. Not everyone realises how important doing things this way is to me. Years of conditioning due to my job.'

She took another bite of the taco as someone began to rap from the stage.

'I never really thought of the long-term,' she said. 'What would happen once I'd sold it on.'

'And everyone has their own agenda. Will relies on a pension — maybe his house is too expensive for him and selling the land would help him. Hugo, of course — he wants to build that access road—'

'He told me he wasn't going to do that,' Bella said quickly.

'Has he played his guitar to you yet? Given you a lesson?' Jorge took the napkin and wiped some mayonnaise from the corner of his mouth. 'These are absolutely delicious but very messy.'

'I . . .' Bella couldn't say anything. An image of them sitting so close, as he showed her the chords, so close she could reach out and touch his face trickled into her memory. It had felt like something then. But was it? Was that just something Hugo did?

She managed to gather her thoughts quickly. 'Are Lenny and Martim working for someone else? They don't seem like the kind of operation that would be able to develop that much land.'

Jorge paused for a moment. 'I am not sure,' he said slowly. 'I can ask . . . but if you're not selling the land, why do you care?'

'Just because, like you, I need to have all the information to hand in order to understand the world around me.' Bella finished her taco as Jorge took out his phone.

'I've been asked to meet some friends in a café near the harbour. Would you like to join us?'

Bella felt suddenly weary. She'd got more information than she wanted, and why did she care whether Hugo was known for playing the guitar to impress women — and what was Jorge implying anyway? 'That's kind.' She wiped her hands on the napkin. 'Maybe another time. I've got work to catch up with first thing — the part-time work isn't really part-time at the moment.'

They both stood up. 'I hope I've been of some help.' Jorge smiled so widely it lit up his face.

'Of course, I appreciate it.' Bella relaxed again.

He touched her arm gently. 'Maybe we can meet for dinner again soon?'

'That would be lovely.' Bella put her rubbish in a nearby bin and Jorge kissed her on both cheeks.

'*Adeus, até a próxima*. Until the next time.' He turned away, then waved as he walked toward the marina.

Bella looked at the taco truck to check out its name so she could recommend it to her friends at the House on the Hill. The woman with the bob who had been arguing with Hugo was chatting to the owner, laughing, then waved and hurried away, almost running towards Jorge, who had turned the corner onto the avenida. As she did, she was joined by the older man she had seen at the restaurant with Lenny and Martim. The same man who had spoken to her outside her house. The same man, she realised, who was in the photograph gazing into her aunt's eyes when he was young and apparently in love.

It was Francisco Lopes.

CHAPTER 16

'I've had some visitors again.' Will had turned up at her doorstep with Deidre, looking drained, so Bella had offered to make him a drink. He leaned back in the chair wearily, rubbing his knee. 'It's getting a bit tiresome and stressful.'

'Is it about the house again?' Bella poured him a cup of tea from a teapot she had found at the bottom of a chest of drawers in the third bedroom.

'Why do they want my house? I've had Lenny and Martim visit me and then this young woman knocked on the door. What was her name?'

Bella was beginning to feel uneasy. 'What did she look like?'

'Young, short hair, well dressed.'

'What did she say?' Her heart beat a little bit faster, a knot of anxiety hitting her chest.

'That she was representing a certain party who was interested in buying the property and the land nearby in order to build more housing on it.'

'Did she leave a card or anything?'

'She tried to give me a card but I said no.' Will looked at the floor. 'This is all feeling a bit strange. You know, she said she knew I'd had an accident and that I must be worried about earning money, and she mentioned my pension and how I couldn't top it up. How did she know that? I've only told the company I work with. And Elena. You and Hugo . . .' He trailed off and looked at her.

'Honestly, it's nothing to do with me.' Bella smiled at him. 'I'd be feeling a bit weird about it too. It won't be Hugo and Elena is an accountant and very trustworthy. Have you phoned the company you work for?'

'Yes, the boss said they don't discuss their employee's business with other people.' He shook his head. 'I feel a bit intimidated. Uneasy.'

'Have you mentioned it to Hugo?'

'No. Do you think I should?' Will stroked Deidre's ears, absent-mindedly. 'I only told you because I know Martim and Lenny have been around to you. I was just worried you may have had some other visitors too.'

'I think you should tell him.' Bella sighed. 'He may know who this woman is for a start.' She didn't say she was pretty certain it was his ex-girlfriend.

'Righty-ho.' Will stood up. 'I haven't worried you, have I?'

'No. It's always good to know what's happening.' Bella stood too.

'I'll go and see if Hugo's in then. Thanks for the tea and biscuits.' He put Deidre on her lead. 'Then I'm off to The House on the Hill for some meditation. Elena is convinced that will help me relax and stop worrying about money. And make my knee less painful. Bye now.'

He walked down to the track and Bella watched him uneasily, hoping she wouldn't get any unwanted visitors herself.

* * *

Bella spent the rest of the afternoon sorting through two chests of drawers in the third bedroom, telling herself that she was being overdramatic if she thought that there was something strange going on that involved Hugo's ex and Lenny and

Martim. It was just people trying to do business, that's all. 'That is all it is,' she told Yin and Yang as they watched her put the last of the old magazines she'd found in a bin bag.

Her phone rang so she wandered downstairs, followed by the cats, getting to it just as it stopped. It was her mother, so she called back straight away in case something was wrong.

'Mum!' She made herself sound bright. 'How are you? Did you just call?'

'Yes.' Her mother sounded excited. 'I've just found something lovely. I was sorting through some old photographs.'

'Oh, I was sorting through some of Aunt Flo's stuff just now.' Bella put the bin bag on the floor.

'Must be something in the air. Anyway, I found some old pictures of that holiday we had with Flo.'

'I thought you'd put them away right after Dad's accident.' Bella walked to the kitchen to get a drink. 'What made you look through them after all this time?'

'You being over there I suppose. I keep trying to picture it and what it's like. I mean, the video calls help but . . . Anyway, what's happening with the swimming pool?'

'Nothing at the moment.' Bella poured herself a glass of water. 'It's just another thing on my list.'

'You loved that pool. I've found some photos of us swimming in it, jumping into it, sitting round it, floating on lilos in the middle of it.'

Bella closed her eyes and tried to remember. 'Can you send me copies on the phone, Mum?'

'Yes, and I think you should make sure you get the pool fixed. So that you can enjoy it before you have to come back.'

Bella sighed, thinking of the ever-growing list of things to do.

'You work so hard, Bella. And even now when you get the chance to go somewhere you're doing two jobs — sorting out the house and your regular job. Cut yourself a bit of slack.'

'It may not be worth my while, spending the time and the money.'

192

'Bella Leonie Creswell.' Her mother's voice changed. Bella never liked it when her mother used her full name. It meant a telling-off was coming. 'You own your own flat in London, you now own Flo's house and land, you have a good job. Do something frivolous for once. And by that, I mean spend some money on something nice for yourself. A swimming pool!'

'But I was going to send some extra money over this month so Dad could have that heat therapy.'

There was a pause. 'Do something for yourself for once, Bella,' she said eventually. 'You help us a lot and we're grateful. But just for once. OK?'

'All right, I'll think about it.' Bella tried not to sound like a sullen teenager. It was her usual response to being called Bella Leonie Creswell.

'Oh, someone's at the door. I'd better go. I'll send on the photos. Love you.' Her mother rang off so Bella wandered outside and looked in the empty pool. She had managed to clear it of most of the leaves and dirt.

The photos arrived on her phone. She studied the first one: Bella and her mum and dad were floating on inflatable unicorns in the middle of the pool. Her father had bright red sunglasses on and was laughing at her mother, who was holding a drenched straw hat that had fallen in the water. Bella was just smiling happily.

Bella sat down at the pool's edge, allowing her feet to dangle in the imaginary water. *It won't do any harm, I suppose*, she thought. *I can make this better for me for a while anyway. And it's not that much money.*

After a few minutes she went back into the house, rifled through the file of information Ignacio had left her and found the details of a man who looked after swimming pools. She rang him and left a message, then decided to put her mind in order by checking in on all the information she'd gathered.

'Oh God,' she muttered, feeling a little sick. 'My spreadsheet has got out of control.' Background information for selling seemed to float out from the screen, joined by numbers from the costs for repairs to 'make it better' and random words like *cats*, *storks*, *Hugo* and *tree* from the *Miscellaneous* section bounced behind them.

Bella covered her eyes. It was all too much. Too much. For a second she even considered selling the land to Lenny and Martim to just get rid of it. Maybe they could make it all better by knocking it down.

One of the cats put its paw on her arm and squeaked.

Bella opened her eyes. 'That bad, am I?' she said softly. 'And I didn't mean it. I don't want it knocked down.'

She decided to amble to the café to see if Hugo was there in case he'd had any more unwanted visits.

'I know it's not strictly ambling, Yin and Yang,' she said, picking up her bag, 'as I have a firm destination. But honestly, I feel my life is like an amble at the moment — because my firm destination seems to be getting further and further away along a windier and windier road.'

* * *

Bella stood in the doorway looking for a place to sit among the late-afternoon customers. Hugo waved at her from behind the counter and pointed at a table that had just been cleaned on the outdoor patio.

She sat down, staring at the sea from behind her sunglasses, trying to get her mind level again. Quiet Julian placed a *galão* in front of her and almost managed a smile.

'*Obrigada*,' she murmured and took a sip, the heat from the glass steaming up her sunglasses.

'*Olá!*' Hugo sat down opposite her. 'How are you today?' He sounded a little hesitant.

'I'm fine.' She studied him briefly. 'Is everything all right?'

'You've spoken to Will?'

'Yes. He's told you what has happened, has he?'

'I'm sure it was my ex, Deanna, who visited him. She is very persistent.' He took his phone from his pocket and scrolled through the messages. 'She has been sending me texts saying that by the time everyone else has sold the land I may as well get on board as the place will never be the same again.' Hugo looked up at her, his face weary.

Bella wanted him to know he wasn't alone. She wanted him to smile again. 'I did have a moment earlier when it all got too much for me and I wondered if it would just be easier to sell. I'm not going to. It lasted the amount of time it took for me to think of it.' She looked up at him. 'This must be getting you down. Especially as it's your ex.'

Hugo stared at her. 'Are you that stressed that the thought of selling the land seemed a good idea?'

'No.' Bella shook her head. 'I meant that I understood Will and the pressure he's under. You must be exhausted by it too.'

Hugo stood and went to the counter without replying. He started to make drinks, banging glasses on the counter and throwing ice into the bottom of them, his face dark and furious.

Bella walked over to him, confused. 'What have I said?'

He carried on concentrating on what he was doing.

'Why don't you sort out what's happening with you and your ex?' she said, trying to sound calm. 'Instead of being angry with me for simply trying to explain how difficult this is.'

He still didn't say anything.

Bella couldn't stop herself. 'I saw her in town with a man. Same name as your great-uncle . . . Francisco Lopes . . . I saw him in the lane a while ago.'

Hugo paused briefly, then carried on making the drinks.

'So maybe we've been drawn into your family spat or something, me and Will?'

'Me and my ex — it's complicated. And what about you? You were the one who got Lenny and Martim over in the first place.' He still didn't look at her. 'Maybe they are all involved together. And your friend Jorge—'

'Complicated with you and your ex?' Bella felt inexplicably hurt. 'Maybe you've just been nice to me so I wouldn't sell *my* land.'

Hugo stopped mixing the drinks and looked at her, shocked. 'No . . . no—'

Bella couldn't stand to be there anymore so threw some change on the table for her drink, then hurried back to the Nest, desperate to feel safe inside its comforting walls.

* * *

The large straw hat was visible as Bella turned the corner into the lane. Even though she couldn't see the short black bob, Bella knew it was Hugo's ex standing under the tree next to her gate.

Taking a breath, she walked slowly over to her. 'The buzzer doesn't work, I'm afraid. Can I help?'

The woman smiled. 'My name is Deanna De La Cruz. Are you the owner of the property?'

'Yes I am. How can I help?'

Deanna took a card out her handbag and handed it to Bella. 'I work in redevelopment and construction. I represent parties who are interested in buying your house and the land around it.'

'Ah, right. I'm not interested in selling the land for redevelopment.'

'It's a lot of land for one house, you know.' Deanna smiled. 'We could build three or four villas on this.'

'No apartments?' Bella looked at the card, wondering if the number on it was the same on the flyer that had been stuck on the tree near Hugo's café.

'There may be a concession for some affordable housing. But this is prime land.'

Bella handed her back the card. 'I'm not interested. But thanks for mentioning it.'

Deanna nodded and put the card back in her bag. 'Not everyone is privileged enough to be left a house by a relative.

196

You would be enabling other people to have somewhere to live — more than one person, a couple or a family.'

Bella looked at the old tile on the post next to the gate with the name of the house on it, painted by her aunt. 'I'm aware that I'm lucky to inherit this. Although, how did you know that?'

'It's my job to know these things.'

'Thank you for your interest.' Bella put on her formal and assertive work voice. 'Should anything change I'll be in touch.'

'You haven't got my card.'

'I know how to get hold of Lenny and Martim. And—' Bella hesitated for moment, but decided to say the name anyway '—I'm sure Francisco Lopes has an office address I can find on the internet.'

Deanna looked like she was searching for the right words, then took her card out of her bag and posted it through the letterbox. 'It's better you go through me.'

'It's not going to change though.' Bella took her key fob out and the gate clicked open.

'Where I'm from, we had to steal electricity to survive.' Deanna adjusted her straw hat. 'I lived in in Lisbon near Belém. Not in a beautiful, Instagrammable neighbourhood. It was a slum. Everyone knows it's a slum. I'm sure you understand my drive to make a lot of money so I never go back to that.'

Bella studied her. Her dress was smart and sleek, her nails scarlet and pristine, her bag and shoes obviously designer. 'I understand,' she said. 'Drive and ambition are admirable. And you deserve to be successful. But I'm not selling my aunt's property for redevelopment. Thank you.'

She turned away and walked through the gate, somehow feeling guilty and angry at the same time.

CHAPTER 17

Bella had booked herself in for an early-morning yoga class so she could get rid of some of the tension she had accumulated before she had to start work. The car park of the House of The Hill was full of class-goers with the same idea.

Taking her yoga mat out of the boot, she walked up into the building, the smell of patchouli and lavender making her more relaxed with every step she took.

'Bella!' Layla came out of the office. 'How are you today? I hear you are getting your swimming pool done. What a lovely idea.'

'How do you know that?' Bella was beginning to get used to the very speedy Lagos grapevine.

'I can't remember actually.' Layla gave her hand a squeeze. 'Off to yoga? I love this time of the morning. It's so busy and buzzy and—'

'What do you mean, we may as well stick together, better than nothing. But friends with benefits?' Elena's voice suddenly echoed through the House on the Hill, clearly audible over the squealing feedback.

Bella and Layla spun around. 'Is that Elena? Which studio is she in? Did you remember to switch off the sound system?' Layla asked Ignacio as he rushed in from the car park looking confused.

'I didn't mean it like that,' Will replied defensively.

Minnie hurried out of the office into the hallway. 'Which room are they in?'

'I was in the atrium.' Ignacio tried to open the door. 'But the door was sticking so I nipped to my car to see if I had anything to oil it in my toolbox.'

'Well, that's what you meant,' Elena said abruptly. 'Is that what you're saying — you're settling for me because you can't be bothered to try to meet anyone else?'

Two students paused as they walked down the stairs. 'Oh dear,' muttered one.

'How interesting,' mouthed the other.

'Why are they standing so close to the microphone?' Ignacio pushed the door again, then began to knock.

'I've been on my own for so long, Elena. I don't want a proper relationship.'

'You were messaging me. "Come and see me, Elena, I miss you, Elena."'

Another student walked into the hallway 'Is everything all right?' she asked.

'It was all getting a bit too much.' Will's voice got louder.

'So, it's not too much when you ask to see me, but when I make one simple suggestion it's all too much?'

The feedback squealed again.

'You wanted to change my curtains.'

'I simply suggested they needed a wash. I'm not trying to move in.'

'I'm very glad to hear it!'

Minnie gasped. 'Oh dear. Oh dear.' She put her hand over her mouth and raised her eyebrows.

'That's not good,' mumbled another student who was walking out of another studio.

'I have a detached villa with its own pool overlooking the sea,' shouted Elena. 'Why would I want to move into your little cottage with the dirty curtains?'

'Well, why were you there all the time?'

There was a collective intake of breath.

'Open the door,' shouted Ignacio, banging it again. 'We can hear you! Everyone can hear you.'

'At the beginning, because I felt responsible. Because I dragged you out of that ditch and shoved you in my car and I probably should have LEFT YOU THERE.' Elena now sounded like she was talking to a small child. 'And then because I liked you. And then because you kept asking me to come round.'

'I don't like everyone knowing my business,' Will shouted.

'What's that got to do with me?' Elena shouted back.

'I'm very confused,' whispered Layla. 'I'm not sure I know what they are actually arguing about. Can you call Elena, Minnie? And can you call Will?' she asked Bella.

Minnie rushed back into the office, while Bella took her phone out of her bag. She rang Will. 'It's gone straight to voicemail.' She hurriedly sent a text.

Can you come out of the Atrium? You are standing next to a microphone that is picking everything up and transmitting it throughout the building.

'It's bounced back,' she whispered, as the meditation class from the next room filtered out into the hall.

'There's no signal at the back of the room. It's very strange.' Ignacio leaned against the door, pushing it with his back.

'I like my life the way it is. The way it was. Before you found me in that ditch,' Will was shouting again. 'And I don't want to sell my house!'

'I don't want you to sell your house. What's that got to do with me? I like my life too. I have my job. I have my friends. My dancing. My birdwatching. If I wanted to just have a sex buddy I'd go on Tinder.'

Minnie was almost doubled up with laughter. 'Go girl,' she wheezed.

'She's going to be so embarrassed.' Layla shook her head.

'They came into the class quite happily together,' mused Ignacio. 'They stood at the back, did the yoga like everyone else. I don't know what happened.'

'Curtains,' laughed Minnie. 'She just wanted clean curtains.'

'Me too!' yelled Will. 'We talk too much. You know too much about me . . .' His voice trailed off.

'So you want me to see you but you don't want us to talk?'

Everyone fell silent and waited.

'Well that way I won't have anyone spreading my private business around,' shouted Will.

There was a pause, and then the sound of footsteps. The door opened, and Ignacio slid to the floor.

'What are you doing down there?' Elena stepped over him and walked through the hall, apparently oblivious to the now quite large audience gathered around her, then disappeared down the steps and into the car park.

'How did she open the door so easily?' wheezed Ignacio.

Bella looked at Layla. 'Is anyone going to tell her we could all hear?'

'I will.' Minnie wheeled her chair back into the office. 'I'm really looking forward to it.'

'I think we'd better leave it to you to break the news to Will,' said Layla quietly to Ignacio.

Bella glanced at her phone. 'You may not need to. The text has now arrived and it says here it's been read.'

Layla turned to the students. 'Perhaps we should all go about our business and not say anything?'

Everyone nodded and within a minute the hall was empty.

'I'd better go.' Bella smiled at Layla. 'Never a dull moment.' But as she walked to the studio, she wondered why Will had told Elena he didn't want to sell his house.

Her phone rang as she drove down the hill towards home. It was her mother, so she answered it, making sure there was a smile in her voice rather than unease.

'Hi, Mum! I've arranged to get the swimming pool done. It's all fallen into place very quickly.'

201

'That's wonderful news.' Her mother sounded strained. 'Listen, lovely, it's nothing to worry about but your dad took a tumble yesterday. He was in the garden and tripped over a paving stone.'

'Oh. How is he today?'

'In bed. We spent eight hours in casualty, but he's OK. Just bruised, fragile and—' her mother's voice cracked '— very, very sad.'

'Oh Mum. I'll come home. I'll book a flight.' Bella began to work out logistics in her head.

'Absolutely not, Bella. I won't allow it.'

'But—'

'No buts,' her mother interrupted. 'It's not serious. It's a blip. You just needed to know, that's all. He'll be up on his feet in no time.'

'How did it happen?' A tear trickled down Bella's cheek but she tried to sound calm.

'He was having a good day and decided to try to walk without his sticks. But he's so unsteady on his feet now he lasted less than five minutes.'

Bella gathered her composure. 'Well, let me know if you need me. We need to make the garden accessible and the downstairs of the house so he can feel less constricted.'

'Sort out things in Portugal first, Bella, and then we will think about that. He's calling. I'd better go. Send me photos of the swimming pool when it's finished.'

Her mother rang off and Bella pulled over, allowing herself to cry, before going home and starting work.

* * *

'It's in pretty good nick actually.' The pool man opened the door of his van. 'Your aunt looked after things very well. I checked our books and we came out to service it only a few months before she passed away.'

'I've heard she loved swimming every day.' Bella had logged on early to a work meeting and was hovering in the doorway, glancing back at the laptop while he got out some paperwork.

'Lovely woman by all accounts.' He took out his phone and looked through his calendar. 'She was thinking of fitting some hydrotherapy jets to help her arthritis actually. I've given it a clean and can get it filled and treated early next week.'

'Oh, I was expecting it to take longer than that.' Bella looked at the pool, imagining herself jumping into it, refreshed by its cool, clear water.

'We've had a cancellation so you're in luck.' He smiled. 'And with this heatwave you'll be glad of it being there even if it's just to dunk yourself in. I'll be round every few weeks to service it while you're here, then we'll discuss what happens after that when your leaving date is confirmed.'

'It sounds lovely.' Bella imagined herself gliding out of the house at sunrise and jumping in to swim for half an hour, then lounging around on a lilo when she wasn't working, after which she'd have a sunset swim before bed.

'I'll see you next week.' He got into his van. 'Have a good weekend. *Até a próxima.*'

'*Obrigada*, thank you. *Até a próxima.*'

As he turned onto the lane, she noticed Hugo waving at her. 'Can I come in?' he shouted.

Her heart fluttered at the sight of him, then she remembered their argument and pulled herself to her full height, in order to look stern. 'I've actually got the buzzer fixed.'

Hugo didn't move. Then she remembered she hadn't answered his question. 'Yes, yes, of course, come in.' She pressed the button to unlock the gate and looked back at the clock on the wall to check how long she had before her meeting.

'I'm sorry. Again,' he was saying. 'I shouldn't have spoken to you like that at the café. There is no excuse.'

'I shouldn't have spoken to you like that. So I'm sorry.' Her face relaxed into a smile.

He looked at the floor. 'It's become very complicated all of a sudden.'

'What has?'

'Just . . .' He paused. 'All that is going on with these developers and my new business idea and wondering what's going to happen to the Nest.'

'Once I'm gone.'

They both looked away this time.

'We really need to be . . .' Hugo looked like he was searching for the right words.

'Friends,' interrupted Bella. 'And good neighbours.'

He smiled thinly. 'Exactly what I was thinking. So, we can support each other.'

'Exactly what I was thinking too. We have to remain on good terms in order to make the right decisions.' Bella was trying to sound brisk, but was just feeling sad, and she didn't know why.

Yes, you do know why, whispered her inner voice.

'You mentioned my great-uncle.' Hugo's voice was quiet. 'I haven't seen him since I was a child...I don't know why he's here.'

'He was driving past not long after I got here. He stopped the car and asked if anyone was living here now. Said something about that lovely tree by the gate.'

Hugo's face clouded. 'How do you know it was him?'

'Because Jorge told me who he was. He was in a restaurant with Lenny and Martim and I saw him with your ex too. It's been niggling me. But now Will is feeling pressurised I thought I'd better say something.'

Hugo shook his head again. 'Why would he be interested in all of this? He has so much money. It's so stupid.'

'It is if he's anything to do with it. But he might not be. All I know is that I've seen him. It may be a coincidence.'

'And it may not be. When my grandmother died and left the property and café to my father and him, he wanted to sell so they could develop the area and make a lot of money. But my father wouldn't. Francisco was furious. My father scratched the money together to buy him out and he disappeared. That was it.' He turned towards the gate. 'I'm sorry, I have to go. I need to find out what's going on.'

'Deanna De La Cruz came here yesterday.' She spoke to his back.

He spun around. 'What?'

'I told her I wasn't interested in selling for redevelopment.'

They stared at each other for a moment. 'Thanks for telling me,' he said eventually. 'I have to go.'

Bella wanted to run after him, but she was almost late, so rushed inside and sat at her computer, logging on to the meeting thirty seconds before it started.

* * *

Bella watched the water tanker as it eased its way through the gates and onto the track, internally jumping up and down with excitement. The swimming pool was now full.

'My own swimming pool,' she told the storks. She had put her bikini on under her clothes that morning, so pulled off the sundress and left it on the floor, then stood for a moment, looking at the reflection of the sun on the water, and trying to decide whether jumping in without checking the temperature was a good idea, or whether she should ease herself down from the steps.

The storks chattered from the roof and Yin and Yang ambled over to see what was going on.

'What do you think?' she asked them. 'The sensible thing would be to ease myself in. But — then there is no sense of occasion to mark the fact I have my own pool I can use every day.'

So she jumped, submerging herself in the freezing water, then swam to the surface, breathless. 'Hasn't had time for the sun to heat it up, has it? Oh well.' Bella lay on her back and floated around for a while, then swam, then floated, and only got out when the skin on her fingers began to crinkle.

She lay on a sunbed that had been stored in the utility room and allowed the midday heat to dry her, closing her eyes and listening to the birds flitting through the trees, and the roar of the sea.

She woke herself up with her own snoring, opening her eyes to find one of the cats sitting on top of her. Rolling over gently to displace the cat, she sat up and checked her phone. She had been asleep for two hours. The midday heat had dried her and her skin was turning slightly red. 'I'm late back from lunch,' she told the cat, standing up and putting her sundress back on, then checked her phone for messages and realised it was Friday. 'I don't work on Friday,' she reminded herself, then sat down again and laughed.

She video-called her mother. 'Look,' she squealed, when her mother answered. 'The pool is done!'

'Oh goodness. Fantastic. Have you been in?'

'Yes. And it was freezing. The sun heats the water, and so it feels like it's fresh out of the fridge at the moment.'

'Never mind. At least you can enjoy it while you're there, now. Have you made it better yet?'

'No. No. There's so much to think about.' Bella's good mood began to ebb away.

'Whatever you decide will be right, Bella. It doesn't have to be perfect.'

'But it's our future.'

'It's your future.'

'But whatever I make from this will go towards helping you and Dad with the house and therapy.'

'It's your future. Not ours, Bella.' Her mother's tone was firm.

'I wish you could come over.'

'So do I.'

'Well, come. Where's Dad?'

'He's at a cricket match. One of his friends has taken him. I've got to go — I'm off for coffee with the girls. What are you up to tonight?'

'I've been invited to a charity function at the yoga place I go to. I'll make an appearance and then come home.'

'Try to enjoy yourself. All work and no play et cetera, et cetera . . .'

'Mum, I've just fallen asleep next to my swimming pool.' Bella moved the camera on the phone around again so her mother could see it.

'Yes, but I expect you'll go inside and do some work even though it's Friday and you don't work on Fridays.'

'I've just got to keep on top of things.'

'Just don't overdo it. Go for another swim!' Her mother smiled.

'I'll send you some photographs and a video just to make you jealous.'

'Thank you. Bye, darling.'

'Bye, Mum.' Bella ended the call and decided to take her mother's advice and go for another swim before she went inside and did some work, even though it was Friday. So she climbed back into the pool and for a moment felt she was sharing it with her eight-year-old self and her parents, with Auntie Flo sipping a cocktail on a lounger under the tree.

CHAPTER 18

Ignacio and Duarte were on plinths in the entrance hall of the House on the Hill, both dressed as John Travolta in *Saturday Night Fever*. Ignacio's wig had listed to the right. Bella resisted the urge to adjust it. In front of them was a sign that said:

Donate two euros to see us dance.

Bella put the money in the hat on the floor in front of them and watched as they gyrated to 'You Should Be Dancing'. After thirty seconds they stopped and resumed their poses.

She grinned and waved, then wandered out into the garden, where a group of children were dancing to 'Me and My Shadow'. Layla was in front of them showing them the moves, while Minnie was filming them on her phone.

'Bella!' Elena waved at her and walked over. She was wearing a suit and her hair was tied up in a neat bun. 'How are you, my dear?'

'I'm OK. Getting there with the house.'

'Yes, there's a lot to do. A lot of responsibility for you.'

Bella looked at her, unsure whether to ask if she was OK, because if she did, Elena would know she had heard her argument with Will over the intercom.

'I now have a functioning swimming pool, though,' she said instead, 'so that is a real bonus. But I can't seem to get going with clearing the fourth bedroom. It's the last one to do, but it's got so much stuff in it.'

'Oh dear. But the swimming pool — that is good news. With this heat too. There is something I wanted to ask you. How is Will?'

'He's OK from what I've seen of him.' Bella tried to sound nonchalant.

'You heard we are no longer together?'

'Ah, OK.' Bella smiled. 'That's a pity.'

'One day he's all over me, the next he wants some space. I have no idea what happened. But—' she leaned closer to Bella '—I'm glad really. I was losing myself — wearing clothes to keep him happy rather than me. I was cooking, Bella. Cooking! Me?' She let out a throaty laugh. 'Oh, the things you will get yourself into when you want to be with a nice man . . . companionship, laughs, being cared about, sex. Sex. That was lovely.' She shook her head. 'But I have realised that this friends with benefits thing is not for me. I need clarity. I am an accountant.'

Bella nodded, smiling, trying to think of the right response.

'And a weird thing you know — he accused me of telling other people his business. He blamed me for people coming round asking to buy his house. Now, that was very hurtful. Ah, here is Jorge.' She waved at him. 'He's been such a help.' She sighed. 'But so very driven work-wise. Always working. Always. You should get on very well. Ha ha!'

'I'm not always working, am I?' Bella said to Elena as she turned to go.

Elena didn't hear her, throwing her arms around her nephew before walking inside.

'*Olá!*' Jorge beamed at Bella. 'And how are you? How are things with the house?'

'I think I'm making enough progress that I can see it now. Although the list of to-dos and miscellaneous items I can't actually quantify is expanding every hour.' The children's dance finished just as Bella was about to ask him about Francisco Lopes and Hugo's ex, and Layla waved at her, hurrying over and giving her a hug.

'Thank you for coming.' She had a scented mist dispenser in her hand. 'I believe in the power of aroma to positively affect our moods.' She held it up and looked at the label. 'This is bergamot and lemon — I just grabbed it out of the cupboard.'

'I must go and be with my aunt, ladies, excuse me.' Jorge shook his head seriously. 'She's putting a brave face on it but the thing with Will has really upset her.'

Layla shook her head. 'Minnie said she was crying earlier. And I think Will just wants to be left alone. Ah, here's Hugo.' She smiled as he stood in the hallway.

Bella had the usual overwhelming urge to run her hands through his thick, dark, tousled hair. She folded her arms instead and smiled as he walked over to them.

'Hello, ladies.' He grinned and Bella's stomach did a little loop the loop. She moved her arms down in case that would stop it. It didn't.

'Thank you for providing the food, Hugo.' Layla squeezed his hand. She turned to Bella. 'I'm relieved we organised this so quickly for the new charity — the final paperwork was all ready to go before Flo passed away. So we all got together over the last few weeks and dotted the i's and crossed the t's.'

'We just couldn't do it until now.' Hugo shifted awkwardly. 'She left such a gap. But now the Nest has some life in it I felt she was somehow pushing me forward.'

'Flo would have been proud.' Layla waved at someone in the doorway. 'I'd better go. Why don't you both have a dance?' Layla took their hands and put them together. 'The salsa is on in the next room.'

'Oh no,' they said in unison. 'I can't dance.'

'You don't have to be able to dance. Just jig around to the music. Look.' She pointed at Ignacio and Duarte, who had climbed off their plinths and were on their way towards the sound system. 'Ignacio is a dance teacher but—' she leaned towards them conspiratorially '—although Duarte is great at tango, for anything else he seems to have two left feet. He doesn't care, he loves it!'

Layla gently but firmly guided them into the room, where Minnie stood behind the sound deck. '"La Bamba",' she announced to the room, then more quietly but still into the microphone. 'Don't look at me like that, Ignacio. The DJ is late and someone had to do it. And if you weren't doing that silly John Travolta living statue thing you could do it instead of mouthing at me to put a bit more enthusiasm into it.'

Layla jumped onto the stage and took the microphone from her. 'You can just play the music, Min,' she whispered, still audible through the sound system. 'Don't worry about announcing it. The DJ will be here soon.' She disconnected the mic and jumped back onto the dance floor.

Hugo caught Bella's eyes. They were still holding hands. 'As we're here, shall we try? I have two left feet.'

'I probably have three.' Bella averted her gaze shyly as they moved backwards and forwards in time to the music, trying to concentrate on the steps instead of the closeness of Hugo.

'Shall we try to do the proper dance hold?' he murmured, putting a hand on her waist and pulling her closer. Part of her wanted to step back and keep him at arm's length, but she couldn't because another long-hidden part of her wanted to move even closer.

The couple next to them executed a couple of exuberant spins, so Hugo attempted to do the same with Bella, who reacted by slowly walking around in a circle.

'I'm rubbish!' she murmured, wanting him to pull her closer again. But if he did, what then?

'That was very elegant.' Hugo squeezed her hand. 'Slow. But elegant.'

Bella felt tiny electric shocks trickling around her body and their eyes locked again for a moment just as the music ended. They stepped back away from each other awkwardly, still smiling.

A brass band playing 'The Floral Dance' blasted out of the speakers. Minnie pressed the buttons, panicked, and picked up the microphone. 'Did you put this on here, Duarte?' she asked as he climbed up next to her. 'What do you mean you are thinking of signing them to your record label?'

'Let's have some *Grease*.' He tried to grab the microphone while scrolling through the songs. 'Here we are. "You're the One That I Want".'

Ignacio tapped Bella on the shoulder. 'Elena has told me you are stuck with Flo's fourth bedroom. It is indeed almost an ecosystem in itself. She put so much in there.'

'It feels like it glows radioactively every time I walk past it. Just like the outbuilding did.' Bella shook her head. 'Once I've cleared it, then I'll be able to see what needs painting or repairing in there.'

'Well, as one of your knights in shining armour, I will gather together some friends and we will come and help you.' He scratched his head. 'This wig is so hot,' he muttered, as it fell halfway down his face.

'That's very kind.' Bella tried to help him put the wig back on.

'We will be in touch with a date.' He took the wig off and wandered off towards a bathroom.

'Excuse me,' Hugo said quietly. 'I want to have a word with Jorge.'

'Have you had any luck with your great-uncle?' Bella looked around to see where Jorge had gone.

'I phoned his office and left a message. He hasn't contacted me. But I don't expect he will.'

Bella went to get a drink.

'You two seem to be getting on very well.' Layla was carrying a plate of canapés around. 'Bruschetta?'

Bella took one. 'Yes. He's a good neighbour.'

'Looked more than a neighbour to me.'

'No more than that. Neighbour and friend.' Bella took a bite so she didn't have to say any more.

'Pity. You look good together.' Layla turned to a group of people behind her. 'Canapé?' she asked, as Bella ambled outside.

Jorge and Hugo were talking, their expressions like stone, then Jorge shook his head and walked away as Elena hurried past. She looked like she had been crying. Minnie took her hand as Hugo followed Jorge back inside.

Bella decided to go home, back to the comforting walls of the Nest.

* * *

The skip was booked to arrive on Monday, so after doing some work in preparation for a big meeting after the weekend, Bella decided to go through the bin bags full of sheets and blankets that had been cleared in the outhouse, in case anything could be recycled before sending the rest to a charity shop.

She picked one up and took it to the shade of the patio so she could enjoy the sunshine instead of working in the outhouse and emptied out the bag onto the floor. Folding everything up neatly, she put it on the table and found a turquoise blue cotton sundress, with tiny white daisies printed on the skirt. She held it to her body, checking the length, and examined the fabric to check for any holes or tears. It was perfect.

'Great-Aunt Flo, you had such style,' she said, pulling it on over her T-shirt and shorts. It felt like it fitted properly and she went up to the bedroom and stood in front of the mirror, twirling around, enjoying the swish of the full skirt, then took it down to the utility room, washed it carefully and hung it out to dry. 'I think I'll keep you,' she told it. 'And look after you as I think you may be quite old.' Then she returned to the bin bag to finish sorting out its contents.

Before going through another bag, Bella went inside to get some water and checked her phone for messages.

We are coming to help you to clear out the fourth bedroom. Send me some dates and times in the next week and we will be there. Ignacio.

She smiled, relieved. Every time she had opened the door of the fourth bedroom and its piles of furniture, boxes and bin bags, she felt anxious and closed the door firmly behind her. It felt like the final frontier, the place where Great-Aunt Flo had put the stuff that even she didn't know what to do with.

Thank you, she messaged back. *I'll check my diary for my work commitments next week and get back to you. Bella.*

Taking her drink outside, she sat for a while in the hammock, closing her eyes and listening to the birds and the sea, until a plane buzzing overhead disturbed the peace. She got up and felt the dress to check if it was dry or not. It was, so she put it on and took it for a walk to Hugo's café.

Putting on her Portuguese language app, she paused under the tree just outside the gate and took her headphones out of her bag just as a car drove along the lane towards her.

'*Olá*,' said the occupant, as they slowed to a halt.

'*Olá*,' replied Bella, absent-mindedly, as she connected her headphones to her phone.

'You are definitely Florence Creswell's niece.'

Bella looked up properly. It was Francisco Lopes.

'Yes,' she said, unsure what to say to him.

'You look just like her.'

'I didn't realise. I suppose I would a little as we are related.'

'The dress,' he said.

Bella waited for a moment, expecting him to say something else but he was looking past her now at the tree. 'Is the tile sign still there on the gatepost?'

'Yes it is.'

He attempted a smile, but it was half-hearted, then he shook his head sadly. 'Have a good day.'

He started the car and drove away without saying anything else. Bella watched as it disappeared around the curve in the lane, confused and unsettled, then walked quickly to the café to see if he'd been there.

Hugo was standing behind the bar making coffee. He beamed at her. 'Hello.' He put the last cup onto the tray and waved at Julian. 'I've had the message about the fourth bedroom. I'm part of the cavalry.'

'Has your great-uncle been in?' she asked.

'I don't understand. Are you all right? You look worried.'

'Francisco Lopes stopped to talk to me in the lane outside the house. He was coming from the direction of your café.'

'I don't know what he looks like now.' Hugo's face creased into a frown. 'I was so young when he argued with my parents I can barely remember him, and they threw all of his photographs away. What did he say? Are you all right?'

'Hardly anything . . . just mentioned this dress, the tile on the gatepost and that I was Flo's great-niece.'

'That's odd. What does he look like? Maybe he was here and I didn't notice.'

'Thick black hair flecked with grey, sad eyes. I've seen him before so I know it's him.'

'Oh yes. There was an older man here in the corner like that. He just ordered a coffee and he kept looking over. That's right . . . I wondered why, and went over to ask if he wanted anything else but he just shook his head and left after only five minutes or so.'

'Why is he hanging around but not saying anything? Have his office got back to you at all?'

'No.' Hugo's face clouded. 'But I'm not having him intimidating you.'

'He looked more sad than intimidating, to be honest.'

'I'll send them an email and I'll phone again too.'

A group of six customers walked in.

'I asked Jorge about him,' Hugo went on. 'He was very evasive. How well do you know him?'

'Evasive? I've met him a few times. He seems nice. He is Elena's nephew so he must be reliable.' Bella shook her head. 'Maybe there's nothing to tell?'

Hugo looked as if he was about to say something, then the group sat down. 'I've got to get on, sorry. Do you want a *galão*?'

'Yes please. Before I get back to sorting things out.' Bella found a table and started to make a list of things to do on her phone, to stop her mind racing with theories about Francisco Lopes and what he was doing.

CHAPTER 19

Bella stood on the patio as the convoy of cars arrived at 9 a.m. on Friday and the occupants got out, marching towards her determinedly.

Ignacio took his sunglasses off. 'Well, Bella, and here we are. Are you ready?'

'Yes?'

Duarte got a steam cleaner out of his car and slammed the door shut, carrying it in front of him. Bella thought it looked like a very large, very ineffective weapon.

'There are a lot of you, aren't there?' she said. 'Thank you so much.'

'We thought we'd make it quick and easy if we all came together.' Minnie took her sunhat off. 'Where's Hugo?'

'I'm here.' He appeared from behind the house. 'I took the shortcut!'

Bella beamed at the sight of him, then turned away and tried to compose herself, annoyed at herself for having feelings for someone she knew she couldn't have. Or anyone, really.

'So,' said Layla sternly, 'lead the way.'

'We'll go and get some refreshments then.' Duarte put the steam cleaner on the patio and walked to the gate with Ignacio.

Minnie and Elena watched them go and sighed. 'Honestly,' they said in unison.

Layla looked like she was going to laugh. 'Shall we start then, everyone?'

Bella walked inside and stood at the bottom of the stairs, staring up.

'Shall I?' Hugo walked purposefully up to the landing. He opened the door a crack and peered in, then shut it dramatically. He looked down the stairs, shook his head and said solemnly, 'I'm not sure we are up to the task.'

'Oh, stop mucking about!' shouted Minnie. 'He's joking, Bella. You are, aren't you, Hugo?'

Bella laughed. 'Yes I know. I shouldn't have let him go first.'

Minnie strode up the stairs brandishing a bin bag. 'Come on, you.' She pushed the door open, nudging Hugo inside.

Layla stood in the living room with a notepad and pen. 'I'll make notes on here, and I've got the lists on the table of furniture, clothes, and miscellaneous.'

'Thank you,' murmured Bella.

Ignacio and Duarte carried in a tray of takeaway coffee and cakes. 'Sustenance!' shouted Duarte. 'We'd ordered them to be delivered to the gate. Excellent service.'

'We haven't even started yet.' Minnie shook her head.

'It will get us prepared.' Ignacio placed the cakes on the table in the living room. 'We will work faster if we are properly fed.'

Elena hovered by the door. She was dressed in an old pair of black leggings and a faded blue short-sleeved T-shirt. 'Who's here?' She put her hands on her hips. 'I can only help if I know who's here.'

'Will is not here!' bellowed Minnie. 'Now get a grip. You are a grown woman.'

'That's not very sympathetic,' she muttered. 'I was always sympathetic to you when you were endlessly crying about all those men.'

'You used to give me a handkerchief, buy me a gin and say *"plenty more fish in the sea"*,' huffed Minnie. 'And say "he's not worth it." So, he's not worth it. Have a blueberry muffin and move on. There are plenty more fish in the sea.'

Elena stood, her face like stone, then shuffled inside and picked up a cake as Minnie walked down the stairs, then put her arms around her. 'He's not worth it. He's not.'

Elena hugged her friend back. Duarte smiled happily and took a sip of his coffee. 'Delicious. Delicious.'

'Is anyone going to help me up here?' Hugo's voice carried down the stairs.

Bella looked at the clock on the wall. 'Well, I suppose we'd better get on?'

Layla nodded. 'Yes we had. We need to get this done today.'

'Then,' shouted Hugo, 'Bella can tick it off her spreadsheet. Although—' he laughed '—she'll probably add more subsections to it once she's seen what's in here.'

'That's why we get on so well.' Layla searched through her phone. 'I've got an app.' She winked at Bella. 'You'll love this. Everyone, to your stations, one . . . two . . . three . . . GO!' She pressed a buzzer and began to giggle. 'Oh, the power.'

* * *

'Gosh, she didn't like getting rid of things, did she?' Bella was going through a trunk full of old paintbrushes, easels and watercolour paints.

'In the last couple of years, no, I think she just slowed down.' Hugo brushed a cobweb from his face. 'I think she just put things in here and felt if she couldn't see them, she'd dealt with them.'

'Do you think any of these can be used again?' Bella picked up an unopened tin of paints.

'Duarte and Ignacio may be able to pass it on to the school they've been helping. If they are useable, they will go to a good home.'

219

Ignacio was pulling an empty chest of drawers out onto the landing. 'Charity shop?' he asked. 'It's in reasonable condition. Someone could make it better.'

'Ah, make it better.' Bella sighed. They had been working for three hours and the room was almost empty. 'There's just that wardrobe over there now.' She looked at it and hesitated.

'Clothes — they can be difficult to deal with when someone's gone. But, getting rid of them, I think, would be regarded by Flo as making it better too.' Ignacio smiled kindly at her.

'OK. Right.' Bella couldn't work out why she felt so emotional when she'd only known Great-Aunt Flo for two weeks oh so long ago.

'Shall we open the door together?' Hugo put his arm around her shoulder. 'I think we are all feeling a bit sensitive. We may see something Flo wore and . . .'

Bella nodded, fighting the urge to cry. Biting her lip, she put her hand on one of the handles.

Hugo did the same. 'Right.' He took a deep breath. 'One, two, three and . . . pull!'

The opened the doors and for a moment they didn't say anything.

'Where have all of her clothes gone?' Bella mumbled eventually, touching the only occupant of the cupboard — a long, green silk dress decorated with tiny bright red flowers and edged with black lace along the neckline and the bottom of the skirt.

'Maybe she just threw everything away when she got ill. All the clothes, I mean.' Ignacio sighed. 'I feel very relieved that we don't have to sort out more.'

'I have a picture of her wearing that.' Hugo laughed. 'The story was she had another argument with my uncle as he was trying to persuade her to sell her house and her land. AGAIN!' He shook his head. 'He used to try it with my parents regularly, but they ignored him. Flo would always react.'

220

'Oh yes. Minnie told me about that. Long before my time.' Ignacio squeezed Bella's hand. 'He was convinced he could make them all rich, wasn't he?'

'The photo was taken the year he parked the bulldozer at the end of the lane. My parents told me about it. Just to provoke us. And he did. Flo was furious.'

'Oh dear.' Bella's eyes widened.

'She was wearing this dress. I remember because she came round for dinner afterwards, which is when my parents took the photo.'

'Minnie says your great-uncle was like a dog with a bone.' Ignacio was smiling and shaking his head too. 'Where is he now?'

'Living in a big house on his own in Quinta do Lago counting his money.'

'Well, we think he's been in Lagos actually,' said Bella, 'don't we?'

'Let's ignore him and his money-grabbing ways, for now anyway.' Hugo looked back at the wardrobe and took the dress off the hanger. 'It smells of lavender. Your aunt loved lavender.' He handed it to Bella. 'I think it belongs in your wardrobe now.'

'I'm not sure . . .' Bella was still feeling emotional.

'I'll just pop downstairs with this.' Ignacio was holding another bin bag and left the room.

'She wanted you to have the house. She'd want you to have the dress too.' Hugo kissed Bella on the cheek.

She felt herself blush bright red.

'Bella!' Elena yelled from downstairs. 'We need you in the garden now to help us sort all this stuff.'

'OK!' Bella turned to Hugo. 'Thank you so much for today. I was getting very overwhelmed. Every time I walked past the room I felt it was pulsating!' She laughed. But then she remembered Francisco Lopes and his sad eyes when he'd stopped at the gate the previous week and began to feel anxious again.

'Why don't you try the dress on?' Layla shouted. 'It looks like it fits you perfectly.'

Hugo smiled. 'Yes, go on. It's a beautiful dress. It deserves to be worn.' He walked out onto the landing and down the stairs.

Bella took a deep breath and went into her bedroom, closing the door behind her. She put it on, didn't look in the mirror and went downstairs to show it to the others.

Hugo walked out of the kitchen as she stood in the living room.

'It suits you,' he said eventually. 'It really . . .'

Bella felt a pull towards him, as if she was being lifted, her feet moving despite her brain telling them not to.

'. . . suits you,' his voice was low and quiet.

'Come on!' Duarte appeared in the doorway. 'We have a picnic set up in the garden.'

'Right,' said Bella.

'Right,' said Hugo.

They followed Duarte outside.

'We used to meet here regularly when Flo was alive.' Hugo sat down next to Bella. 'We'd all bring food and sit here and chat and enjoy one another's company.'

'Oh, happy days.' Layla sighed. 'It's lovely to be here doing this again.'

'And seeing you in that dress — it's as if Flo is here some-how too.' Ignacio poured himself a glass of wine. 'To Florence Creswell. And to Bella Creswell, who is making things better just by being here.'

'Hear, hear.' The table echoed with the clinking of glasses.

'When my parents were alive, they were always talking with Flo about organic farming, and how they wanted to spread the word.' Hugo took a piece of bread and spooned some salad on his plate. 'They kept reminding themselves that they were so lucky to live here.'

Bella looked at the guests sitting around the garden eating and chatting, the swathes of red bougainvillea hugging the

222

wall of the house now a deep, rich crimson, the cherry tree in the garden heavy with lush green leaves, pots of bright flowers she had carefully brought back to life, the storks preening on the nest, the cats sitting patiently at her feet, and the tree outside the gate gently waving to and fro in the breeze.

And she realised last time she had anyone round for a party was when she had been at university. Which was a very long time ago.

CHAPTER 20

Hugo was striding out of the sea, pushing his hair out of his eyes, droplets of water glistening down his chest.

A bang nearby made her take a breath. Half-awake, she heard a dog bark in the distance. Bella looked around, trying to work out where the noise was coming from.

'Stop it,' someone shouted. 'We can't do it again.'

Bella tried to speak, but felt she was standing in a rainforest rather than the dunes, the sound of a macaw calling startling her. The dog barked again.

'Shhhhhh . . .'

'We can't go that way.' The voice seemed to be shouting at someone else now.

'Keep your voices down.'

'If I was her I'd call the police with all this noise. It's not even 7 a.m.'

A cat licked Bella's nose, and there was a clicking outside.

'We just need to walk down to the beach and around and then we can see them. I think they're near the lagoon.'

'See what?' mumbled Bella.

'You are making too much noise. You won't only wake Bella up, you'll scare those birds away.'

Bella opened her eyes. Yin or Yang was sitting on the pillow next to her, purring. The ambient rainforest track was still on. And there were birdwatchers in the garden again.

She climbed out of bed, opened the door and walked out onto the balcony.

'Hello?' she shouted, looking around. She couldn't see anyone. 'Hello? I know you're there. I can hear you.'

'We're not in your garden,' someone shouted.

'Well I can hear you, so you're somewhere.'

There was a brief muttering until someone stepped out from behind a bush next to the gate. It was Hans, the leader of the group.

'Hello.' He waved, sheepishly.

The storks looked at him and began clicking. Bella grinned. It sounded like disapproving tutting.

'You're not the only one there. I could hear the rest of you.'

About ten other people shuffled into view, silently, looking at their feet like naughty children.

'Why are you standing outside my gate at this time in the morning?' Bella folded her arms. 'I've got a busy day ahead so was having a bit of a lie-in.'

'There's a rare bird,' said Hans. 'We think it's on your land. We have been following it from Alvor. But we don't want to come in, it would be trespassing.'

'On my land? That sounds fun.' Bella waved at all of them. 'Just come in. Don't trample over the vegetable patches though.'

There was silence. 'Are you sure?' Hans called.

'Yes.' Bella laughed. 'It's all part of the fun, isn't it? And my Great-Aunt Flo let you in occasionally, didn't she?'

'Occasionally.' Hans beamed.

She beckoned them in. 'I mean it, just come in. I haven't seen this bird, but if it hasn't gone by the time I'm dressed, will you show it to me?'

'Of course, Bella, of course.' They all walked up the track.

Bella watched them happily, then closed the window and went downstairs to feed the cats, who were weaving around her feet and chirping. 'Well, that was an interesting start to the day. Maybe I'll see the bird,' she said, spooning out their food. Then she went back upstairs to shower so she could see the rare creature before she had to start work.

* * *

'So,' she ambled up behind Hans.

'Shhhhhh,' shushed everyone else.

'Sorry . . .' she whispered. 'I wondered where the bird was, given it's in my garden.'

'Over there.' Hans handed her his binoculars, which were still around his neck. Bella didn't notice and put them up to her eyes. He coughed.

'Shhhhhhh,' shushed everyone else.

'Sorry.' Bella handed them back so he could take them off. He then gave them back to her.

'Over there, on the tree right next to Hugo's place.'

'Ahhhh.' Bella smiled. 'That is beautiful. It's sort of purple.'

'Isn't she just?' sighed Hans. 'It's a purple heron. They are just here in the spring normally, and further east.' He smiled at Bella. 'Nothing — nothing — beats the sight of a bird like this on a summer's morning.'

'How long will it — sorry, she — be there for?'

'Who knows? She could just fly off at any time. You have to enjoy the moment.'

'I never imagined that I would get so excited about a little bird sitting on a tree.'

'This place does that to you. Plus, perhaps, having storks as lodgers.'

Bella laughed.

'Sshhhhhhh,' they all said again.

'Sorry, sorry. I've got to go and do some work before work,' she whispered to Hans.

She handed him back his binoculars and crept back into the house, then made herself breakfast and sat at her computer to catch up with her assignments and admin.

* * *

'OK, everyone.' Jules was trying to look upbeat from her section of the screen on the Zoom call. 'This is Philip, from Head Office. He's keen to meet you all in person, but as a lot of you are working from home today, he's decided to join the Zoom just to say hello.'

'Hello,' said a voice. It came from behind a photograph of a yacht. 'Dodgy internet means I seem to only do audio at the moment. Hello, I'm Philip. It's nice to meet you.'

'Hello. Welcome,' they all said brightly.

'Just pretend I'm not here,' he said. 'And hopefully the connection will improve, and I will become visible.'

'Let's start the meeting so we can all get on with our allocated tasks.' Jules picked up a pen and ran it down a pad. 'We've got some deadlines coming up this week, so we need to be on top of it. Shall we just give everyone an update on where we each are? We'll start with you, Lil.'

The rest of the group talked about what they were doing and when they would finish their tasks. Bella was busy making notes when she felt something moving underneath the table. Both the cats were sitting next to her, so she looked down. It was one of the young storks.

She and the bird stared at each other for a moment and then it began to peck at her foot.

'Ow!' she squealed, then put her hand over her mouth.

'What was that?' Lil peered out from the screen.

Everyone, including Bella looked around, confused, shaking their heads.

'So, finally, Bella. Where are you on the Lomas project?'

'The input from Fred and Magenta is due in today and once I've collated that, the report will be with you by 4 p.m. tomorrow as agreed.'

The stork pecked her foot again. Bella took a sharp intake of breath but tried to remain expressionless.

'Ah,' Philip said. 'There's been a change of deadline. We'd like it by midday tomorrow.'

'Midday. When was that decided?' Bella started to look through her notes.

'Just before the meeting. The clients have brought forward their deadline, so we have to bring forward ours.'

'When's their deadline?'

'Thursday.' Philip's face appeared on the screen. 'Excellent, the signal is fixed.' He smiled, but his eyes didn't.

'If that's the case, why do you need my report earlier? It will be in plenty of time.'

'I need to look at it before it goes to them.'

'Right.' Bella checked her timetable and diary. 'It just used to go to the department head — that's now Jules — and then to the clients.'

'Yes, but I need to look at reports now too. Is it a problem? I know you are part-time currently. Are you able to keep on top of your workload?'

'Yes.' Bella was beginning to get irritated but tried not to sound it. The stork pecked her foot again. 'I had all my work timetabled in.' She didn't mention the extra hours she was doing just to keep on top of everything. 'But this has changed very suddenly.'

Philip tried to smile again. 'I know this is last-minute, and I have had to move my diary around to accommodate this. But it's come from further up than me. I do apologise.'

There was a soft knocking at the door. 'Excuse me . . .' It was two of the birdwatchers.

'May we use your lavatory? We weren't expecting to be out so long,' the older of them, a lady with white curly hair, almost shouted. 'Bladder problems. Ageing. What can you do?' She shook her head and guffawed.

'Yes, of course.' Bella beckoned them in, deciding it was easier and quicker than directing them to Hugo's café down the lane. 'There's one the other side of the utility room. Just go through the kitchen. I'm actually on a work meeting . . .'

'Oh, sorry, sorry,' they shouted, almost tiptoeing past. The older lady waved at the screen as she went. 'Don't mind us . . .'

'For someone supposedly so quiet, you get a lot of visitors,' said Jules. 'Last time it was a woman and a dog — and noisy storks outside.'

'They're birdwatchers.' Bella tried to return the conversation to work. 'I will be able to get the report in when you asked, but is it possible to have more notice next time?'

'Yes.' Philip folded his hands and looked kindly out of the screen. 'There are a lot of changes going on in the background. It will settle down very soon and this is less likely to happen again.'

A loud clicking sound came from the door. It was one of the young stork's parents. From a distance, thought Bella, the storks were elegant and beautiful. Closer up, they were rather large.

'What's that noise?' Philip unfolded his hands and looked confused.

'It's the storks that live on top of the roof outside,' one of her colleagues said.

'Ah . . .'

The stork walked inside the house. Bella held her breath as it edged closer. The stork under the table continued to peck her foot.

'There's a stork in the house!' shouted the younger birdwatcher as she walked in from the kitchen. 'Quick, Marge, finish your wee and come out here!'

'It's in the house?' A range of sounds came from the work meeting. Bella shouted 'ow' and jumped up as the young stork pecked her foot a little harder.

'There's a young stork under the table too, Marge,' yelled the birdwatcher. 'Do you need any help getting them out?'

'Yes please.' Bella edged back. The young stork followed her. The adult stork clicked more loudly and moved into the centre of the room, so it was visible to the entire meeting.

More noise came from her workmates. 'That is so beautiful!' exclaimed Lil, drowning out everyone else.

Marge was now standing in the living room. She took out her camera and began snapping photographs.

'I need help to get them out!' Bella could hear her voice rising. 'I have work to do. I'm in a meeting.'

The younger birdwatcher was now brandishing a broom she had found in the utility room, stepping towards the birds as if she was going to brush them outside. 'There you go,' she was saying softly.

The adult stork continued to click. The younger stork was sticking close to Bella's foot.

'That young stork is too used to you,' Marge said sternly. 'It thinks you're part of the family.'

'Well I am!' shouted Bella.

For a moment there was silence. Then the adult stork moved forward and started clicking again.

'Right! Enough!' Marge clapped her hands. 'Out. Out we go. You belong outside. Come on!' She glanced at her friend and Bella. 'Do it too. Come on!'

They both began to clap and walked towards the adult bird, while the young bird followed Bella. Once the adult was outside, Marge took the broom and gently put the handle between Bella and the younger bird and encouraged it to follow its parent.

'There you go.' She leaned the broom against the wall. 'Right, come along, Mary. Let's leave Miss Creswell to her work. Toodle pip!'

Bella stood in the middle of the room watching the storks waddle across to the outbuilding and Marge and her friend waddle towards the orchard.

How can I ever look like I'm on top of my work ever again? she thought.

Sitting down, she plastered a wide smile on her face. 'So, apologies. Where were we?'

'That's the noisiest quiet place I've ever come across,' murmured Jules.

Bella didn't respond, trying to focus on her work rather than the impression she may have made on Philip from Head Office, and planning how much time she would need to spend outside her normal hours to really get ahead on her assignments.

CHAPTER 21

Bella watched the pick-up truck drive away with the skip, then walked around the house admiring the space that she had created, and the sense that she had somehow 'made it better'. But the 'making it better' had revealed chipped floor tiles, possible damp patches and quite a lot of missing plaster. The cats followed her around the rooms till she sat down on the floor of the living room, then they climbed on her lap. She stroked their heads, looking around, and took a breath — everything that needed to be done seemed to be superficial. *It's getting easier*, she thought, closing her eyes. One of the cats started to purr, and then so did the other one, so she listened to stereo contentment for a few minutes wondering how she had managed to live without cats for so many years.

Glancing at the clock on the wall, she went over to her computer and opened her spreadsheets, but the columns and words looked more like symbols and lines than anything she could make sense of, so she closed them again quickly, rubbing her forehead. She walked outside. The storks were standing on the roof, bright white against the blue of the sky. 'There's still so much to do,' she told them. 'I can't stay much longer. Real life is beckoning.'

Have you ever thought that this is real life too? Her inner voice was sounding reasonable. *Yes, your job and your flat are in London. Your parents are just outside. And you can't be far away from them for long. But — but — there may be another way.*

Bella rolled her shoulders and ignored the voice, deciding to take a swim in her very own swimming pool that she had 'made better'. She put on her swimming costume, grabbed a towel and walked outside past what she now called the 'ambling picture'. *Is that what this is?* she thought, *planning on doing something important and useful, but going for a swim instead?* She smiled, stepping onto the patio, the tiles warm under her bare feet, then strode over to the pool and climbed in, pushing herself off through the water, and with each stroke and each breath felt the spreadsheets floating away into the air.

After her swim, she fell onto a sunbed and dozed for a while, enjoying the heat on her back and the singing of the birds, then stood and headed back into the house to try to make sense of the spreadsheets and do some more work, even though she was part-time and it wasn't one of her official working days.

* * *

'Hello!' a man's voice shouted from the gate.

It was Jorge. He was dressed in shorts and a T-shirt and didn't look like he had come from work.

Bella waved. 'Come on in. Do you want anything to drink? I've got some homemade lemonade that Layla gave me.'

'No, no thank you.' His face was serious, and he couldn't meet her eyes. 'I am on my way back to Lisbon for a week or so.'

'Oh, lovely. A holiday?' Bella smiled at him, but he didn't smile back.

'Not quite. Bella. Can we sit somewhere? I have something I need to explain.'

'Of course. Shall we sit in the shade under the tree? Is everything all right?'

They sat down.

'What do you need to explain?' Bella was beginning to feel uneasy.

'I got myself involved in a situation that has got a little out of hand and I need to apologise.' He still couldn't meet her eyes. 'About your house. About the land . . .'

'Right.'

'I came to Lagos to get ahead, move up the ladder and make money so I could go back to Lisbon and make lots more money.'

'Yes?'

'And then, just after you arrived, I met a woman through a mutual friend . . .' He shook his head and sighed. 'I have been an idiot and I'm sorry.'

'Sorry about what?'

'She persuaded me that — no, I allowed her to persuade me because I wanted to believe her.' He shook his head again. 'She works for a property development company, and they are looking for land in this area — it's become very popular. She said there is a shortage of housing, and we need to do something about it, but we could also make a lot of money as we did.'

'Is this lady connected to Hugo at all?' Bella shifted uncomfortably.

'Yes. They were together for a while. It ended very acrimoniously and now I wonder if some of this is because she is still angry with him.'

'Ah.'

'And she is not interested in me. You know, Bella.' He looked at her now, his eyes intense. 'When you arrived and I saw you for the first time at the bar I thought . . . I found you . . . I mean . . . I liked you immediately. A lot.' He scratched his head and stared at the table. 'So please do not think that all of the chats we had were because I wanted to use you to get to the land. It's just she swept in and turned my head. She's very intense and . . . I was flattered. And saw the chance to make some quick money.'

'Go on.' A shred of anger was curling its way through her body.

'She said, why shouldn't we make lots of money from this? These are only three little houses. My company could build a lot of properties on it, or even three much better houses, she said, and I'd get a slice of it for helping to persuade you to sell. And I would be set for life. I wouldn't have to worry about money anymore.' He looked at her again. 'My father died when I was very young, and my mother always struggled and worked hard to make sure me and my sister could stay at school, so we could get a good education. But it was hard, so hard.' He shook his head. 'And I don't want us to be like that anymore. It felt like I could jump to the front of the queue rather than edge my way forward from the back.'

The anger dissipated for a moment. 'I understand that.' Bella looked away for a moment, unable to meet his gaze.

'And she knew. How did she know? It turns out she has been talking to my friends — some had already moved down from Lisbon. She targeted me.' He shifted awkwardly in his seat. 'She knew that Elena is Hugo's accountant, and when she and Will started to become friendly, she persuaded me to tell her about his situation. That's why Lenny and Martim were around so much talking to him.'

'Why are you telling me this now, Jorge?'

'My actions have upset Will, and they have very much upset Elena because he wonders who has been passing on information about his personal circumstances.' He began to talk more quickly, the words spilling out almost angrily. 'And when Hugo asked me if I knew anything at that charity function, I realised it had gone too far. I saw my aunt cry because she had argued with Will. Hugo said that Lenny and Martim and his ex — who I thought was interested in me—' He shook his head. 'Anyway, that they were beginning to intimidate you all and were they anything to do with his great-uncle Francisco Lopes.'

'Are they?'

'She works — or worked — for his company. That's all I know.'

'This all seems a bit personal, doesn't it?' Bella stood up. 'Hugo's ex wants his farm, Francisco Lopes — is he still angry with Great-Aunt Flo? I mean—' she sat down again '—It seems so irrational.'

'Money, money, money,' Jorge said quietly.

'That's what Hugo said when I first met him.' Bella sighed.

'So, I am leaving for a while. I have told them all sorts of things I shouldn't have, and I am sorry. Sorry doesn't make up for it, but I am.'

He stood and held his hand out. Bella looked at him for a moment, waiting for the anger. But there wasn't any.

'I am very ashamed. I shouldn't have started, but when you told me about your parents and your situation it struck a chord and I should have stopped then. But I sort of got swept away with the whole thing.'

'Have you spoken to your aunt? Or Will? You need to put it right.'

'I am on my way to Will's now. I'm not sure he will be as kind as you, but I deserve it. As for my aunt, I'm planning on telling her quickly then jumping in my car and driving off into the distance.' There was half a smile on his face. 'But wait till she tells my mother.' He shook his head. 'Oh dear.'

He kissed her tentatively on the cheek. '*Adeus*, Bella. Good luck with everything. And I'm sorry. So sorry.'

He turned and walked back to the gate.

Bella went to the postbox and opened it, retrieving the card Deanna had put in it when she'd met her. She took it into the house and put it on the table, trying to plan what she wanted to say to the woman. But her thoughts were too tangled. She was too angry to plan anything. So she picked up the phone and, when it went straight to voicemail, said the first thing that came into her head.

'This is Bella Creswell.' Her voice sounded even and assertive. 'I believe you have been using underhand tactics to try to persuade me and my neighbours to sell. This is unprofessional, unethical, and actually a little bit on the creepy side.' She enjoyed saying the last few words, sensing that glamorous, sleek and ambitious Deanna would hate being called 'creepy'. 'I may well phone the police.'

She rang off, then found the number of the office of Francisco Lopes and left him a message asking him to call her.

Then she put on a sundress, grabbed a sunhat and walked down to the café to see if Hugo was there.

* * *

He was sitting outside looking at his phone when she arrived.

'I've just had an email from a potential investor about my business plan.' He waved the phone at her excitedly. 'I think this is the beginning of something wonderful, you know. The charity is getting going and now this!'

'That's just lovely.' Bella smiled at him, wondering whether telling him about her conversation with Jorge was a good idea.

He stood up. 'Is everything all right? I thought that with all the clearing and the progress you were making with the house, you may look a little bit happier than you do right now.'

'Shall we walk for a moment? I need to tell you something and I don't want anyone to hear.' She began to walk towards the beach.

Hugo caught her up. 'I'm starting to worry, Bella.'

'No, no, it's not that bad. It's unsettling and somewhat private.' She took a breath. 'So, Jorge has just been to see me and has told me that he's been giving information about Will to your ex.'

'What?' Hugo stopped walking.

'These people are really keen on our land, Hugo. And—' she turned to face him '—she works — or worked — for your great-uncle.'

'I knew he was behind this. I'm going to drive to his office now and get this finished.'

237

'I've left Deanna and your great-uncle messages. Maybe they'll stop now. Perhaps you shouldn't waste your time travelling to see him.'

'This is so stupid. He knows I won't sell. I don't know why they are doing this.'

'Maybe they thought they could persuade Will and me to sell. I have no emotional connection to the house, after all.'

'Don't you?' He almost smiled.

Bella didn't answer. 'I have to go home and do some work.'

'You said "home".' Hugo smiled again.

'I've had a bit of a stressful afternoon, so not too much teasing please.' Bella couldn't help herself. She smiled back as her phone buzzed in her bag. 'I didn't hear it ring,' she muttered, listening to a voicemail.

'This is a message for Miss Bella Creswell,' said a female voice. *'I am ringing on behalf of Francisco Lopes. He has asked me to inform you that he has no interest in buying your land or that of your neighbours in Lagos and has no business connection to anyone who may be approaching you about this matter. Thank you.'*

Bella repeated it to Hugo. 'Unbelievable.' He shook his head. 'What are those clowns trying to do?'

'I don't know, but maybe they will stop now that he knows one of his employees — or ex-employees — is getting a bit carried away with herself.'

'Maybe.'

Someone called him from the restaurant.

'I have to go back to work,' he said. 'Thank you for making the call. It probably was better coming from you than me.'

'No problem. I'll get back myself now.'

They paused, looking at each other briefly, then they both nodded and walked off in opposite directions.

CHAPTER 22

Bella lay in bed the following day, feeling slightly lighter. 'Didn't realise how much all that stuff about Will's house was affecting us,' she said to the cats, who were sitting peacefully at the end of the bed.

Switching off her ambient rainforest soundtrack, she put her feet on the floor, enjoying the sensation of the cool tiles and wondering whether to put the air conditioning on later. It felt as if the day was going to get much hotter. Grabbing a quick shower, she put on her swimming costume and walked outside. The sea roared, the birds sang and the storks sat watching her as she climbed down the steps into the water.

When she got out, she made herself a cup of tea and sat in the shade of the tree for a while, before standing up and tidying around some of the bougainvillea bursting from the window boxes on the ground floor.

Back inside, she opened the wardrobe and decided to put on the blue sundress that had belonged to Flo, went downstairs switched on her computer and logged on, preparing to tick a number of items off her to-do list.

Her phone buzzed and she checked the message.

Join us for breakfast at Hugo's, Bella? We all decided it would be lovely to meet before we start our day. Duarte

Bella checked through her diary. Her first meeting was at ten thirty. Thinking about the fact she'd worked till 8 p.m. the previous night she decided she'd already done two hours' work, glanced over at the 'ambling' picture, smoothed down her dress and typed a response.

What a lovely idea. I have to leave by ten but can be there in a few minutes. Bella

Excellent news! See you very soon.

She grabbed her bag and ambled down to the gate, pausing under the tree in the track to check she had remembered her keys. Birds chirped above her in the tree's tangled branches, hidden by the lush green leaves, its roots stretching out towards the entrance to the lane. Only one side of the storks' nest tile was visible behind it, and she pondered arranging for some of it to be cut back but put her arms around it instead. 'Gorgeous tree,' she murmured, turning and walking towards the beach.

As she walked over the dunes towards the café she paused, enjoying the sea glittering under the sunlight.

Her friends were sitting at a long table outside that faced the beach.

'Here she is!' Ignacio waved at her.

'Hold it!' shouted Bella, feeling a sudden urge to capture the image for ever. 'I just want to take a picture to send my parents. Say cheese, everyone!'

'Cheese!' they all shouted.

'Thanks.' She took the photo and sent it to her mother then went over to the table. 'What's the occasion?'

'No occasion.' Layla stood and moved a chair for her. 'We just decided it's a beautiful day and we live in a beautiful place and we should take more time out to enjoy it.'

'Absolutely right.' Minnie touched Ignacio's cheek. 'And it will stop these two constantly rehearsing their living statue routines every time they have a spare ten minutes.'

'It's called having a passion.' Duarte took a sip of a fresh orange juice. 'Talking of which, I've been thinking more about Hugo's charity and businesses idea.'

'Yes, but isn't the idea of being a living statue that you just stand still a lot?' Minnie's face was deadpan.

'There is more to it than that, Minnie!' Ignacio folded his arms and stared into the distance.

Elena shook her head. 'Duarte, I say this with love, but you have the attention span of a bumble bee, flitting from one thing to another to stop yourself from being bored. How much money have you spent on those John Travolta costumes?'

'I can have more than one passion.' Duarte sounded petulant.

Bella sat down. 'Well, meeting you for breakfast is a lovely idea. I can't stay too long though.'

'Neither can I.' Elena leaned back. 'I have a lot of appointments with clients today.'

'What would you like, Bella?' Hugo stood in the doorway, clearly busy.

'Avocado on brown toast with tomatoes, an orange juice and—'

'A *galão*,' he interrupted, smiling. 'Coming up.'

Quiet Julian was delivering the food to the group as Will walked over from the dunes to the bottom of the steps with Deidre, who was trying to pull him up to the café on her lead.

'Will!' shouted Ignacio. 'How's the leg?'

'Much better.' Will held up his stick. 'Hopefully won't need this anymore soon.'

Deidre barked and then whined.

'You can't go on the beach at this time of day, girl,' he told her. He looked back up at the group. 'I just wanted to say hello. Duarte messaged me to tell me you were here.'

'Come and join us.' Minnie pointed at a chair. 'You can move that one over.'

He looked sheepish. 'I'm not sure . . .' He glanced at Elena, who was very focused on her phone.

She jumped as Minnie nudged her and grabbed her phone. 'Are you an adult?' Minnie asked.

'Work,' muttered Elena.

Minnie nudged her again. 'Sort it out,' she whispered. 'Goodness knows what you see in an old hippie like that, but you've been miserable since that argument.'

'I heard that.' Will almost smiled. 'Everything was closing in on me and I panicked.'

'I'm so embarrassed and angry about Jorge,' Elena said quickly, still unable to look at Will directly.

'Go for a walk,' whispered Minnie. 'Go . . .' She stood and gently pulled her friend to her feet, walked her down the steps and planted her next to Will. 'Life is too short. And I think all this needs to be private this time. Or should I give you a microphone like you had at the yoga class?'

Deidre clicked Elena's hand and her face cracked into a smile.

'Shall we?' asked Will.

Elena nodded, and they walked slowly back over the dunes towards Will's house.

'Thank God. She's been so miserable.' Minnie sat down and picked up her glass.

'Are you working today, Bella?' Layla took a bite out of a croissant.

'Yes but starting a bit later as I was working till late last night. I think I deserve a bit of a treat.'

'We should do it more often.' Layla squeezed her hand.

'We should. It's such a lovely café, and you are all such good company. What a wonderful start to the day.'

'How is the house looking now?' asked Ignacio.

'It's good. It's mainly decorating from now on. Structurally fine apparently. I've got to sort out the land at the back of the house, but Hugo may be able to help with that. So, I think I can say I have "made it better" although . . .' She shook her head. 'I don't know if I've "made it better" enough?'

'Ah, the end is in sight.' Ignacio picked up his coffee.

'Yes. It's going to be a beautiful spot for someone.' As soon as the words came out of Bella's mouth, she felt a lump in her throat, and looked up.

Hugo was standing in front of her with her drink. Their eyes met for a moment. Then they both looked away.

Bella cleared her throat. 'I can understand why Great-Aunt Flo loved it so much.'

Her phone began to ring, so she rummaged around in her bag, trying to concentrate on that rather than why she was feeling so strangely emotional all of a sudden.

'Hi, Mum!' she said brightly.

There was silence at the end of the phone.

'Is everything all right?' Bella's stomach lurched. 'Excuse me.' She stood up and walked down onto the beach.

'Your father had another fall.' There was silence again. 'He's getting more and more frustrated and more and more angry and our whole lives are about that now.' Her mother's voice sounded flat. 'And I'm finding it difficult to cope. There. I've said it. Finally.'

'I'll come home. I'll come home today.' Bella turned towards the café. 'I should be closer to help you. It's not fair.'

'It's not fair on any of us, including you.'

'We need to change things though, Mum, don't we?' Bella waved at the others. 'Tell Hugo I'll pay him later,' she shouted, then hurried up back towards the house.

'I don't want you to come home.'

'I'll come home for a few days.' Bella forced herself to sound upbeat. 'Help out. And I'll pop into the office to show my face to my new boss. I've got a review booked in for this week and we can do it in person.'

There was a pause. 'We need to do something,' her mother said eventually. 'You're so organised, you'll see whatever it is that we can do to get us on our way and then go back to Portugal.'

'I've got to come home sometime.' Bella was standing under the tree again. 'This is a temporary project, remember.'

'But I don't think you're ready to finish it yet, Bella. So, this is just for a few days.'

Bella watched the storks gliding across the treetops in the distance towards the Nest, as Yin and Yang wandered down the path towards her. 'Just for a few days, Mum. I can't be here for ever. I'll let you know when I've booked my flight.'

She ended the call and took a deep breath. 'This wasn't supposed to happen,' she told the cats. 'Whatever this is, this—' she pointed at her heart '—this was not supposed to get involved in the decisions this—' she pointed at her head '—has to make.'

'Bella!' Hugo was running up the track towards her. 'You forgot this.' He handed her a box with her breakfast in it and a takeaway coffee.

'Ah, thank you.' She smiled at him, relieved he was there. 'I'm glad you're here. Can you keep an eye on this place for me for a few days? I've got a family emergency.'

'Oh, I'm sorry to hear that. Of course I'll look after it.'

'I'll ask Will to feed the cats. They're used to him.'

He touched her hand. 'Are you all right?'

She bit her lip. 'I'm used to this kind of family emergency,' she said. 'But I'm usually very close by when it happens.'

They looked at each other.

'It's difficult being pulled in many different directions.'

'Yes.' Bella nodded.

'Keep in touch.'

'Yes. I'll let you know when I'm coming back.'

'Good,' he said.

'Yes,' said Bella.

'I'd better get back to work.'

'Thank you.' She held up the coffee cup and nodded.

'You're welcome.' He nodded back and turned away, then strode back towards the café.

Bella walked into the house, turned on her laptop, logged on for work and spent the rest of the day organising her trip home and her face-to-face meeting with her new boss.

* * *

She finished packing just as the sun set, deciding to go and sit on the roof for a while before she went to bed to try to get some rest before leaving for her early flight.

She stepped outside. In the distance Lagos glowed, vibrant and full of life, the beach bars dotting the bay like lanterns, the windows of the apartments and villas along Meia Praia flickering with light.

Sitting down, she pulled a blanket over her shoulders and looked at the crescent moon surrounded by hundreds and hundreds of glimmering stars hanging like a canopy in the sky. The muted sound of music pumped quietly from a café inland, and the waves crashed rhythmically on the beach.

The cats followed her out and lay under the chair. She glanced down and murmured, 'Will's going to be feeding you for the next few days, guys.' Then she looked at the storks' nest. 'I think you can look after yourselves.'

Pouring herself a glass of wine, she sat and watched, the chatter in her head slowing down. *How are we going to manage now with Dad . . . I have to sell this place soon so I can be closer. Lurching from one crisis to the next with the parents . . . What will it be like for someone else to live in this? What's going to happen to you two?* She looked at the cats and felt something unravel in the pit of her stomach. *You two, this place . . .*

She shook her head. *No . . . no . . . I'm just stressed.* She almost gritted her teeth. *This was always a business proposition. The cats were always temporary. They will live with Will and it will be fine. Fine.*

The lights of Hugo's café began to dim, and then disappear, and Bella pictured him locking up and walking along the track back to his house. Her stomach lurched again.

Telling herself firmly she would only be away for a few days, she looked back up at the sky. *I'm only passing through*, she thought. *I've nearly made it better. It must be better enough soon.*

Opening her eyes, she took a sip of wine and her mind calmed again, lulled by the stillness around her. She put her glass on the floor and pushed the chair back to recline, closed her eyes and listened for a while, breathing slowly in and out in time with the sea.

Bella didn't remember going downstairs, but she was standing in the kitchen looking for the cats. But they weren't there. A tiny dog she didn't recognise wandered in and sat next to the table.

'Hello?' Bella said. 'Are you related to Deidre?'

The dog ignored her and trotted back into the living room.

'I'm not sure I like it, to be honest,' said a female voice from the other room. 'I think we'll have to gut the whole place and start again. I mean, the shell of it is fine, but it's so old-fashioned.'

'What? Sorry, who are you?' Bella hurried into the living room. A middle-aged woman with curly grey hair was taking photographs of the room, while a man was knocking the walls.

'You're right, babes.' The man took his sunglasses from the top of his head and cleaned them on his shirt. 'I bought it knowing that. But, you know, it's in a great spot.'

'Can we get rid of those storks?' The woman wrinkled her nose with distaste.

'Not yet. But leave it with me.'

Bella walked up to them. 'What are you doing in my house?' she asked, but they didn't seem to notice she was there. 'Why do you want to change it after all the work I've done? I've nearly made it better.'

The dog started to bark, then purr, then snort.

Bella opened her eyes. She was sitting in the middle of a vista full of stars, glittering and shimmering and shining, surrounding her with pinpricks of light, as if she was sitting in the sky. She heard the purring again and opened her eyes.

Only this time she was actually awake. The cats were stretched out, purring noisily, and she was lying under the blanket on the reclined chair, looking up at the stars, not in them. And she'd just had a bad dream.

'Oh.' She put her hands down and stroked Yin and Yang, their fur warm and soft, realising she had just had a nightmare. And then she began to wonder how she could make sure that when she sold the house, the new owners wouldn't knock it down. Or get rid of the cats.

Unwrapping herself from the blanket, she got out of the chair, picked up the wine and the glass and went inside, set the alarm for 6 a.m., and attempted to go to sleep.

* * *

Bella lay with her eyes wide open, the alarm ringing in the background. She couldn't seem to get herself out of bed. Her body felt like a stone, heavy and hard. She rolled out of bed, hurried into the shower and tried to wake herself up by turning the water down to lukewarm. Putting on her clothes, she brushed her hair and put her make-up on, the alarms still ringing in the background to make sure she felt some sense of urgency, rather than the kind of dread that made her want to shut the doors and hide away from the world. The kind she hadn't felt for years but knew would one day come back.

Putting her phone in her bag she walked onto the landing. Her suitcase was next to the door, ready for her to pick up to take to the car. Glancing at the door to the roof terrace she paused for a moment, then pushed it open and walked up the steps. The sky was a misty grey, the moon still visible high in the sky, a pink glow hovering over the sea to the east. The sea was quiet and calm and the storks were standing next to the nest, preening.

Wishing she hadn't taken one last look, she hurried inside, locked the door, ran downstairs, put the cat food in the bowl for when Yin and Yang woke up, picked up her bag, locked the door behind her and put the case in the boot of the car. Then she turned on the engine and drove down to the track, the house getting smaller and smaller in her rearview mirror. She stopped next to the tree, got out, locked the gate and drove away again. But this time she started crying.

'Stop it,' she shouted to herself. 'You're coming back in a few days. It must be because you're overtired and worried about Mum and Dad. Not because you're sad to leave the house. It's a house, Bella, not a person.'

She switched on the radio, turned the music up as loud as she could to drown out her thoughts and accelerated from the lane onto the main road.

CHAPTER 23

'We've made a decision, Bella.' Her mother sounded in control again. 'Do you want another biscuit?' She held out a plate of digestives.

'No. I've had three so far, Mum.' Bella took the plate and put it back down on the table. 'What decision?'

'We're selling the house.' Her father took a sip of tea. 'Jan and Frank next door are selling up, and Mr Francis over the road has decided he's going to buy a house near his son in Scotland.'

'But you love the house and the garden. Are you sure?'

'We love it too, darling.' Her mother was smiling but it didn't reach her eyes. 'This house is too much for us now. Our oldest friends are leaving. We'll buy a small flat or a bungalow with a smaller garden.'

'Doctors say warmth will help the joints, so we'll go somewhere modern and well insulated that's cheap to heat.' Her father took a biscuit from the plate.

Bella sat back and looked outside at the garden, nurtured by her mother and father all through her life, memories of them tending it and sitting in it and dozing in it playing like a film in her mind.

'It'll also take the financial pressure off.' Her mother sighed. 'It means I won't have to take extra shifts and your dad won't worry about the tiny amount of money he gets paid for doing those sports reports.'

'I can stop marking the exam papers.' He tried to smile. 'Rest. Enjoy . . .' He glanced out at the garden, then closed his eyes for a moment.

'Where will you move to?'

'We don't know.' Her mother frowned. 'But we'll work it out. It's an adventure!'

'Has something happened?' Bella asked. 'Apart from all these falls you've been having recently?'

'Well, apart from being told it's not going to get any better, and slowly worse, no.'

'Right . . .' Bella managed to order her mind into focus. 'Once I've got rid of the Nest that will help you financially. I don't need the proceeds from it. I'm working and I have a good job, and if we use that money wisely we can do something about the heating here and adapt it — there are grants to help — and you won't have to move.'

Her mother put her hand on her daughter's arm. 'No. Thank you. But no. Don't spend all that on us. You matter too.'

'It's bound to help with something for you, though.' Bella felt herself go rigid. It was the only way she could stop herself thinking of the dream she'd had when she was on the roof terrace. 'It's just bricks and mortar, Mum. And I have to do something practical with it.'

'You sound so happy when you are there.' Her father leaned forward.

'But I don't live there.' Bella was beginning to feel exasperated. 'I live in London, near you. And being near you is the most important thing to me.'

'It shouldn't be, though, should it?' Her mother was staring at her.

'What do you mean?' Bella felt herself bristle.

250

'Your need some love and fun in your life. Not just work and supporting us.'

'My life is fun.' Bella couldn't think of anything else to say.

'When you're in Portugal,' her father said firmly. 'Here it's all work and career-obsessed boyfriends.'

'Well . . .' Bella looked at them both. 'I think that's a bit simplistic. But none of us can go on like this. I've got a meeting at work tomorrow and then we can focus on selling the Nest and your living arrangements.'

'Whatever you say, Bella.' Her mother finished her biscuit. 'We've loved seeing the photos you've been sending. You've made such an impact on the Nest. And your friends look lovely. And that café on the beach . . .' She smiled. 'Who is that handsome man standing next to the shy-looking young man in the last photo you sent? I'd love to meet him.'

Bella's heart fluttered and she folded her arms. 'Must be Hugo and Quiet Julian. What photo?'

'You took it yesterday morning. I didn't see it until after I'd phoned you. What's the deal with him?'

'Deal?' Bella picked up her bag.

'Anything going on?'

'We are just friends. And neighbours. That's it.' She stood up.

'Hugo?' Her mother looked confused. 'I thought he was older.'

'He's Hugo's son, Mum. Also called Hugo.' Bella didn't want to keep repeating his name. In the near future, he would be nothing more than a nice friendly memory from an interesting interlude. She didn't want to keep thinking about him or talking about him. Because there was no point. 'Well, I'd best go. I've got to check in on my flat — my home — and get myself ready for work tomorrow. The taxi's here.'

She hugged her parents, she took her luggage and went out of the door to the cab.

* * *

251

Bella walked swiftly in through the modern entrance to her block of flats, all glass and metal, with artfully placed large green pot plants dotted on plinths and a sculpture made of recycled plastic bottles hanging from the ceiling of the atrium. In the past she'd barely noticed them, as she had generally been rushing in or out, but today, as she waited for the lift, she looked around. Someone, she realised, had made an effort to make it look, and feel, welcoming.

Deciding to make time to appreciate her surroundings more when she moved back, Bella pressed the button to her floor. 'When I'm back,' she said out loud, feeling suddenly flat. No more storks on the roof, no more Yin and Yang purring next to her ears in the morning, no more Deidre running up to say hello, no more Will, no more Hugo . . .

No more Hugo.

She told herself to get a grip, managing to suppress the sudden and increasingly regular desire to cry and reminding herself that when the Nest was sold there would be no more responsibility.

The lift doors opened opposite the door to her flat. A wave of weariness overwhelmed her as she unlocked the door, put her case down, locked herself in and crawled straight into the welcoming warmth of her own bed.

Someone was talking outside. Bella put a pillow over her head to muffle the noise. 'Birdwatchers again,' she mumbled, rolling over, keeping her eyes firmly shut.

'And now, ladies and gentlemen, my rendition of "Come On Eileen" on traffic cone and my own beautiful voice.' A loud cheer greeted this announcement as an unknown man began to hum through the cone.

Realising that there were no birdwatchers outside, and this was just the usual night-time noise in London on a busy main road, Bella checked her phone. It was 2 a.m.

Pouring herself a glass of water, she opened her blinds to locate where the impromptu performance was coming from just as a police car pulled up and moved the group along. She climbed back into bed, managing to get back to sleep until a delivery lorry began reversing into a bay behind a shop across the road, beeping as it did. Bella checked her phone. It was 6 a.m.

How did I manage to get any rest? she thought irritably, drifting off into a listless doze until seven thirty, when her alarm went off.

She took her dressing gown out of her wardrobe and went to the kitchen to put the kettle on, then remembered to switch on the hot water so she could have a hot shower. She stared out of the window over the rooftops of London, the ever-changing city landscape she'd gazed at for so many years.

She wondered which part of the Nest Yin and Yang had slept in, and whether the storks were awake yet. She hadn't seen the geckos for a few days but pictured them behind the chest of drawers in the living room preparing for a new day. And she thought of Hugo. She tried not to think of Hugo, but as she got ready for work, she couldn't stop thinking of Hugo.

She tried to focus on what she was going to say during her review at work, and what she had to do to help her parents. But all she could think about was Hugo.

Climbing into the shower, she switched the temperature to cold, and forced herself to stop thinking of Hugo. For a few moments she was able to think about how cold the water was. And then she thought of Hugo in his wetsuit doing yoga on the beach.

I live here! she told herself. *I love this flat. I own this flat. I have earned this flat through my hard work and dedication and I can't be far from my parents. And my job, my career is here. I can't fall in love with a man in another country.*

She turned the temperature back up to hot, pretending to herself she hadn't just thought of the word, *love.*

Getting out of the shower, Bella took a couple of deep breaths, preparing for a day that was about her job and her parents.

'The job and my parents, the job and my parents,' she chanted, so when she finally left the flat to get the tube to work, her mind was racing with all the problems she had to solve involving those things, and those alone.

* * *

Bella's phone pinged with messages every few minutes. She tried to ignore them, her mind now full of her parents and how, for the first time, she'd really seen how they felt. Years of both them and Bella putting a brave face on, meant they had never acknowledged the effects that the accident and its aftermath had had on the three of them.

Making the most of it, she thought to herself, sadly. *Trying to keep things the same. The same house, the same place. The same neighbours. But . . .* A slow panic began to flow through her body. *The neighbours are leaving, the house is too big, and they will never have enough money to have a nice, easy life. No matter how much I throw at them.*

Numbers whirred through her brain again. Sell the Nest. How long would the money realistically last from the sale? If she couldn't sell, how regular would the rental money be? How much time would it take her to manage it?

Bella tried to focus on her spreadsheets to get her thoughts in order. But there was a voice whispering to her from somewhere.

But someone else will be living in it, Bella. Not you . . . someone else . . . Remember that dream . . . someone else . . . not you . . .

Her phone pinged again, and then it rang.

By now her heart was pumping uncomfortably, so she took a deep breath. Opening her messages, she saw several from Lil.

I know you're coming in today for a face-to-face with Jules. They've just announced yet another restructuring out of the blue. I thought you should know.

She's stressed and NOT dealing with it well. It's been dumped on her too.

Talks of job losses. Redundancies. Never saw it coming.

254

Didn't want you to walk into the middle of this without knowing.

Bella's heart began to race faster as she scrolled through messages from other colleagues telling her the same thing. Among them there was one from Hugo and one from Will, which she decided to file away for later. 'I can read them at the airport,' she mumbled, putting her head back and closing her eyes, trying to calm herself down.

She pictured driving up to the Nest, the bougainvillea in full bloom, the scarlet of the flowers tumbling over the window boxes and trailing to the floor. Her breathing slowed slightly.

She put the phone back into her pocket, focusing on getting the review meeting done and then getting on her flight.

* * *

Walking through the entrance hall of the shiny office block in Canary Wharf, Bella tried to summon up the sense of pride she used to feel every time she stepped inside. She had a good job with a good company, and she loved it. She used to feel she was in the epicentre of the world, right in the middle of everything.

But today she didn't feel like that. It felt like a shiny office block in Canary Wharf. And that was it. Rifling through her memory file, Bella attempted to alight on something that would motivate her, because it sounded like things were changing and she might have to fight for the job she had loved so much. But all she could think of was the money she'd lose if she left. How would she help her parents? How would she live? What would she do?

She tapped her security pass against the lift and walked inside, counting to ten as it began to move.

The door opened and she plastered a serene smile on her face. Scanning the room, she couldn't see anyone she knew.

Then she remembered, it was one of her team's working-from-home days.

'Bella!' Jules waved and walked over to her. 'How lovely to meet you at last in person.'

Bella shook her hand. 'You too. Thank you for being so accommodating with my temporary work situation.'

'Not at all!' Jules began to walk to a meeting room. 'You are an extremely valuable member of the team, so it's no surprise my predecessors ensured you got the support you needed. They really couldn't have done without you.'

She closed the door behind them, and they sat down.

'So, how are things going in Portugal, Bella?' She picked up a carafe of water. 'Would you like some?'

'Yes, please.' Bella's throat was feeling dry. She decided she had become unused to air conditioning and took a sip of her drink, then put it down. 'They are going well. In fact, the six months are almost up.'

'Six months?' Jules looked confused.

'The terms of the will stated I could not sell or rent the property for six months after I took possession of it. And I had to "make it better".'

'Ah. That's vague.'

'Yes it is.' Bella shook her head. 'I have made it a bit better, but there's no benchmark, no tick list, nothing.'

'So, that means you will be back soon?'

'Yes. And I would like to return to full-time work.' Bella felt sick, and then surprised that she felt sick.

'We would love you to. But—' Jules looked strained. 'We've just been notified of some more restructuring. It's all very sudden. And so I can't tell you anything.'

'Restructuring?' Bella pretended she hadn't already heard about it.

'Yes. I've nothing concrete to say really. Just rumours at the moment. So I'd rather say nothing.'

'Right, I understand.'

'So, we'll just do the performance review as agreed?'

256

Bella nodded. 'Of course.'

'Well, as I have only been in this job for almost four months, I've referred to my predecessor's notes on your work while he was here. It is full of praise. No negative issues at all.'

Bella relaxed slightly.

'However, since you went part-time and have been in Portugal, there have been some issues. Deadlines missed.'

'By an hour.' Bella felt herself bristle. 'Twice.'

'Yes, but it's an essential part of your job.' Jules smiled. 'It's just to flag up, that's all, and—' she scanned through her paperwork '—I've noticed you haven't volunteered for extra tasks the way you did in the past.'

'It's difficult when you're part-time to take on extra work.' Bella sighed. 'In fact, I'm actually doing a full-time job in part-time hours at the moment.'

'Are you sure that isn't bad time management due to your change in circumstances?'

'My time management has always been excellent. I think it's the new structure of the department that's the issue. Teething problems.'

Jules lowered her voice. 'Bella. The reason you were allowed to take a long holiday, then go part-time and work from Portugal was because you are a real asset to the company. We didn't want to lose you. But . . .' She sighed and frowned. 'The people in charge now are not the same people. They are looking for a different way of doing things and putting pressure on people like me to put pressure on people like you.'

'Oh. Um . . .' Bella's stomach began to flip nervously.

'I'll be frank — reading between the lines, they are looking for excuses to ease people out. And I think maybe you're one of them.'

'What? After all these years?'

'That's not what they see.' Jules looked almost defeated.

'The extra hours I've worked for this place, the sacrifices I've made to make sure things are done on time. The commitment I've given—'

'I know. I'm just—' she leaned forward again '—It's not good at the moment. I'm really not happy with all of this but I need my job.'

'Me too.' Bella tried to control the anger in her voice, but as she said it, she glanced out of the window and saw a bird flutter onto a tree. She wondered what the storks were doing now.

'You need to ramp it up, Bella. Fight for your job.'

'But after all of this. They want to ease me out?'

'Reading between the lines.'

'I've given so much to this company.' Her voice was low. 'It's meant I could help my parents. But my last boyfriend told me I was married to my job. What a cliché . . .'

'I'm sure we can work it out, Bella?' She tried to sound positive.

Something snapped inside her. She stood up. 'No. No. No — I'm not having this. Sorry, it's not your fault. If they are offering redundancy, I'll take it.'

Jules looked up at her. 'Please, don't be hasty, Bella. I know you've had a lot going on and a number of things to deal with.'

'No.' Bella smiled despite how she was feeling. 'We've been trying to keep things level for so many years — my parents and me — and we have, but it was always going to change. The cracks were always going to show. And what's the point of the status quo when it's not working anymore?' She glanced at the clock on the wall. 'So, I've got to go. I've got a plane to catch.'

And she turned and walked out of the door, wondering what she'd just done, but somewhere inside her she knew that whatever it was, it was the right thing.

She took her phone out of her bag and called her mother. 'Mum, you and Dad are coming to Portugal for a little holiday. You deserve it. A break from everything just for a few days, and then we'll get everything sorted out. We'll sort out accessibility and help at the airport for Dad. I'll be in touch with dates when I get there.'

Then she went back to her flat, checked out flights for her parents, and switched everything off again. 'I've got you,' she said to the living room, 'And I've got the Nest. I may not have a job very soon . . . but I've got you.' She closed the door behind her and locked it, then took the lift down to the lobby and walked to the tube. At the entrance, she sent a message to Hugo and to Will.

I'm coming back today. A little earlier than planned. Bella.

CHAPTER 24

As she switched on her phone at Faro airport, several messages arrived all at once.

Glad you're coming back early. Shall I get you some food? Will

Good news. Is everything all right? Shall I get you some food? Hugo

Do you know anything about the bulldozer? Will

There is a bulldozer parked outside the gate of the Nest. Do you know anything about it? Hugo

I saw Martim hanging around. He said they were going to cut down the tree just outside your gate as they plan to build an access road at the end of the track to some new housing they will be building. It will impact the tree's roots and make it unsafe. Will

Bella began to panic.

I spoke to Lenny and told him he could not cut down the tree outside your gate as the roots will have grown under your wall and probably are on your drive. So they have left the bulldozer there. I don't know why they were going to use a bulldozer. Hugo

It is a public holiday, so they've just left this bulldozer right next to your tree. Will

I am contacting my great-uncle. He must have something to do with this. Hugo

Don't worry. We will sort it out. Will

Don't worry. We will sort it out. Hugo

Bella stared at the messages, temporarily unable to think, until the seat belt sign pinged off, and she was forced to get up. When she rang Hugo and Will as she walked to passport control, the calls both went to voicemail. She left the same message. 'I'll be home in just over an hour. Food would be great. Thank you.'

And as soon as she got through customs, she almost ran to the car park, got in her car, and drove along the motorway to Lagos.

* * *

Bella looked up at the bulldozer, her heart racing, waves of anxiety coursing around her body, combined with beats of anger she'd never experienced before. How could a piece of machinery make her feel so angry?

Manoeuvring so close to the front of the vehicle it would be impossible to move it without flattening her car, she got out, took her bottle of water and airport sandwiches, locked the car door and searched for a way to climb up onto it.

The sky was a bright, incandescent blue, and the sound of children laughing in the distance drifted over from the beach. A low steady rhythm bumped from Hugo's café.

She'd sent Hugo and Will a message as soon as she'd got to the end of the track.

I'm here. Dealing with this bulldozer.

The thought pushed her up, her foot finding the running board next to the driver's seat. Then she climbed onto the front and sat down. At the end of the drive stood the Nest surrounded by pots full of red and orange bougainvillea, the swimming pool glistening silver next to it. There was no storks' nest on the chimney of the outbuilding. She couldn't understand why it wasn't there anymore. Why would the storks leave and take it with them?

She closed her eyes and breathed, trying not to cry. 'I've only been gone a couple of days,' she said to the sky.

A dog barked in the distance. She opened her eyes as the cats climbed up towards her. 'Oh. Hello . . . Thank goodness you're all right.' Her shoulders shook as tears dripped down her cheek. 'I can't believe this is happening, Yin and Yang! It's a nightmare.' Weaving around her they purred, their tails brushing her arms as they did, then lay down and settled down either side of her, like guard dogs.

Deidre arrived, followed by Will. 'Ah. Bella. Thank God.' He shouted from the end of the track. 'I'm so glad you're back. What are you doing up there?'

'I'm protesting,' she shouted. 'They can't cut down this tree. It's my tree. Well, it's not. But it was here when Great-Aunt Flo bought the Nest and it's not going anywhere.'

'Sitting on the bulldozer is not very rational though, is it?' He stood next to it and looked up at her.

Bella felt a surge of excitement so strong it started from her toes and coursed through her whole body. 'I know! It's fantastic, isn't it? I didn't know how powerful being irrational felt until this very moment.'

Will stared at her for a moment then burst out laughing, doubling up and holding his stomach. 'Oh dear . . . oh dear . . . Bella . . . you looked just like Flo then.'

Bella watched him then began to laugh too, wiping her tears from her cheeks as she did.

'How long are you intending to stay up there?' he asked once he'd calmed down.

'Until they get here.'

'Tomorrow morning? Really?'

'Really.' Bella tried to sound defiant, but her rational side was making an appearance.

'Have you thought about the logistics and practicalities?' Will asked. Deidre began to bark at her. 'You can't go up there too, girl.' He pulled her back.

'What if I need the loo?' mumbled Bella. 'I hadn't thought of that . . .'

'I was thinking about food and drink actually, but that's a fair point.'

'They aren't knocking down this tree.' She was impressed at how assertive she sounded.

'I know — they won't. I phoned up the council — the Camara — and asked about new housing here. They hadn't had any requests for planning permission. Hugo has gone through the planning meetings — there's nothing there. It's all a bit odd.'

'This seems like a deliberate act of vandalism to me,' Bella shouted. 'Sorry, I didn't mean to talk so loudly. I'm just . . . A lot has happened in the last forty-eight hours.'

'Hugo has driven over to his great-uncle's offices near Tavira. He's sure he's got something to do with this. He tried to get rid of this tree years ago after he and Flo split up.'

'Why would he try again?'

Will shook his head. 'It seems very irrational to me.'

'The storks' nest has gone.' As the words came out of her mouth, a lump formed in her throat.

He shook his head. 'Could be anything.'

But Bella could see he didn't mean it. 'Can you ring Hans the birdwatcher? He may know why storks leave their nests quickly.'

'Sure I will.'

'And I have an idea,' Bella said slowly.

'You want me to get people here, don't you — make a noise, get the press, all that?'

'Yes please.'

'I'll make a few calls. I'll be back soon.'

As he began to walk away Bella could feel herself panic. 'You are definitely coming back, aren't you?'

'Yes I am. Now don't move too much — you'll fall off.'

Bella looked down. She was surprisingly high up. Then she looked at the cats, sprawled next to her as if sitting on a bulldozer was the most normal thing in the world. 'Maybe it is for you,' she said. 'But it's a first for me.'

She checked her watch. It was now 8 p.m. The bulldozer was facing west, so she took the tuna and egg sandwiches she had bought at Gatwick airport out of her bag and ate them, waiting for the sun to set so she could watch the sky turn slowly from blue to pink to black.

'Right.' Will was hurrying back up along the track. 'We're going to get some company. That means that when you need to stretch your legs, feel like you might fall off, or require a—' he held his fingers in the air as if they were inverted commas, '—"comfort" break, you will be replaced on the bulldozer by a proxy.'

'Oh. Thank you.' Bella put the empty sandwich packet in her bag. 'What about the press, social media?'

'All of this will be recorded ready for when the Terrible Twins arrive.'

'Fantastic.' Bella looked at him. 'I came straight from the airport and climbed on here without thinking. I was so annoyed. Could I get down for a comfort break?'

He nodded. 'Go on. I won't climb on myself — my knee's still not right — but Deidre here will make a lot of noise if anyone we don't want here arrives.'

'Thank you.' Bella thought for a moment. 'This isn't going to be very elegant.' She rolled over onto her stomach, disturbing the cats, who jumped down onto the ground irritably. 'How do you make that look so easy?' she muttered.

'Is that the best way?' Will moved forward, looking worried, as Bella grabbed the windscreen.

'I don't think so,' she wheezed, dangling her left leg down over the bonnet. 'It's higher than I realised.'

Will moved to the side of the bulldozer. 'Just drop down slowly and I'll somehow catch you.'

'I'll hurt your knee,' squealed Bella, losing her grip and landing with a thud onto a row of white flowers.

She managed to stand up. 'This is between us,' she whispered to Will, before hurrying down the track to the house.

She unlocked the door and stepped inside over the newly scrubbed floor, and up the wooden stairs recently painted brown, running her hand over the now smooth and brightly tinted banister.

This was my aunt's sanctuary, she thought. *I won't let anyone intimidate me or her memory.*

She went up onto the roof terrace to see if there was any trace of the storks' nest. But it had gone completely, as if someone had picked it up and taken it away. She hurried into the bedroom and put Flo's dress she had found in the fourth bedroom on as if it was a suit of armour. 'If I'm going to fight like you, I'd better look like you.'

Making sure the front door was firmly locked behind her she rushed down the track towards Will, Deidre and the bulldozer.

'No one here yet?' she said, clambering onto it again.

'The cavalry is on its way.' He smiled. 'With things to sit on, thankfully. I recognise that dress. It's one of Flo's, isn't it?'

Two cars rumbled down the lane towards them. 'I can see them!' Bella said as the cats settled down next to her again. 'That was quick.'

'Well, this is important.'

The cars pulled up. Layla, Minnie and Elena got out. Elena hovered at the back and pretended she couldn't see Will, even though he was standing next to the bulldozer. John Travolta and one of the Bee Gees got out of the other car.

'Ignacio and Duarte have been indulging in competitive living statue-ing,' said Minnie, rolling her eyes.

'Is there a competition?' Bella asked.

Both men were carrying some fold-up chairs towards them.

'No. No. It's just them. Being men. Being twits.'

'Ahh.' Bella smiled.

'I brought the drinks.' Elena waved. 'They are in a cool box in the car.'

'Can I help you get them?' Will followed her.

'I also have some binoculars and blankets that I use for birdwatching. You can keep a lookout from up there.' She handed Bella the binoculars. 'And we'll be ready for them.'

Bella used them to scan the horizon, moving from the Nest to the beach and then across to the lane, where Hugo was loading something into his car. Her heart flipped happily as she watched him get in it and drive towards the Nest, wondering why he was driving rather than walking.

'Glass of wine?' Duarte was holding a bottle and a plastic cup. 'You may as well. Only one . . . don't want you getting too relaxed and slipping off!'

Bella looked at him. Twenty-four hours ago, she would have said no because it was not a very sensible thing to do since she was currently preparing to spend the night sitting on a bulldozer. But that was the Bella of yesterday. This was the Bella who was actually sitting on the bulldozer.

'Why not?' She smiled at him.

He grinned. 'I'm so very proud of you.'

Hugo's car turned down the track. He parked, got out and took something out of the boot.

'They stole the storks' nest.' He held it up so everyone could see. 'And put it behind a tree in my garden. Mateus found it. I wondered why he was standing there, so went to check.'

Everyone stopped talking.

'Why would they do that?' Bella asked. 'They obviously wanted you to find it.'

'They are trying to unsettle us,' Will shouted angrily. 'And they won't. This is ridiculous.'

'They trespassed on my property and trespassed on yours. And made it obvious.' Bella could hear her voice rise. 'I'm going to ring Lenny. I've got his number. Just to ask if it was him.' She took her phone out of her bag and searched through her contacts list.

'My great-uncle wasn't around.' Hugo's voice was angry. 'They said they'd pass the message on.' He shook his head. 'This is very odd. Not businesslike. And Will says no planning permission for anything close by.'

'His number is out of service.' Bella took a breath, then caught Hugo's eye. 'Shall you ring your ex-girlfriend or shall I?'

'I'll do it.' Hugo took his phone out of his pocket and walked to the end of the track.

'I'm going to ring Jorge,' shouted Elena. 'He'll know how to get them. He's been let off very lightly for his duplicity, so he'll have to help. I'll make him,' she almost snarled.

Bella looked through the binoculars again. A group of people appeared to be waddling down the lane, all with binoculars and many with foldable chairs. One of them paused and looked through their binoculars, then waved. It was Hans with the birdwatching group.

Bella waved back and felt a tiny surge of excitement.

'I told them someone was trying to take down your tree!' Elena shouted. 'We are birdwatchers. We love trees!'

Bella looked back at the house. 'I want the storks back. It's not the Nest without the storks. It's not *O Ninho*.'

'We will put the nest back on the roof.' Ignacio picked it up from the floor.

'This will only have happened in the last forty-eight hours.' Elena followed him up the drive. 'They may just be temporarily displaced.'

'The ladder is in the outbuilding.' Bella threw the keys down to Layla. 'Thank you.'

Quiet Julian arrived with some of his friends. 'Hugo told us to close the restaurant early.' His voice was almost audible. 'So, I put the word out, and here we are. I will take some films and put them on social media. I need a hashtag.'

'Save the Nest,' shouted someone.

'Stop wanton destruction of trees,' shouted someone else.

'Partay time,' the voice came from the back of the crowd. Everyone turned around and tutted. 'Sorry . . .' the voice said. 'Got carried away.'

'Save the house that Florence left?' Will looked pleased with his idea.

'They are trying to knock down the tree, not the house,' Minnie replied reasonably.

Hugo reappeared, his phone in his hand. 'Yes, well, I think they were hoping that the tree is just the start.' He looked up at Bella. 'May I join you?'

She smiled down at him. 'Please do.'

He got into the driver's seat. 'There's not enough room for us both on the bonnet.' He reached his hand out and Bella took it, wanting to pull him up so he could wrap himself around her and they could sit staring at the sky and the beach in the stillness. Just them and the stars and the waves.

Someone started playing 'Lovely Day' on the guitar, and one by one the crowd began to sing.

Hugo squeezed her hand. 'Well, at least we are keeping ourselves entertained.'

'Did you get through to Deanna?' asked Bella.

'I'm afraid I did.'

'Afraid?'

'Her perspective is . . . Well, she felt the need to tell me what she feels are some home truths. I felt the need to tell her some too.' He sighed. 'It was about time. But unpleasant to hear.'

'Oh dear. Was she not very nice about you?' Bella remembered Gino's last text, telling her she was too focused on her work.

'Well, no. But also, about what she was trying to do.'

'Go on.'

He looked up at Bella, his chocolate-brown eyes full of sadness. 'She lived in a slum. She got out. She has made a life for herself. She is driven. She saw what I had and wondered why I needed so much space. She saw houses where our trees and vegetables are.'

'I understand. She told me something like that herself.' Bella nodded.

'She got a job working for my great-uncle and that's when we broke up . . . and she began to see big houses where our land is, rather than apartments and small villas . . . She got drawn into making a lot of money. Because to her, money is freedom.'

'And she wants to be free of her past. Free of worrying about money.'

'She can't understand why we want our houses rather than the money. And she and Lenny and Martim have got carried away.'

'That's one way of putting it.'

'So, Lenny and Martim decided to try to intimidate you. Slowly drive you out. Because who wants all this trouble if they are renting a property out? And who would want to buy anywhere when they find out what they are doing?'

Bella's jaw set hard. 'Those three were trying to frighten me . . .' she shouted so loudly that everyone stopped singing and looked over.

'They are trying to intimidate me. And Will. And Hugo,' she shouted.

Julian pointed his phone at her. 'Say that again,' he said. 'But don't say their names — slander, libel, defamation of character — got to be careful.'

'They are trying to intimidate us!' shouted Bella. 'And they won't!'

Everyone cheered.

'And your great-uncle? She works for him.'

Hugo's face almost contorted with fury. 'He will not answer my calls, my visits. He is a coward, and he is hiding.'

Bella heard the sound of a truck in the distance and looked through her binoculars. Her whole body tensed. 'It's Lenny and Martim,' she whispered.

'They are coming!' shouted Hugo. 'Lenny and Martim!'

Everyone gathered around the bulldozer. Ignacio and Duarte watched from the roof of the outbuilding. Julian played the theme from *The Good, The Bad and The Ugly* loudly from his phone.

Bella laughed. She couldn't stop as she watched Lenny and Martim walk down the lane and turn into the track. She laughed till she started to splutter, then laughed again.

'I'm not sure that's the best way to approach this.' Hugo looked confused. 'We need to be assertive, angry, determined . . .'

'I'm sitting on the front of a bulldozer. There are two men putting a storks' nest back on the outbuilding of the Nest, a large group of people gathered around me, and these two men have no idea, do they?'

'They don't, no.' Hugo smiled.

Lenny and Martim strode determinedly towards the corner.

Bella watched, waiting, wondering how they'd react. 'Hello!' she shouted, waving.

'What are you doing?' Hugo looked worried.

'Taking control,' she said.

'Here they are, everyone,' she told the group. 'Are you coming to join the party?' she shouted to the men, who were now standing at the end of the track.

'You are on our property,' Martim shouted. 'You are trespassing. Please get off.'

'Well, you were on my property trespassing, weren't you? So no.'

'No we weren't.'

'Yes you were. You stole the storks' nest.'

'No we didn't.'

'Oh yes you did.' Bella waved her arms. 'Everyone, after me . . .'

'Oh yes you did,' the crowd shouted in unison.

'Actually, you did.' Hugo leaned out from the cab of the bulldozer. 'I've just had one of those Ring doorbell systems installed and I've got a recording.'

Martim looked at Lenny. 'You told me there wasn't any CCTV!'

'There wasn't last week.' Lenny sounded petulant, like a sulky child. 'So don't blame me.'

Will pushed himself to the front of the group. 'There is no planning permission for any building along the lane.' He waved his stick at them. 'So why are you trying to dig it up and take down that tree?'

Martim took a deep breath and tried to smile. 'We are just businessmen trying to make a living. We are working with a consortium of other parties. We assumed the planning request had been sent in.'

'We don't believe you,' shouted Bella.

Lenny stalked towards the bulldozer. 'That is very expensive equipment. You must get off it now.'

'No. Go away. I don't trust you.' Bella folded her arms, just as she heard another vehicle drive down the lane. 'Hold on, we've got a visitor.'

Through the binoculars, she saw a Jaguar park around the corner. Francisco Lopes climbed out.

She leaned closer to Hugo. 'Your great-uncle has arrived.'

'He has?'

'Get out of the cab, please, so I can take this away.' Lenny grabbed Hugo's arm.

'No.' Hugo moved back inside, so Lenny yanked Bella's leg.

'What are you doing, man?' Martim was trying to pull his friend away.

'This is expensive equipment. And we are renting it. These idiots will damage it.'

271

Julian held his hand up and began filming on his phone again as Minnie took hold of Lenny's hand. 'Leave them alone,' she shouted, 'you big bullies!'

'What the hell is going on here?' Francisco Lopes stood in the shadows, the moon illuminating his face briefly before it was obscured by a cloud.

'Ah, my great-uncle makes an appearance at last.' Hugo stared at him. 'What do you think you are doing setting your people onto us like this?'

'This is nothing to do with me.' The group parted and he walked forward. 'This land is hard to develop. Too many environmental issues, access issues, it's difficult to build on, some of it is a flood-plain. And there will inevitably be a day when a rare bird nests here and the paperwork around that will not be worth the trouble. Why would I waste my time on a money pit like this?'

'You tried before.' Hugo held Francisco's gaze.

His uncle didn't reply.

'I saw you with these two.' Bella pointed at Lenny and Martim. 'On more than one occasion.'

'Deanna De La Cruz — my now ex-employee — was trying to build up a case to persuade me to invest. I thought about it. But I said no. I said no more than once and—'

'So they don't work for you?' Hugo's voice was getting louder.

'I didn't say that. They don't anymore. What the hell did you think you were doing?' Francisco turned his attention to the builders.

'We decided to set up on our own, have our own project.' Martim was beginning to sound embarrassed. 'Get her out.' He nodded at Bella. 'Buy the land, and then find an investor.'

'So all this about the tree and the access was a lie?' Bella looked at the people around them. 'Get this bulldozer away from my house.'

'It's just a tree.' Lenny said. 'Just a tree that will fall down one day anyway.'

272

'It's not *just* a tree,' Hans shouted. 'Living things are part of that tree. Birds, insects — only a few months ago we spotted a lesser-crested netherbird nesting there.' He winked at Bella and whispered, 'I made that up.'

'You will not touch that tree.' Francisco's voice boomed and everyone fell silent.

No one said anything for a moment.

'Florence loved that tree.' Francisco's voice was lower now. 'We used to meet under that tree. I would watch her amble down the path towards me in one of her colourful dresses.' He looked at Bella. 'I recognise that dress . . .'

'But you tried to knock it down?' Hugo looked confused.

'Oh, I did.' He almost laughed. 'She never had any money, you know. And I decided in my arrogant way that if she sold the house and the land I could build properties on it and she would have all the money in the world to have the kind of life I thought she deserved. With me.' He turned to Hugo. 'Your parents were the same. Living hand to mouth. Just like our parents before them. And I didn't want that. I thought they deserved better. I watched them all working themselves into early graves.'

'But my parents loved it here,' Hugo said softly. 'It's not all about money. They had enough — they would have liked a bit more, I suppose but they were a part of this place and the sea and the fields . . . That was them. Not what you wanted.'

Francisco looked up and smiled at Bella. 'You, sitting on that bulldozer. She did the same thing when I got so angry I hired one. I just wanted to show her. I wanted her to want what I did and I was furious.'

'This is making me sad.' Elena took a handkerchief out of her pocket.

'Then I went away and I became rich and I didn't speak to my family and I lost Flo. And then she died.'

He didn't speak for a moment, then took a breath. 'And one day I drove past and I saw you.' He looked into her eyes. 'Flo had told me what had happened to your father. "I just wish I could make it better," she'd said. And for just one moment, I wondered if I bought this off you, I could help you. So when Deanna mentioned the idea to me, I agreed to talk to these two.' He looked at Lenny and Martim. 'But I knew it was wrong, and I said no. You get this thing away."' He pointed to the bulldozer. '"And if I hear anything about you trying to get past building controls and putting anything on this area, I will go to the police".'

Someone clapped their hands at the back of the crowd.

Everyone turned around. It was Deanna De La Cruz.

Hugo shook his head angrily. 'What are you doing here? What business do you have here?'

She moved forward slowly, her eyes on his. 'This . . .' She stopped, then looked at Bella. 'This was not my idea. This is too much. I got carried away, but this is an act of vandalism. How will I ever be successful as a property developer if I get caught up in this? You idiots! It's all over social media and the press.'

'You didn't say that,' Martim sneered. 'You were all for getting information and using it.'

'I was, I admit it.' She winced, then spoke to Hugo. 'I feel it was partly anger with you. I wanted you to be like me, and you aren't, and . . .' She shook her head then smiled. 'You being you was why I wanted you in the first place.'

Bella tried not to look at Hugo. She was too frightened to see his reaction.

'Well, that's done now.' Hugo's voice was even but firm. 'Thank you for your apology and openness. The way you have behaved has been hurtful and underhand. I hope you have learned from it.'

Deanna nodded then spoke to Bella. 'I met your aunt a few times. She was a force of nature.' She looked at the floor. 'Money, money, money.' She shook her head, turned around and walked away.

There was silence until she was out of sight.

'To *O Ninho*!' shouted Duarte, who began to clap, and then everyone joined in. Hugo got out of the cab and helped

Bella slide down from the bonnet. Lenny climbed inside and switched it on and it lurched backwards, knocking into Bella's gate. There was a collective intake of breath until he jolted forward and drove off.

Something fluttered at the top of the tree, and a large brown bird with soft white feathers tinged with blue hovered above it for a moment before flying away.

There was another collective intake of breath, then silence until Hans said, 'Was that what I think it was?'

'I think it was,' someone else said. 'I have never seen one here before.'

Hans gripped Bella's hand and beamed. 'Oh, Bella. If that bird is what we think it is, no one will be able to build on here anyway. That is a rare, rare bird, and once I have contacted the relevant societies, the red tape involved in trying to move forward with any building will drive even the most patient developer quietly mad.'

'Oh? We seem to be a bit of a magnet for shy birds.' Exhaustion suddenly swept over Bella and she rubbed her eyes.

'I was worried there for a moment.' Minnie stepped forward. 'Oh . . .' She pointed at the floor. The sign for the Nest was on the ground, shattered.

Francisco stepped forward and picked the pieces up. 'I'm sorry.' He handed them to Bella. 'I remember when Florence painted this.' His voice cracked. 'I hope this hasn't caused you too much distress.'

Bella took his hand, but she couldn't find the right words. Then she remembered the old photo she had found in the chest of drawers in her bedroom. 'Florence kept a photograph of you both standing under this tree,' she said softly. 'You looked so happy. You must have meant a lot to her.'

Francisco Lopes stared above her head, unable to speak.

'Thank you for stopping them,' she said eventually.

He looked at Hugo and nodded. Hugo nodded back, and Francisco turned at walked up the track towards the lane.

'Are you going to go after him?' Bella asked.

Hugo shook his head, then put his arms around Bella. She felt safe and secure. And until that moment she hadn't realised that she hadn't felt safe and secure for a very long time.

Duarte and Ignacio were following Layla from the house. 'The nest is back where it belongs,' she said.

'I'm so sad about the tile.' Elena looked like she was going to cry again.

Ignacio smiled. 'Leave it with me. Are you all right, Bella? It's nearly midnight. You must be exhausted.'

'I think I just want to go home.' Bella looked at the Nest. Yin and Yang were sitting expectantly on the drive.

'Shall I walk you there?' Hugo asked.

'No, thank you. I think I need to shut out the world for a few hours.' She turned to the group. 'Thank you all for your support. It means a lot to me.'

Then she turned towards the Nest and walked home.

CHAPTER 25

Bella woke up to the purring-cat alarm of Yin and Yang sitting either side of her ears. She looked at the clock on the wall. '6 a.m. . . . 6 a.m.? Why have you woken me so early?' Rolling over, she tried to get back to sleep. Then her brain kicked into gear. And she sat bolt upright in bed.

You asked for redundancy. What were you thinking?

What are you going to do? What about your parents? What about money?

What were you thinking? What were you thinking? What were you thinking?

There was a clicking noise outside, followed by the fluttering of very large wings.

Bella jumped out of bed, opened the blinds and then the doors and stepped onto her balcony. The storks were standing on the roof of the outhouse as if they had never been away.

Bella waved at them. 'Hello, old friends!'

Then she glanced down at the outhouse and suddenly everything became clear.

Make it better, she thought. *I know how to make it better.* She looked at the cats. 'All this time I've been trying to make the house better, but it's not the house. I can use it to make it better.' She clapped her hands excitedly, went downstairs, made herself a cup of tea and took the laptop out into the garden. Then she opened all of her spreadsheets and deleted them one by one. Then she created two more and called them:

Renting out my London flat

Mum and Dad — the outhouse, thermal therapy in the pool.

She leaned back and smiled, then opened another one and called it:

Job search

Then she deleted it, deciding that, for a few weeks at least, she could allow herself to just go with the flow at her current job until everything changed and she would just have to see what happened after that.

She walked into the house and picked up the print that was still on the table by the door and read it out loud. '*The amble by its very definition does not have to have an actual firm destination, often fizzling out in a café, on a beach, or in a shop en route. Although it isn't really en route as you are not actually going anywhere. You are ambling.*'

Then she made herself some breakfast, took a shower and unpacked, logged on again and composed a letter officially requesting redundancy should it be on offer, then decided to walk to the beach before logging on again to start her proper working day.

Putting on her headphones, she switched on her Portuguese language app, then listened to the birdsong and waves instead. Music drifted from Hugo's, so she went inside the café hoping to see him. Bella knew she had something to say, but still couldn't formulate the words. She just wanted to see him.

'Ah!' Quiet Julian waved at her. 'Bella. You are quite the social media star! Sit down and I'll bring you a *galão*.'

'Hello. Thank you for everything last night.'

Julian blushed. 'It was nothing.' He walked behind the counter.

'Is Hugo here?'

'It's his day off. His manager will be here soon. I'll bring your drink over.'

Bella went outside and sat down, staring at the beach, watching people walk past, her mind at last quiet.

'Here. On the house.' Julian laughed. 'I have always wanted to say that.' He sat down opposite her and showed her his phone, scrolling through his social media feed. 'I don't think Lenny and Martim's property development dreams will get very far after this.'

Bella laughed as she read through the posts, watching videos of her and Hugo sitting on the bulldozer, Ignacio and Duarte putting the storks' nest back on the roof, Layla holding the ladder, Will shaking his stick, Hans looking through his binoculars, Elena crying into her handkerchief, and Minnie with her arms around her.

'Goodness. It's like a film.'

Another customer came in. 'I have to go. Enjoy.' Julian touched her hand gently before standing back up. 'What an unforgettable adventure.' His voice was almost at full volume.

Bella leaned back and took a sip of her coffee, wondering if it was too early to call her parents and tell them her idea.

* * *

'We can adapt the outhouse, Mum. It's really light and airy. If you didn't want to live here, you could both come over and have very long holidays here. The garden is lovely. Dad and you could help me with it.'

'What about your job? It sounds wonderful, but what about your job?'

'I can rent out my flat in London. And there may be redundancies on offer. If not, I'll leave and find a way . . . I know I'll be fine.'

'What about work visas and all that?'

'It will be fine. I'll work it out.'

279

'Your dad is having a lie-in. He's a bit low about us selling the house, even though we know it's the right thing to do.'

'Come over for that holiday. Just to see. You'll want to stay.' Bella looked at the clock. 'I've got to start work, Mum. I'll call later.'

Bella rang off and logged on to her work account. She had a Zoom meeting and wanted to get ahead after the upheaval of the past few days. She took her computer outside and began to work.

'Hello,' she said to the assembled faces on the screen, then carried on as normal, taking notes and participating in the meeting as if nothing had happened.

'Bella.' Lil leaned forward. 'Is that a donkey behind you?'

Bella looked around. 'Oh. Mateus, I didn't see you there.'

The donkey snorted and nodded his head.

'Bella.' Lil smiled. 'I don't think Mateus understands. But . . . has he got something tied round his neck?'

'Has he?' Bella got up. 'Oh yes. There's a collar with a letter attached.' She took the envelope and opened it.

Bella. Will you join me for a late breakfast? Mateus knows where to find me. Hugo.

Bella's heart skipped a beat. In a nice way. 'Um . . .' She looked at the screen. 'I've just got to go . . . Carry on . . . Bye.' She waved at her colleagues, then switched off the computer, put it in the house, locked the door and followed Mateus across her vegetable patch, through her orange grove and along the hedge, where they both squeezed through the gap.

'You To Me Are Everything' drifted from a speaker close to the house, where a picnic was spread on a blanket on the floor.

Hugo stood in the doorway and smiled at her. 'Thank you for coming.' He smiled shyly, not moving.

'Thank you for inviting me.' Bella smiled at him expectantly.

'I have something to say.' He still didn't move.

'OK.'

'I don't want you to leave. I don't want you to sell or rent the house out — and not because of anything apart from the fact that if you do, you won't be there. And I won't like it if you're not there. I like it when you're there. I didn't like it at all when you were away, even though it was only a couple of days.' He looked at her. He still didn't move.

'I realised what my aunt meant when she said I had to "make it better".' Bella began to walk towards him. 'She didn't mean the house, she meant make it better for my parents, and make it better for me. And making it better means staying. I'm not going anywhere.'

He still didn't move.

'Because if I go, I won't be near you, and that won't be better for me, it would be worse. So, I'm staying. Because I want to be near you.'

Hugo moved towards her. 'I want to be near to you. Very near to you.'

'Good.'

They were standing in front of each other. Hugo held his hand out. Bella took it and he pulled her towards him, wrapping his arms around her and kissing her, long and lingering, then running his hand down her spine and kissing her neck and shoulders.

'What about the picnic?' she asked, as he led her inside.

'It can wait. We're in no hurry. No hurry at all.'

CHAPTER 26

Bella sat under the tree and looked at the house. Its newly painted walls glowed white in the sun, the deep red bougainvillea cascading opulently from the window boxes, the blue wooden door scrubbed and cleaned and brought back to life.

The cats lay sprawled on the terracotta tiles on the patio and the storks flew back and forth from the nest on the roof of the bright yellow outbuilding.

'So?' Hugo sat next to her. 'Do you think you've "made it better"? I mean, the house.'

She lay her head on his shoulder. 'Who knows. But I like it . . . Actually, I love it.'

'How does it compare to your spreadsheet?' Her father nudged her with his walking stick and laughed.

'Spreadsheet?' She looked up at him and smiled. 'What's that?'

'It is beautiful. Great-Aunt Flo would be so proud.' Her mother put a tray on the table and handed Bella and Hugo tall glasses of homemade lemonade.

'I was hoping it was beer o'clock!' Will wandered over from the barbecue next to the swimming pool, followed by Deidre wagging her tail happily. Elena walked out of the house carrying some plates and put them on the table. She and Will sat next to Bella as Ignacio and Minnie carried a bowl of lemons they'd picked from the orchard over.

'Quite a crop.' Ignacio beamed.

'More than enough for some gin and tonics.' Minnie looked at them all. 'Are we sitting on the floor now?'

'I think,' said Ignacio, joining the others, 'if our knees can take it this is where we get the best view of the house.'

Minnie shrugged. 'Well, if that's the case.' She held Ignacio's hand and sank down.

Francisco leaned back in his chair and closed his eyes, smiling.

Layla closed her car door and joined them, handing Bella a bunch of lavender. 'I picked this from my garden this morning. I just love the smell of it.'

Bella buried her nose in the flowers and breathed them in. 'Clean and clear and happy,' she said.

Layla sat next to Minnie. 'You should be proud of yourself, Bella.' She looked around. 'You took that leap and you're starting again.'

'I'm proud and frightened at the same time.' Bella edged closer to Hugo. He squeezed her hand as Duarte's car edged up the track.

'He's driven down from Cascais today.' Minnie watched as he parked. 'Said something about having to get something important.'

'*Olá! Boa tarde!*' he shouted, climbing out of the car. 'I'm sorry I'm late.' He took a bag from the back seat and walked over towards them, pausing to look at the house. '*Muito muito bem. E lindo.*' He touched Bella's shoulder. 'It's lovely. It's beautiful. It's perfect.' He sat down next to Elena. 'Can you pass this to Bella?' He gave her the bag, which she passed along the line until it got to Bella.

'It's from our friends Alice Mathews Simal and her husband Luis. They are artists. She sold her house in London many years ago and has made her life here. Just like you.'

'Alice — she created the ambling print?'

Duarte nodded and Bella took a picture and a tile out of the bag.

'Only you haven't sold your house in London. So not exactly like you.' Duarte was still smiling.

She looked at the picture. In the middle it said, 'Bella Creswell learns the art of the amble.' And it was surrounded by tiny blue patterned Portuguese tiles. In the corner was a signature: *Luis Simal for Bella.*

Hugo laughed. 'I think you may have officially learned to amble, Bella.' He took her head gently in his hands and kissed her.

Bella's heart fluttered happily.

'There's something else.' Her dad nudged her with his foot. 'I'm dying to see what it is.'

Bella took it out of the bag and unwrapped it. It was a blue, yellow and white tile, with the words '*O Ninho*' painted in the middle, storks soaring through the sky around the letters.

There was a note stuck to the back of it. She took it off and looked at it.

To our homes and all they mean to us. Alice

No one spoke.

Bella stood and looked at the house. *This belongs to me*, she thought. *Or do I belong to it?* Then, walking to the gate, she felt light and free as if she was floating in the air, and stood where the shattered tile on the wall used to be.

'Here,' she said, turning around. 'It needs to go here. Can anyone help?'

They all gathered around her and watched as Hugo handed her a screwdriver and some screws. 'I was mending the table, so I've got these with me.'

She looked at him.

'You can take it from here.' He smiled encouragingly at her.

'Can I help?' Francisco guided her hand to the wall and squeezed it tight.

She slowly fixed the tile, then stood back and turned around. Everyone cheered, and Bella turned again, looking along the drive to the house, then edging backwards until she was standing under the shade of the tree that stood outside the Nest, its roots stretching out along her drive and up the track to the road. She put her arms around it, picturing Florence and Francisco, imagining them together and what could have been. 'I wish you could have both made it better,' she whispered. 'For yourselves.'

'I have found my nephew again.' Francisco ran his hand along the tile. 'I'm now the trustee of his charity. It should have been Flo, but . . .' He took a breath. 'It's given me a new lease of life. I have something back to remind me of the love of my life. So—' He took Bella's hand and kissed it. 'You have made it better. You have made it better for all of us.'

Bella put her arms around Hugo as Duarte handed out glasses of champagne.

One of the storks flew from the outhouse roof and landed in front of them, stretching its wings wide. It shook its head and seemed to stare at Bella.

Bella smiled. 'Hello Sally. Or Harry.'

It turned around and flew back to the roof, where the other storks were standing, watching.

'Look!' Bella pointed at them. 'All the family is here joining in the celebrations. We're all here. Here at the house that Florence left.'

Duarte gave her some champagne and she held it up. 'To Flo.'

'To Flo,' they repeated.

Bella smiled. 'Thank you Flo for making it better. Thank you.'

THE END

ACKNOWLEDGEMENTS

Writing a book is not as solitary an occupation as I first thought. Yes, I spend a lot of time thinking and imagining and creating (or making things up and writing them down!). But, with every step, the people around me have supported me, enthused about my books and encouraged me along the way. And as they are part of it too, I want to thank them.

I'll start with Heather Cox — we recently chatted about how, many years ago, when I decided to finally write that novel and thought it would be a good idea to set it in Cyprus, where I had been a whole three times, she asked why, when I had lived in Portugal and spend a lot of my time there and actually knew it very, very well. 'Why aren't you setting it there, Chris?' she had asked, not unreasonably, thus edging me along the path of setting my first Portuguese Paradise novel, *The House That Alice Built*, in Cascais near Lisbon.

This book is my fourth of that series, and I don't think I'll ever tire of that beautiful country that has so captivated me. Portugal-wise, I'd also like to thank John Cox and Dee Sale for being basically brilliant too.

More thanks go to my uni friends and their chaps — Jill, Sandi, Sue, Loui, Mark and Mike, for being there for me for so many years, and being part of so many accidental adventures. Also, the wonderful Lizzie Chantree, with whom I run our Writing Buddy sessions, my friends and writing pals Deborah Stephenson and Tony Fisher, and all who attend the Writing Buddy sessions at Fête Grays Yard in Chelmsford, plus Laura and her team, who have such a lovely café and meeting space. A lot of this novel was written there.

There's also my friend, artist Judith Dawson in Portugal, fellow Lagos fans, including Alex and Chris, and all the familiar faces I bump into when I'm visiting that make the place such a wonderful, inspirational and vibrant place to be.

To all my friends and workmates, who are funny and kind and adventurous and imaginative and are inspirational just by being themselves — thank you. And to Jean and Meryl for telling me how much they like the books.

Thank you to the team at Choc Lit and Joffe for making my writing dreams come true, and the Tasting Panel.

THE CHOC LIT STORY

Established in 2009, Choc Lit is an independent, award-winning publisher dedicated to creating a delicious selection of quality women's fiction.

We have won 18 awards, including Publisher of the Year and the Romantic Novel of the Year, and have been shortlisted for countless others. In 2023, we were shortlisted for Publisher of the Year by the Romantic Novelists' Association.

All our novels are selected by genuine readers. We are proud to publish talented first-time authors, as well as established writers whose books we love introducing to a new generation of readers.

In 2023, we became a Joffe Books company. Best known for publishing a wide range of commercial fiction, Joffe Books has its roots in women's fiction. Today it is one of the largest independent publishers in the UK.

We love to hear from you, so please email us about absolutely anything bookish at choc-lit@joffebooks.com

If you want to hear about all our bargain new releases, join our mailing list: www.choc-lit.com/contact